Beyond December

MICHAEL EHRET

Scrivenings
PRESS
Quench your thirst for story.
www.ScriveningsPress.com

Copyright © 2024 by Michael Ehret

Published by Scrivenings Press LLC
15 Lucky Lane
Morrilton, Arkansas 72110
https://ScriveningsPress.com

Printed in the United States of America

All rights reserved. No part of this publication may be reproduced, stored in a retrieval system, or transmitted in any form or by any means—for example, electronic, photocopy, or recording— without the prior written permission of the publisher. The only exception is brief quotations in printed reviews.

Paperback ISBN 978-1-64917-426-0

eBook ISBN 978-1-64917-427-7

Editor: Suzie Waltner

Cover by Linda Fulkerson, www.bookmarketinggraphics.com

All characters are fictional, and any resemblance to real people, either factual or historical, is purely coincidental.

Scripture quotations are taken from:

- The Holy Bible, New International Version®, NIV®. Copyright © 1973, 1978, 1984 by Biblica, Inc. Used by permission of Zondervan. All rights reserved worldwide.
- The ESV® Bible (The Holy Bible, English Standard Version®), copyright © 2001 by Crossway, a publishing ministry of Good News Publishers. Used by permission. All rights reserved.

NO AI TRAINING: Without in any way limiting the author's [and publisher's] exclusive rights under copyright, any use of this publication to "train" generative artificial intelligence (AI) technologies to generate text is expressly prohibited. The author reserves all rights to license uses of this work for generative AI training and development of machine learning language models.

To my sister, Jody Prestine:
You were the first one, outside of my wife, who believed in this
crazy dream of mine.

Chapter One

Zak Cooper awoke in heaven.

December held northern Indiana in its clutches. According to his radio alarm, an ice storm from north of Chicago was descending and would hit the area in time for the Friday afternoon rush. Likely dangerous for Chicago. But in Oak Hill? Typically, an inconvenience, but not much more.

Zak snuggled underneath a down comforter and curled around the woman he loved. Had to be heaven.

He traced the outline of his wife's face. Even asleep, Kay's beauty stirred him, and he rose on his elbow to breathe a kiss onto her cheek.

"Mmm." She turned into his arms, settling them both back into their bower.

"Good morning, my love," he whispered. "Storm coming. Got to start planning coverage."

Her hand teased the hair on his chest as he inhaled the aroma of their life together—intimacy in a scent.

"Andy will cover the traffic. Jeannie on the reaction. Mick—"

Kay laid her finger against his lips.

He kissed it. "Okay, love. You go back to sleep." He pulled back the covers and edged toward the side of the bed. Before his feet touched the sure-to-be-cold floor, he made a mental note: long johns.

Her hand slid down to his stomach and tickled him. "Where do you think you're going?"

Her soft voice melted his resolve. As she pulled the covers back over him, Zak rolled onto his side and returned to her embrace, his mouth finding hers and closing over it.

Deadlines could wait.

IN THE SHOWER, Zak savored his morning coffee and the hot water. Warmth on the outside, warmth on the inside. His mind at work, he turned off the spray and made a mental note to ask Jeannie to check the homeless shelter. This might be a suitable time to pull out that feature he'd written on OakHill's new town manager. A few fresh quotes and photos should do it.

"Do you like the coffee?" Kay called from the next room, interrupting his planning.

"Uh, yeah, I guess." He peered around the doorjamb to where Kay sat at the kitchen table with her cup of tea. "Was something different?"

"Apparently not."

Today, the coffee was just a caffeine delivery system. "A new brand?"

"No, same old same old."

As he dried, he tried a new tack. "You added some cocoa to the grounds. I knew something was different. It's my job to notice things, you know. It was fine."

"Well, Mr. 'It's-My-Job-To-Notice-Things,' there was no

cocoa either. The other day, I read in a magazine that adding a quarter teaspoon of cinnamon to your coffee grounds can help reduce your cholesterol."

Zak stepped into the hallway, towel in hand. Shivering in the morning chill, he reached back to grab his bathrobe from the door hook.

He put on his best scowl. "You know I don't like estrogen-enhanced coffee. Plain, black. No cream, no sugar, extra caffeine. None of that froufrou hazelnut almond mocha—"

"You said you liked it." Kay smiled over her cup.

"I said it was fine." He walked to the coffeepot and draped his towel on a dining room chair as he passed. He wrinkled his nose over the pot.

"You tricked me." As he moved to the bedroom with a fresh cup, he wagged his finger. "No more cinnamon."

"It's good for your cholesterol."

Women. Wives, specifically.

He could get used to the taste of cinnamon. If she thought his health was at stake, Kay would never give up.

She followed him into the bedroom. "You going to get dressed?"

"No, *Mother*, I thought I'd go to work in my bathrobe."

Snap! The end of the damp towel Zak had left on the chair connected with his exposed calf.

"Stop it." He leaped onto the bed as Kay pursued him. "Brat." She took aim again. "Hey."

"Maybe you'll learn to not leave your stuff lying around."

Kay snapped the towel once more but missed by a mile.

He grabbed the weapon, locked her in his arms, and pulled her onto the bed into a tangled fit of laughter, limbs, and towel.

"You've got to dress." She extricated herself from the pile. "You're already late. Sloan will have a cow."

"Sore loser." Zak hung his robe on the hook in the closet

and grabbed his clothes, including the long johns, in case he needed to do any outside reporting.

"Someone needs to be the designated adult."

As Kay picked out her clothes, he crossed the room, slipped behind her, wrapped his arms around her waist, and held her close.

"I love you, Katharine Renee Sharp Cooper. I love you like pizza. Like peanut butter. Like ice cream. I love you like NBA basketball and *How the Grinch Stole Christmas*. You are all my best things rolled into one."

"Like *The Grinch*? I am touched." Her hand caressed his cheek. "You have such a way with words."

"Well, I am a writer."

They stood there until the ticking wall clock broke through Zak's reverie.

"Criminitly! Look at the time."

Zak charged around the house like a pinball, racking up points on every bumper. Cell phone here. Car keys there. Briefcase back here. In between, he threw his clothes on.

"Don't forget about the meeting at church tonight." He paused to pull on his coat. "Assuming the ice storm doesn't shut things down, want to meet there and catch dinner after?"

"Sure, that'll give me time to pick up some Christmas gifts at the mall since my last appointment is at the coffee shop on the highway."

"It's supposed to be a bad storm, you know. Ice and all. Why don't I just bring carryout home after the meeting?"

She tucked in his shirttail and straightened his turned-up collar. "I'm already practically going to be at the church. It'll be fine."

"Call me if there are any issues. Promise?"

She smiled. "I promise, Zee."

He raced down the hallway and grabbed his wallet off the

top of the microwave. "Speaking of *The Grinch.* It's on tonight. I forgot to set the DVR. Can you do it?"

"The app on your phone not working?"

He blinked and grinned.

From the hallway, she laughed and shook her head. "I'll take care of it, love. Now, go."

"Thanks, hon. See you tonight."

"Go." She shooed him toward the garage. "Go, go, go. Give Sloan a hug for me."

Laughing, Zak turned, punched the garage door opener, ran to the Jeep, and climbed in. As he pulled out, he began to plan the A-1 layout.

He was three blocks from home before he realized he hadn't said goodbye.

Chapter Two

Zak stood at his desk, drained a cold cup of coffee, and mentally flipped through his five ongoing stories.

"Sloan, I needed that story ten minutes ago. Where is it?"

Two in editing. Vince's dull recap—he refused to call it news—of the school board meeting and a roundup of twenty or so minor fender benders due to the storm. Save those for tomorrow's print edition.

Two others nearly complete. The mayor's press conference regarding the street clearing delays and a man-on-the-street full of storm quotes. People did love to talk about the weather, especially snow. Both would create great online traffic as those who made it home safely browsed to see what happened to those who didn't.

That left only Sloan's apparently epic account of the Calhoun County Dog Show—a piece only written because of Mick's killer shot of a young girl, about five, walking a Great Dane. He should've made it a feature shot, with a few lines, but Sloan claimed he had an angle.

"Sloan!"

"You can't rush art, Zakary." Sloan's nose rose in the air.

"I'm trying to rush you, not art."

Consistently pushing against his deadlines, Zak's assistant editor and general assignment reporter would get no storm coverage.

As predicted, the ice storm had settled over the area, closing schools and creating havoc.

And Kay was out there in it. As a realtor, she could set her own schedule. He'd asked her to cancel that appointment, but she'd just laughed. Stubborn woman.

At least she'd made it to the coffee shop in Templeton. She'd be safe there.

Speaking of coffee ... Zak grabbed the nearby pot and poured a—fifth? —cup for himself. Without the cinnamon, thank you.

"Now or never, big guy. Send, Sloan, send."

"Hitting send now, Zakary."

That meant another five minutes.

"Don't mess with the lead." Sloan's ego was as inflated as his word counts.

Hello? Pulitzer Committee?

Kay's advice from when he'd accepted the editor position surfaced. *Make a conscious effort to appreciate Sloan's abilities, if not the man himself. It's hard to be passed over for a job.*

Well, it wasn't hard to understand why.

"You should have my story." Sloan stood and stretched like a prize fighter loosening tight muscles. "I gotta hit the can. I'll be right back if there are any questions."

Zak already had one. Why me?

He refreshed his screen and "dogshow21" appeared in the queue. At twenty inches. He'd asked for fifteen, max.

Appreciate, appreciate, appreciate.

Maybe the lead would redeem it.

"Baxter Maximillian VonKlepp, the prize miniature schnauzer and companion dog of Greta VonKlepp, Oak Hill, was succinct when asked about his win in the Calhoun County Dog Show.

"Woof. Woof, woof, woof."

Zak closed his eyes and blew out a sigh. Okay, then. *Cancel the call to the Pulitzer Committee.*

With a flick of his mouse, Zak highlighted. Deleted. Paged down. And zip, another six inches of doggie doo from Greta about the breeding of "Baxie" disappeared into oblivion.

"Ah! Fourteen inches, even better."

After a spellcheck, Zak added a headline and subhead, revised the cutesy lead, did a final spellcheck, and he hit *send.*

"Love this job."

"Is that because you get to destroy others' work?" Sloan's voice cut through the air behind Zak's right shoulder. "You cut my lead. I worked hard on that."

He winced. How had he not heard Sloan return? "Tweaked it, Sloan. Just tweaked it."

"You cut it, Zakary. You always do." He sounded like a toddler deprived of his favorite toy.

"Sloan—"

"This is not your beloved *Sun-Times.* This is Oak Hill. Tiny little middle-of-the-cornfield, Oak Hill, Indiana."

Sloan's arms tensed at his sides, and his fists clenched. "Greta and all her friends, many of whom own businesses that advertise in this barely-afloat paper, will be loo—"

The phone on Sloan's belt rang. He snatched it from the holster. "What is it?"

How could anyone get so overwrought about a dog show story—a badly written one at that?

What we have here is a failure to communicate. No, a failure to appreciate.

But Sloan's face—intent on the caller's information—made Zak pause. Breaking news? Maybe "Baxie" gets bumped anyway?

Sloan spun to his desk and grabbed a pad of paper.

"Right. Templeton Road, between County Road 4 and County Road 6. Right. Yes, of course, I know the hill, Barry."

So, it was the local Deputy Dan. Zak opened a file on his computer and motioned for Sloan to sit.

Sloan shook him off.

"Are you serious? How many?"

Zak peeked at Sloan's notes. *Tour bus of Miracle Mile shoppers hit by drunk college kid. Ten fatalities. Ten other serious injuries. Others minor injuries and walked away.*

He knew he shouldn't, but he smiled. He loved deadline news. He'd need to rebuild the front page—and Baxie was definitely gone.

Sloan grew quiet. Zak looked up to find Sloan staring at him.

"Of course, he's here. He's the editor. Yeah. No wait. Is the road closed?"

Zak stood.

A new storm-related lead story in the works. Who was available to cover? Vince Conover was at his desk browsing the Internet. Zak whistled and motioned him over.

"What'cha got, boss?" Vince didn't bother moving.

"No, Barry." Tension filled Sloan's words. "No, that's your job."

Sloan held out the phone, his face hard. "Barry needs to talk to you. Accident on Templeton." He dropped his gaze as he handed over his phone.

Zak took the phone and glanced at the clock. Fifteen minutes to deadline.

~

AFTER PARKING on the berm of the closed highway, Zak stomped on the Jeep's emergency brake and leaped out.

"Are you insane?" Sloan screamed, exiting the vehicle. His eyes darted from Zak to the fast-approaching officers and back to Zak. "How many cars did you force off the road?"

Ignoring him and the hollering investigators, Zak ran toward Kay's crumpled sedan in the median, barely registering the bus on its side. Why hadn't she stayed at the coffee shop?

"What do you think caution tape is for?" Sloan's voice pierced his concentration.

Zak forced it away. Why had he let Sloan come? After talking to Barry and discovering Kay had been involved in the accident, he agreed to anything to get on the road.

"You could have got us killed too."

Zak spun so fast Sloan couldn't keep his feet on the slippery road as he tried to avoid a collision. But it didn't matter. Zak's right hand connected with his assistant's jaw.

Sloan went down.

"She's not dead."

He turned back to the car and peered inside. Glass, snow, blood—lots of each. But no Kay.

"Zak!"

He whirled at the voice, arm cocked.

"Whoa. Zak, it's me. Sheriff Sanders." He held out his palms. "Barry."

"Where's my wife?" His voice sliced the night. He needed answers. Right now.

"Zak, let's get a hold of—"

Zak stepped in close enough to smell the sheriff's stale coffee breath. "My wife, Barry. Where is she?"

Barry moved back a step. "As I tried to tell you before you hung up, she's been airlifted to St. Joseph's. But Zak—"

"In South Bend? That's an hour from here. More in this weather." Zak stomped toward his Jeep, throwing a "sorry" over his shoulder, as Sloan stood from the road slush.

Barry grabbed Zak's arm. "Let me take you. Reg can finish up here." His voice was quiet and calming.

"Absolutely not." Zak shrugged away. He didn't need anyone's help. *He* would find her.

A hint of movement in the scrub beyond the mitigation fence along the road caught his attention. What was that? Was someone over there?

Still staring in the scrub, Zak said, "Where did you say Kay was?" He pivoted toward the sheriff again.

"St. Joseph's. Airlifted there. But Zak—"

"You're sure?"

"Of course. That's my job."

Zak glanced back to the side of the road. Most likely a swirl of snow. "Then I need to get there." He strode toward the Jeep.

"Zak, let me take you." Barry caught up to him. "I have an emergency vehicle. Lights. Sirens."

Zak considered only a few seconds before tossing his keys at Sloan's feet. "Leave it in *The Gazette* lot."

His mind plagued by worst-case scenarios and his body tired from the somnolent effect of the warm car, Zak hesitated when Barry pulled up to the ER entrance. During the drive, he'd called Mick, Kay's brother and his best friend, and their pastor, Dave. Both were on their way. But he'd find her first.

"Car 2, what's your 20?" The dispatcher's voice came over

the radio as he opened the patrol car door. During the drive, Barry had listened to the reports as they filtered in.

Zak opened the car door.

"Hang on. I'll be right there," Barry called after him. "Dispatch, this is Car 2. I'm at St. Joseph's in South Bend. What'cha got?"

He waved Barry off. While grateful for the ride, he refused any more delays. At least an hour, maybe ninety minutes, had already passed since Kay's airlift.

"Car 2, Reg is finished at the FATAC. Uh, Sloan White wants to press charges against Mr. Cooper."

Zak gestured obscenely to the radio, slammed the door, and marched to the emergency room.

Zak's cell phone pinged as the door into the emergency room slid open. He snatched it from his pocket, stepped into a puddle of water, and slipped. "What the ...?"

As he scrambled to catch his balance, his phone crashed into the puddle with an unmistakable *crack*. Not bothering to waste time to check the screen, he snatched it up, shoved it into his pant leg, and strode to the registration desk.

"Sorry about that." A harried woman behind the desk waved a hand at the wet spot. "Things are a little wild here tonight. Jamie, find a mop and clean that up." She turned to Zak. "What's your injury?"

Zak wiped his feet on the carpet. "Um. Sorry, what?"

"Are you injured?"

The ER was packed. People filled every available chair and most wall space. Doctors poked and prodded. Nurses scurried from patient to patient, arms full of clipboards. It was like a scene from the old *Chicago Hope* emergency room. "No, I'm not injured, but—"

"Jamie, where is that mop?" She glared over his shoulder.

"Look, I just want to check on the status of—"

"Miranda, this guy's throwing up."

He turned toward the voice.

A panic-stricken young woman, a girl really, stood in the waiting room, wide-eyed.

The woman at the triage desk, apparently Miranda, sighed. "Volunteers. God love 'em," she muttered, then plastered a fake smile on her face. "Hang on, Betsy. Be right there."

Zak leaned forward "My wi—"

"Sir, this is Emergency. If you're not injured or here to check on a patient, you'll need to go to the hospitality desk near the main entrance. Take the elevator up one floor and follow the signs. We're swamped." She stood and hurried toward the terrified volunteer. "I'm sorry."

Still feeling the effects of the drive, Zak hurried to the bank of elevators and pushed the call button. The doors of the elevator behind him opened, and he stepped in before pressing the button for Lobby and Admitting. The doors closed but instead of rising as he'd expected, the cab began to descend.

Great. This car must have been heading down already. Hang on, Kay.

He poked the Lobby button two or three more times and waited for the car to complete its downward slide before going back up. Kay would be okay. Hurt some maybe, probably, from the looks of the car, but okay.

When the elevator opened in the basement, Zak exited before remembering he was headed up. In front of him hung a sign. *Morgue Holding Area.* The pungent odor of death told him where he was just as well.

As a cub reporter on the police beat in Chicago, Zak had

often encountered death and its recognizable smell—an unforgettable mixture of sulfur and rotting flesh.

As he stepped back into the car, the pneumatic doors to the room *pfffd* open, and a kid pushing a gurney came through.

"Hold the elevator, please!" he called.

Zak almost let the door close so he could be on his way, but a woman's wrist hanging over the side of the gurney stopped him. A charm bracelet circled the wrist. With half of a mizpah heart. And a little airplane from Kitty Hawk, just like—

Zak reached for the chain around his neck. The one with the other half of the mizpah heart. Kay's gift to him on their tenth anniversary.

The heat rising in him and a lack of oxygen fuzzed his brain, and the floor rose to meet his face.

Chapter Three

Zak came to long before he let on.

What was the point?

He could tell from the whispered voices who was there. His best friend and Kay's brother, Mick, and his wife, Dreama. Pastor Dave, of course. They'd want to comfort him with platitudes that would offer no comfort.

All trying to make sense of the nonsensical.

"Zak? Are you with us, Zak?"

That was Dave. How long would they keep trying to rouse him? Could he wait them out? Would they just wander away if he pretended long enough?

"I don't think he can hear you, Pastor. He's still out."

Mick's voice sounded rough, gravelly, probably from crying. At least he had Dreama to lean on.

"Well, the orderly said he banged his head a good one when he hit the floor," Dreama chimed in.

The shock of Kay's death hung over the room like the brain fog of a too-early morning wake-up from a sound sleep. Only no one was asleep. As predicted in junior high, he was officially King of the Dead.

He thought of his two nicknames. Zee came from Kay, of course. She always said it was cute that both their nicknames were the first letters of their names. But King of the Dead he wore deeper—and unwillingly.

Zak chanced a slight opening of one eye, just as Mick reached for the arm of the bedside chair to lower himself into it.

"We're all stunned," Mick said.

Time passed in silence. What was there to say? "I'm sorry" wouldn't cut it. If he heard "She's in a better place," it would drive him mad. And if anyone piped up with "Well, God must've needed another angel," Zak would come out of his feigned unconsciousness and thrash them within an inch of their lives.

Right now, he did not care what God wanted. God took away his life and that would have to be answered for.

"You give and take away," that chorus from church that he used to love, rattled into his brain. How could he have liked something so annoyingly repetitive?

"I thought it best to ask Barry Sasser to stand watch outside the door," Dave said. "As word gets around on the prayer chain, folks will want to come down, and Zak would not want that right now, I'm sure."

Zak let out a too-audible sigh and wished he could take it back. His time to hide was ending.

"I think he's starting to come around, PD," Dreama said. "He might be trying to speak, I'm not sure. I can't make it out."

Zak stirred in his best imitation of someone coming out of unconsciousness.

Dave leaned closer. "Zak? Zak? Are you okay? Are you with us?"

He stirred again. Blinked his eyes open. A performance that deserved an Oscar.

Mick snapped his fingers in front of Zak's face.

When Dreama slapped Mick's hand, Zak almost laughed. But any humor died in his throat as she then kissed the backs of his fingers. "Zak?" She spoke softly. "Come back to us, Zak."

They didn't understand. He didn't want to come back. Not to a life without Kay. He wanted more than anything to be gone too. She was dead. His life was also over.

He no longer had a home. He lived in a house, but it would never be home again—never had been really. Kay had been his true home.

Why couldn't everyone go away and leave him alone? That's what he wanted. But they wouldn't leave. Not unless he made them. So, he opened his eyes.

"Go home." The words burned his throat and came out low.

Mick laid his hand on Zak's arm. "You want to go home?"

The question made sense but wasn't what Zak meant.

"Doc Rawlings wants you to hang out here for a while because of the concussion and all."

He turned his head toward Mick, but only saw Kay. He tried again.

"I want you to go home. All of you. Just go." Then he closed his eyes again.

Pastor Dave cleared his throat. "We want to be with you. You need us and we need you. We're all trying to deal with Kay's loss together. It just seems best to—"

"I know what's best for me, PD. I can't do this right now. I can't face this today." He opened his eyes. "I need to be alone with God right now. Talk to Him, probably yell a little —inside."

Dreama gazed at him, lips pursed. She wasn't making the purchase.

He scrambled. "Dreama, honey, I can't right now. But you'll all be with me in prayer. Besides, you need to be home with the kids. They need you too."

Bingo. He'd knocked that one out of the park. Her Mommy gene was going crazy, and she wanted to get home to hold Satchel and Jazz close.

Dreama got into his face. "Your BS isn't working. I want you to know that." Her voice was low, but full of compassion. Yet the struggle in her eyes told him he was right.

"Go, Dreama." He inclined his head toward the door. "They need you. You know I'm right."

She held his gaze a moment before taking Mick's hand and walking toward the exit.

"We'll be back tomorrow." The statement was more like a warning than a promise. "This is going to be hard for us all, Zak. Don't shut us out. We need each other."

Pastor Dave nodded his head to indicate he'd be following her in just a moment. As the door closed, he eyed Zak. "She's right, but you know that."

Dave bowed his head and close his eyes in a silent prayer. Then he lifted his head again. "I'm going to pray with you and then leave you alone as requested, but we *will* be back tomorrow. We aren't walking away."

The older man laid his hand on Zak's shoulder and the warmth in his touch almost made Zak cry, but he pushed the emotion down and endured. Kings didn't cry.

"Father, we do not understand anything that has happened tonight. So much suffering. So many in pain. But our brother and friend is hurting like he never has before."

"Like he has too often before." Zak stiffened and edited the prayer internally.

Dave went on, emotion choking his words. "We ask that you inhabit his mind and provide comfort—comfort and rest. We don't ask for answers, because there aren't any that will suffice. Right now, we only ask that you walk this road beside us and that you never leave us."

With the prayer over, Dave opened his eyes, and the compassion in them brought tears to Zak's.

"Barry is in the hall," Dave said. "He'll stay until visiting hours are over. He's watching over you."

Dave grabbed his coat off the chair and headed for the door. Before he reached it, he swiveled back around.

Zak bit his tongue.

"Oh, Barry also convinced Sloan to drop the charges, so there's that." Dave dipped his head and looked down. "You know I lost my first wife early, right?"

Zak had forgotten.

"You don't get over it. Not really. But you can get *through* it. With help."

Zak stared at the pastor whose preaching he'd listened to for the past ten years. He could not recall a single word from those sermons that offered him comfort now.

The pastor's shoulders slumped and he turned back toward the door.

"Dave?"

The man turned toward him again, eyes expectant.

"Would you ask Barry to come in? On your way out, I mean."

ZAK'S REPORTER mind never shut off. He did not want to hear Barry's report, but he listened anyway, the reporter in him taking mental notes according to the time-honored journalist's fact-gathering technique he'd learned in college. The Five W's and an H.

Who? Katharine Renee Sharp Cooper.

What? Dead, D.O.A., deceased.

Where? Behind the wheel of her Honda Accord. On the crest of the hill on Templeton Highway. Beneath the wheels of a tour bus that hit a sheet of black ice and slid sideways on the road.

When? December 11, 2021, 6:34 p.m.

Why? Drunk driver. College student from Templeton University on his way from one Christmas party to the next. Because of his excessive speed, he'd lost control of his car on the icy road and slid into the bus, which slid into the Accord. Contributing factor: Deceased was on her cell phone.

She'd tried to call him because the roads were worse than she thought. He'd made her promise to call.

In the end, her death was his fault. He shouldn't have let her go.

How? Her neck snapped when the bus slammed into her Accord. She had internal injuries, as well, but the neck injury did her in.

"Her death was quick." Barry didn't lift his face from his notes.

She'd been alive—barely—when airlifted but not when she arrived at the hospital.

So far, twelve people from the bus had also lost their lives. Several others were recovering. College Boy had walked away with only a few scratches and a broken pinkie finger on his right hand.

Zak's editor mind kicked in and assessed the story's value, clicking each item that made it newsworthy. Multiple fatalities?

Check. Alcohol involved? Check. Perp still alive? Check. Tragedy near Christmas? Check. Deceased well known in the community? Check.

Yep, front page news for sure. This story would sell papers. Photo on the front. Package it. Follow the story for several weeks, maybe months, while the kid is chased through the court system. Experts—and local pundits—would debate the safety of phones in cars. Lawsuits were already being filed against the bus company. The angles were unlimited.

Zak came out of his trance, his chest heaving. Tears soaked the front of his hospital gown.

The editor was efficient. All business.

The husband was falling apart.

OVER THE FIRST couple months after Kay's death, Zak did all the right things. Accepted condolences. Allowed people to say the trivial, occasionally painful, things people say when a loved one died. Smiled weakly. Demurred when insensitive clods asked if he'd remarry one day. Pretended not to notice when divorcees and widows tested the waters. And sank deeper into his grief.

Zak's assistant editor had adequately, if begrudgingly, kept the paper functioning until Zak's return—which was too soon, but what else did he have to do? If he had to spend another day roaming his house with memories of Kay in every nook and cranny, he'd drown in his grief. The *Gazette* became his reprieve.

Coworkers tiptoed around him, not talking about their spouses or their fun family times. Finally, and happily, they moved on and assumed Zak had as well.

He attended church but took no part in the services. He filled his spot in a pew—but not their pew. Though he stayed in the presence of God's people, by degrees, he stepped away from God. He'd abandoned Zak that December night. If God didn't need him, then he didn't need God either.

Chapter Four

When Zak saw Kay—or rather a woman who resembled Kay—across the sanctuary of Zion Community Church one Sunday, he tried to ignore her. Except the woman sat in their pew—right side, five rows back from the front, on the aisle.

The exact place Zak had not sat in twelve weeks.

The woman, whoever she was, kept stealing glances at him. His heart pounded out a barely discernible "what if" beat.

He couldn't help but recall, as he often did, the movement he'd noted, but not investigated, along the berm of the highway that night. While the police reports hadn't mentioned anything regarding the berm, his mind toyed with the inconsistency frequently.

But then he'd remember the hand on the gurney.

Today wasn't the only time he'd caught a glimpse of Kay. He'd seen her days after her funeral but dismissed it blaming his grief and lack of sleep. Besides, he still occasionally saw a woman who reminded him of his long-deceased mother.

This woman had, however, sat in their pew.

As the congregation stood and Pastor Dave gave the benediction, Zak moved out of his pew and strode to the back of the sanctuary. His nerves were as jangly as the guitars in R.E.M.'s "Losing My Religion" as he exited out a side door. But he kept moving toward the other end of the narthex. Sonny Joldersma, who patrolled the halls looking for the youths skipping out on the service, intercepted him.

Sonny sidled up to Zak and leaned in. "Caught the Sasser boy in the back hallway—with a girl."

"Good, that means he's healthy." Zak winked at the Elder of the Day.

As he tried to pass with a smile and a nudge, Sonny grabbed his elbow.

Zak tensed. The service would let out at any moment, and when the narthex filled with people, finding one new person would prove difficult.

"Speaking of healthy"—Sonny said in his transplanted Southern drawl—"Sharon and I have been worrying about you. Praying for you. How are you getting along? I mean since the incident."

Zak closed his eyes. The incident. Is that what everyone was calling it?

The organist played the closing music. In moments, the doors would open, and people would exit. Zak's breathing shallowed. Would the usual lie help him break free?

Zak scanned the lobby. "Oh, Sonny, I'm doing well. Fine, I guess."

"Considering."

"Yes, considering." Screaming at an elder would not be good form. "I do appreciate your prayers."

People pushed through the doors, filling the lobby and exiting to the parking lot.

Sonny kept his hold on Zak's elbow. "Well, Sharon and I

were wondering if you'd like to come over for dinner one night here soon?"

Anything. Anything, just turn me loose. Zak grabbed Sonny's hand to shake it—and to break free.

"That'd be nice. Tell Sharon to give me a call." Zak searched the lobby as people headed for the exit in droves. He'd missed her. He turned away from Sonny and headed for the door, dejected. Would he get another chance?

"Sharon's cousin will be in town next week," Sonny hollered as Zak sprinted for the parking lot. "Thought you might like to meet her. She lost her husband a year ago."

Zak grimaced as he left the building. Great. Another matchmaking opportunity he'd failed to see coming. Joy.

He stood in the parking lot, looking left, then right, then left again. Nope. He didn't see the woman anywhere. The opportunity passed and he headed for his car, disappointment filling his gut.

A week and a half later, he stood on the sidewalk outside *The Gazette* when the mystery woman drove past in an Accord —though hers was gold, not silver like Kay's had been.

Although Kay had preferred the gold one, Zak had talked her into the silver because the color was sportier.

He ran after the car but was moments too late as she turned left at the next light and disappeared.

While strange, Zak again dismissed the sighting as a coincidence. A yearning of the heart. But he daydreamed about Kay all evening before settling into a restless sleep.

Throughout the next several weeks, he'd see a Kay about every other week. In the grocery. At the park. Going into the women's room at church. Some were women who reminded him of Kay, but some were ... more.

He played the "Spot the Kay" game, a morbid Where's Waldo-esque compulsion. Then, at times during the day, he found himself *searching* for her. Anticipating her. The sightings comforted him, made him feel less alone.

One day in mid-April, Zak sat at his desk. With the sightings increasing to nearly every week, he wondered if his obsession with seeing Kay was healthy.

How could remembering the good times and seeking some semblance of normal be unhealthy?

Although he saw Mick every day, Zak didn't share his concerns. Once or twice, when they were talking about Kay, he'd almost mentioned seeing her. Had Mick noticed the woman at church who looked like her too? But the notion that his sightings were special—just for him—silenced the question. He feared talking about them might threaten their existence.

He tried to guess where he'd spot her next and, like a boy with a crush, had written a list of places to go where he might "accidentally" run into a Kay.

Zak blinked and glanced up from his desk, where he was supposed to be working on tomorrow's news budget instead of tinkering with his list. He needed to get a grip. Standing, he crumpled the list and tossed it into his wastebasket.

Everything in his office—from the photo on his desk to the ugly chair Kay had forced him to remove from the house to the Bill the Cat stuffed animal on the shelf—reminded him of Kay.

"I've got to get out of here." He dialed Mick's extension.

"Yaas, boss?" his brother-in-law drawled.

Zak smiled despite his mood.

"How 'bout some lunch, oh enslaved one?"

"Sure. What's the matter?" Mick's tone took on a concerned edge.

Zak lowered his head. Mick was a good friend—and more. He ought to tell him. Maybe at lunch. "Oh, you know. Just chasing ghosts around the office. I think some pie would help, though."

"Pie is never a bad thing." The worry in Mick's voice vanished. "I'll be in the hall before you hang up the phone."

Zak chuckled and hung up. He grabbed his coat from the coatrack—another Kay touch—and headed for the door. But he backtracked and retrieved his crumpled list from the wastebasket.

After opening the sheet of paper, he smoothed it flat on his desktop. Then he folded it in quarters and tucked the list into his inner coat pocket.

The paper warmed his heart like a small blanket, shielding it from the bitter cold of the world.

AT LUNCH, he almost told Mick about his Kay sightings. But as they talked about sports, work, church, and music, he held back the confession. Sharing her with her brother went along the lines of talking about their lovemaking. Neither of them would be comfortable with the discussion. So, he held his secret close.

When he got home for the night and scrounged through old VHS tapes for their wedding video, he wished for someone he *could* talk to. Someone who would listen to his grief. Be a shoulder to cry on. With his mother dead and his father presumably dead, Zak needed a confidant. Gram was gone. He was an only child. No cousins. No extended family.

Kay had been his world.

He had a new understanding of the word *bereft*. Each day he lived "deprived of somebody or something loved or valued." He "lacked in something desirable or necessary" and was "filled with a sense of loss."

"That would explain why your photo appears in the dictionary next to the word," he said to nobody. As a word guy, some days were harder than others.

Apparently, the wedding video had disappeared the same way one sock sometimes vanished in the wash. He gave up his hunt and opened the "Recordings" menu on the TV. A foolish comedy would occupy his time—and his mind.

"How the Grinch Stole Christmas" appeared on the device's menu. Recorded the day of Kay's death. Well, he *could* use some Seussian, three-sizes-heart-growing encouragement.

He held a soft spot for the Grinch. In many ways, he related to the misanthropic nature of Dr. Seuss's character that always reminded Zak of an evil Muppet.

As he clicked on the title, he flashed back to asking Kay to record the show. He berated himself for the eleventy-hundredth time for such a lamentable conversation. Their final exchange had no profession of undying love. No last kiss. Not even a common, everyday "I love you" on the way out the door.

He'd give anything to relive that day. Maybe, with a different approach, he'd change the outcome.

But no, the last words he'd shared with the woman who was his life's breath had been about recording a television show that played every Christmas on one station or another. With the show available on DVD, he could have bought it and watched the special in the heat of July.

Oh Kay, I miss you so.

Three quarters of the way through the show, as little Cindy Lou Who was safely tucked back into bed, a news crawl popped up at the bottom of the screen. Zak's heart froze.

Fatal multi-vehicle accident outside of Templeton. Details at the newsbreak. Stay tuned to Channel 16, your friend for life.

Zak gripped the remote but couldn't make his fingers function. His mind screamed, "Turn it off," but his body refused to listen.

The news anchor for Channel 16 appeared on the screen, her face a study of practiced empathy. "Tonight, a Christmas tragedy on the Templeton Highway and another shocking reminder of the importance of naming a designated driver. For the story, Trey Lawrence is on location."

As the scars on his heart ripped open again, the tangled mess of Kay's silver Accord and all the other vehicles involved, including College Boy's Chevy, filled the screen. While he'd seen still photos in the paper, this was the first time he'd viewed the live scene of the accident. Red and blue emergency lights flashed in the background. One glimpse of the cars, and it was clear no one could have survived. Yet College Boy had.

Zak's gaze riveted on the Accord, hungry and terrified for any glimpse of Kay in the wreckage or along the road.

"Excessive speed and alcohol certainly played a role in this tragic scene." Trey's report registered in the fringes of Zak's mind. "Back to you in the newsroom, Scout."

Zak's fingers finally obeyed his commands, and he shut the TV off.

He sat in his recliner, his brain hovering far from the reality of his body.

"Hello, darling."

Zak screamed and bolted from his chair whirling toward the voice.

"Oh." He exhaled, relief flooding through him. "It's only you, Kay. You scared me to d ..."

He rubbed his eyes, but she remained standing before him. How? Had his grief finally pushed him over the edge?

"It *is* you, isn't it?"

Chapter Five

After Kay's unexpected—what should he call it? Appearance? Zak dug out the pamphlet from Wyatt's Funeral Home about grief counseling. Inside was an invitation for a free get-acquainted session from Dr. Harley Culp.

Though she hadn't stayed long that night, the fact—could he even call it that?—she'd materialized had shaken Zak. He didn't believe he was losing his mind, but he had seen—and talked with—his wife five months after her death.

He was sure that was not a part of the grieving process.

Part of him wanted her to visit again. He tried but couldn't conjure her at will. He'd walked around the house while focusing on her. He even watched *The Grinch* again, but when she hadn't returned after the news break, he'd shut the show off and gone to bed with a mixture of relief and disappointment.

Two nights later, he'd entered the sunroom and found her curled in her favorite chair reading a book. They had a short, tentative conversation.

The next morning he had another brief, decidedly normal, encounter over coffee.

As he entered Dr. Culp's office, he determined to find out if his experience was normal. But he wasn't at all sure how to explain.

Zak sat in one of the two chairs across from Harley's desk. Since Kay had always chosen the left seat, he'd opted for the right one. Too bad there wasn't a couch to lie down on.

The office was decorated in what he assumed was an attempt to make occupants comfortable—and comforted. Warm colors. Overstuffed chairs. Generic framed photos of people expressing various positive emotions.

When Dr. Culp walked in, Zak's comfort vanished and his apprehension rose. What had he gotten himself in to? Nevertheless, the counseling session went well until near the end when the reporter in Zak asked Harley if he'd ever lost anyone close. The counselor admitted he had not.

"So, your advice is based on head knowledge, not heart knowledge, Dr. Culp." Zak filed the counselor's advice in his mental recycle bin. "You assume it works, but you don't really know, is that accurate?"

Harley gnawed on his pencil eraser, which further increased Zak's distrust. If the good doctor couldn't cure his own nervous tics, how could he cure anyone else?

"Just because I've not put this advice into practice myself, doesn't mean it doesn't work. Clinical studies as far back as 1969 as well as research from Dr. Kubler-Ross, whom I'm sure you've heard of—have shown there are roughly seven stages of grief that ea—"

"Kubler-Ross listed five stages, didn't she?" The reporter in Zak couldn't let the factual error pass.

"Yes, she did, but other researchers expanded on her studies. I tend to agree with the seven stages: Shock and Denial; Pain and Guilt; Anger and Bargaining; Depression,

Reflection, and Loneliness; The Upward Turn; Reconstruction; and Acceptance or Hope."

Dr. Culp paused.

Zak nodded. Where would the doctor place him on the spectrum?

"Now, each person won't go through the stages in the same order or over the same length of time," the doctor said, "but many people do process death in similar, yet distinct, ways."

"Similar, yet distinct?" Zak rested his left hand on the arm of the adjacent chair. He wanted to pursue this line of questioning but wondered how much he could—should—share.

One thing still concerned him, but it was pointless, almost silly, to bring it up. Surely it was innocent, and completely understandable, given his situation.

The doctor cleared his throat and began his wrap-up.

"Zak, you're making positive strides toward working through your grief. You're moving through the stages—a little back and forth yet between denial and bargaining, but that's to be expected. But remember, it's only been five months. Give yourself some space—some grace. Grief isn't a short process."

Zak stared at the man, his chin resting in the palm of his left hand, but said nothing.

"On your way out, Joyce will give you a handout about the seven stages of grief," Dr. Culp continued. "For our next session, I'd like you to read over that sheet and find where you think you are. It may be in-between two stages. That's okay. I'd also like you to share your best memory of your life with Kay."

Zak raised his finger to answer, reconsidered, then rose.

"Was there something else?" Harley smiled. "If not, I'll see you again in two weeks."

"Just one other thing," Zak glanced to his left as he returned to the chair. "You mentioned people go through similar, yet distinct phases of grief."

"Yes. Your denial phase, for instance, may be longer or shorter or more intense or less obvious than mine—"

"If you had any."

"Naturally. As I was saying, though our phases would not play out the same, we both would go *through* the denial phase in one way or another."

Harley gathered his notes and began to stand.

"I'm talking to her." Zak hadn't intended to blurt the truth out.

"Talking to whom?"

"Kay, of course." Zak gave the doctor a wry smile. "Is that distinct or is it fairly normal?"

Harley sat back down and picked up his pencil and pad.

"It can be normal," he said. "When you say, 'I'm talking to her,' what do you mean?"

"Have I just become interesting, doctor?"

Harley circled his hand in the air.

Zak sighed. "I mean just that. I'm talking to her. Asking her what I should have for dinner. Pointing out idiocies in the TV commercials like always. Asking what it's like—being dead, I mean. I'm *talking* to her."

"Is she talking back?"

"Would that be distinct?"

When Harley didn't answer, Zak sat, glanced left again, then down to his lap. He tapped the arm of the chair. Some misdirection was in order. "No, of course not, Harley. How could she? She's dead."

Harley leaned back. To better appraise Zak? "Yet you're talking to her." The doctor resumed chewing on his eraser.

Zak sighed. This session was officially off the rails, and he needed to find a way out before he said too much. "Occasionally, yes, but not every day." *Not yet.*

"Why do you think you're doing that?"

If only Zak hadn't exposed his vulnerability. His emotions. It was silly, he knew, but he had the impression he was telling tales out of school on his wife.

He fidgeted in his seat.

What would Harley believe? What would get Zak out the door?

"Maybe because there isn't anyone else to talk to. Because I miss her." Zak turned his face away from Dr. Culp and toward the empty chair.

"Because I love her." He drew in a sharp breath.

A small red light on the phone sitting on the far corner of Harley's desk blinked. Harley grabbed the handset and punched a button before turning his back to Zak.

"Please ask them to wait, Joyce." His lowered voice did not prevent Zak from hearing his side of the conversation. "Yes, I understand. I'll just be a moment."

Harley hung up and looked at Zak. "I'd like to see you again next week."

Coming had been a mistake. "Why? Do you think I'm losing my mind?"

"I doubt it, but I believe you would benefit from discussing this further." The man shifted in his chair. "Talking to a deceased spouse is not unusual, particularly with couples who have been close or lived together for many years. In those cases, it's sort of a habitual response."

Did Harley consider him one of *those* cases?

The doctor's eyes held a challenge, but also a depth of compassion he'd overlooked in his rush to judge the man. Zak pulled a tissue from the box in front of him and dabbed at his eyes. Tears were never far away these days. Yet his reporter's mind could not leave a detail unexplored.

"Spill it, Harley. You've left a 'but' hanging in the air."

The counselor seemed to wrestle with his thoughts for

several moments. Searching for the right thing to say or deciding what not to say?

This is not a good pause.

When Harley looked at Zak again, he'd made his decision.

"But if it progresses? If she talks to you or if you see her?" Harley searched Zak's face. "That could signal larger problems. That—"

"What kind of problems?"

Harley hesitated again. "Let's talk about that next time. For now, know there's also a phenomenon sometimes called bereavement hallucinations. Perceptions of something or someone who is not really there. Particularly in cases of a loved one's traumatic, unexpected death."

Zak squirmed.

"There's nothing necessarily wrong with them, and the experiences are very common and ..."

"And what, Harley?"

He set down his pencil, interlaced his fingers, and leaned across the desk. "And usually benign."

"Usually?" Zak swallowed.

"Yes, usually."

The red light on the phone blinked again.

"Read the material Joyce gives you and assess yourself—honestly. And don't forget to set another appointment for next week. I'm sure the paper's Employee Assistance Program or insurance will cover it."

Zak inhaled deeply, trying to get his ducks realigned. He couldn't afford to fall apart—not now. He was almost out from under Harley's scrutiny.

There would be no more appointments, particularly none the paper's insurance would pay for. The last thing he needed was for Sloan to discover Zak was seeing a shrink. Small town newsrooms were notorious for their inability to keep secrets.

Besides, he wasn't losing it. Harley said so.

"Thanks, Harley. I'll be all right—and I know where to find you, if not."

"Give it a couple days thought, Zak. See you soon?"

Zak smiled noncommittally and walked out the door.

"Well, you almost blew that." Kay said from behind him as the door closed.

Chapter Six

As always, driving into Oak Hill Cemetery stirred angry, frightful memories Zak Cooper needed to forget. He reached across the interior of the Jeep searching for Kay's hand —for the comfort it represented.

It wasn't there. *She* wasn't there.

In the two weeks since the appointment with Dr. Culp, Zak had talked with her many times. The conversations were always too short. He didn't try to understand it.

Whenever he tried to touch her, it was like she wasn't there —even though he could see her. He didn't reach *through* her like in a *Casper the Friendly Ghost* cartoon. But she was always just beyond his reach.

As he pulled next to the town founder's place of prominence inside the cemetery gate, the towering granite slab topped with a Celtic cross, he shivered and not merely from the chill.

He stared at the large marker, the site of the childhood prank that had earned him the King of the Dead nickname. A dare, and a silly one at that. But at the time, it had been too real, coming only months after his mother's death.

"Dare me? Dare me to do what?" Zak had asked Q that day. His friend's real name was Aaron Quiesling, but only their teachers called him that.

He and Q stood in front of the cemetery gates, two blocks down Fisher Street from Montgomery Elementary.

"Dare ya to go into the cemetery, stand on top of Ol' Montgomery's tombstone, and holler 'I am the King!'"

"Why?" Zak leaned back and crossed his arms over his chest.

"Because," Q said with a finality that mocked the question as ridiculous. "Because, Zak, I think you're a chicken. *Bawk. Bawk. Bawk.*"

Zak wasn't afraid of anything, which Q well knew. Still, he wasn't about to let a dare go unanswered—even a ridiculous one.

"You're on." Zak angled toward the entrance. "You coming?"

"Nah." Q feigned disinterest. "I can see from here whether you do it or not—and you won't, 'cause you're chicken."

"Suit yourself, Quiesling." The emphasis on Q's last name earned him a single finger salute.

He strode toward the monument, faking a confidence he didn't possess. The crunch of gravel under his feet brought back memories of his mother's burial in this cemetery. Truthfully, he was more than a little creeped out by graveyards. But if Q realized that, Zak would never hear the end of it.

His mom had died of breast cancer. Shortly after, his father left Oak Hill—and Zak—and no one had heard from him since. His dad wasn't dead, as far as Zak knew, but he may as well have been. Gram certainly wished he were.

Distracted with thoughts of his parents, Zak approached the tombstone. He climbed up and gave Q a thumbs up. He linked his arm through the lower circle of the cross and leaned out over the slab.

"I am King!" Zak pumped his fist in the air above him. "See? No big—"

"Ready to die, King Zak?" A voice rasped behind him as the owner of it grabbed his ankle.

Zak screamed.

Not the oh-man-don't-walk-up-on-me-like-that yelp he gave when Gram surprised him in the hallway. No. This was a girlie-girl scream that came from the bottoms of his Red Ball Jets to the top of his Cubs baseball cap.

He was not ready to die.

Zak leaped from the stone, still screaming, and fled down the gravel road.

Q's laughter stopped him. "Zak Cooper. King of the Dead," Q had crowed, along with the ankle-pullers—more of Zak's buddies, including Mick. Q had set the whole thing up as a joke.

But that scream—the one he could never live down—and his resulting nickname had echoed through Zak's life ever since. The deep scar had never completely healed.

Even though no one called him that anymore, the moment had implanted itself in his memory where it festered and grew —and deepened. On that long-ago March afternoon, Zak had realized he and everyone he cared about *would* die. Like his mother and for all the good he was now, his father—regardless of how much, or how well, he loved them.

Zak buried his face in his hands as the memory receded. Now the Kingdom of the Dead included his wife.

Zak stuffed down the pain once again, shifted the Jeep into

drive, and headed for his weekly destination. Serenity Park, Quadrant 3, Plot 4.

Serenity. That's rich.

About halfway into the cemetery, a few rows past his mother's grave, Zak parked along the narrow road and turned they key off. He inhaled a deep breath, opened the door, and placed his feet on that gravel once again.

He leaned back into the Jeep and picked up the small potted fake geranium that sat on Kay's seat next to his well-worn copy of Tolkien's *The Fellowship of the Ring*. Holding the book brought him an indescribably delicious pain. Each night, he and Kay had read the trilogy to each other regularly, chapter by chapter.

She found the tale endlessly engaging, and he enjoyed the bookish foreplay.

Overwhelmed by grief, Zak sank into the driver's seat and called out again to a God he wasn't sure he believed in anymore.

Lord, this cannot be your plan. Your Word says you will not give us more than we can handle.

He wiped the tears from his cheeks.

You lied. I cannot handle this.

With effort, Zak bit down the mounting dread, stood again, only this time on the Jeep's running board, and smacked his head on the upper frame.

"Ow!" He dropped the pot on the gravel and reached for the crown of his head. "How many times will I do that before I learn?"

"So far, one thousand forty-three by my count," said the familiar voice.

"Ha-ha. Very funny, Kay."

"It's nice of you to come by so often, darling, but it's not necessary. You could read to me anywhere."

"I know." Zak knelt to pick up the flower. "But what would the groundskeeper think if I didn't brush the snow off your headstone and replace the fake flowers every now and then?"

Even though he couldn't touch her, hold her hand, seeing Kay again salved the wound her death had opened in his heart. He needed his wife—had always needed her. She healed him in ways no other human could.

After replacing the weatherworn, fake daffodils with the geranium, Zak returned to the Jeep, climbed inside, and picked up the book. "Where did we stop last time?" Zak stifled a yawn.

"Never mind," Kay said from the passenger seat. "I already know the story, and there can't be a lot of fun in it for you, anymore."

The catch in her voice as she turned away, confirmed that Kay needed him as much as he needed her. At least for this moment.

"That's not why I'm reading—you know that's not it." Zak reached his hand out to caress her hair before stopping in midair.

"I'm ... I'm tired, that's all. Busy day at the paper. Sloan and Mick got into another argument. Waxman called a special meeting to ..."

As she turned back to face him, the snare of her eyes gripped his heart. The love reflected there sliced through his defenses, which were never strong when it came to her. He moaned quietly, covering it with a cough.

"Never mind, Kay. What happened today doesn't matter. I'm here now. Where were we?"

She held him in an intense gaze until he fanned the pages of the book.

"You were almost to where Frodo looks into the Mirror of Galadriel," Kay said. "I've always loved that line about how the mirror shows what was, what is, and what is yet to be."

Sometimes Zak tried to run from the places his mind took him, knowing no good could lie there. But he never ran for too long or too far.

WALKING through the front doors of *The Gazette* each day was safe, almost normal. Every man embraced a dream that sustained him, and this paper was Zak's. With Kay more or less gone, he had even more reason to live for his work. He stood in the entrance to the newsroom and inhaled deeply.

"Nice of you to stroll in with half the morning gone already, Zakary."

Zak exhaled and shifted with a thin smile toward his assistant editor.

"But don't fret," Sloan said. "The crisis is under control, as usual. Although, if you had bothered to look at my budget yesterday—like I asked—this could have been avoided."

"Good morning, Sloan." Zak tried to ignore the man's peevish attitude and avoid his laborious explanation of what "this" was. "How was your weekend?"

With a huff, Sloan slunk away, moving from one imagined crisis to the next. The man didn't smoke, but his constant harping and complaining spread secondhand angst in his wake.

Charles Waxman, the paper's publisher, had passed over Sloan for the editor position and hired Zak. Sloan possessed no people or management skills. His news sense was good, though he tended to overcompensate for a paper the size of *The Gazette.*

Sloan must have missed the lessons in kindergarten about being nice. He should have been let go by now. But in a show of extreme cowardice, Waxman had made it clear four years ago that Sloan came with the job and since he was the assistant editor, he was Zak's responsibility.

"I don't want that ferret racing into my office every day with a new complaint," Waxman had said. "Deal with and handle him. I won't fire him, nor will I demote him. He's good and he's loyal—but he's a pain in the patoot. The paper wouldn't be what it is without him."

Upon hearing the stipulation, Zak had almost declined the job. But his better sense had overruled his pride. If he could overlook his officiousness, Sloan was dedicated and knew his craft. After four tense months of learning how to work with each other, they eased into a pattern they were both comfortable with. Sloan detested Zak and his ideas, and Zak tolerated Sloan.

"Good morning, boss." Nancy Lopez, Zak's much appreciated and underpaid administrative assistant, grinned. "Coffee's on your desk, but since you're so late, you'll have to reheat it—yourself, of course."

"Of course. On Sloan's team today, are you Nancy?"

Even though she was twentyish years his senior, she stuck out her tongue like she was a pre-teen girl.

"*Pfft*. If I were, you wouldn't know until they pulled your red pen from your back."

Zak chortled and entered his office, which reminded him of every editor's office he'd seen in every movie made about newspapering. Three-quarters high glass walls, with his name and *Editor* etched into the glass door.

After closing the door, Zak sat at his desk, took a gulp of cold coffee, grimaced, and swallowed. He would not give Nancy the pleasure of watching him nuke his cup.

As much as he loved his job, being in his office made him think about Kay and the hole she'd left in his public life, as well as his private one. In an instant, his excitement from the start of the new day dissolved. He took his glasses off, cupped his face in his hands, and surrendered once more to his grief.

"Don't cry, baby, this chair isn't that ugly." Kay sat in the chair and crossed her legs. "It really does need to go, though. Overstuffed is so not you. Besides, whoever sits in it feels small and insignificant."

Looking up through his fingers, Zak sighed and wiped his moist hands on his pant legs. "You asked me to get it out of the house, so I did. You never said I couldn't bring it to work. It has to be big enough to go with this humongous metal desk of Rob's."

Rob York, the paper's editor before Zak, had ordered a desk roughly the size of Rhode Island. For Rob, size really was everything. Big was okay. Bigger was better. He ruled the paper from his office, holding court behind his desk and handing down pronouncements.

Zak preferred a more collegial management style—functionality over form. Big certainly worked in the right time and place, but he preferred subtler techniques. Waxman was amazed at the results Zak had coaxed out of Rob's beleaguered staff in a brief time, but the boss hadn't yet approved his request for a new desk.

"Why don't you let me fix this office up?" Kay said. "A new coat of paint, a few plants, a few paintings, a couple of knick-knacks, a new desk chair ...."

"You leave my chair alone, woman." Zak pointed at her. "It was my father's, and you know it."

"It's no wonder your back hurts. That chair was an antique before the word ergonomics existed. At least let me repair the leather."

When he spun around to pick up the day's proofs from the top of his credenza, Zak smiled. "Okay, but no knick-knacks. Painting and plants, yes, but no knick-knacks, Kay."

"And no froufrou colors." He looked over his shoulder. "I can't ... Kay? Hon?"

He sank into his chair. He never knew when to expect her or when she would leave. Never a hello or goodbye—just like that last day.

You're all around me, darling, even when I can't see you.

Zak lowered his head into his hands, losing himself again in memories.

"Hey, boss. Lunch today?"

Zak glanced up and smiled, glad for the distraction of Mick's regular morning visit. Shaking the past loose, he invited Mick, along with his customary powdered donut, to sit.

"I'd love to go to lunch, my portly pal, but I can't." Zak grimaced. "Big editors meeting today. Budgets, forecasts, belt-tightening, dire threats of imminent closure—you name it, we got it."

"As if Waxman would ever close this place."

"Nah, but management has to shake the bones every now and then to appease the gods of chance." He opened his calendar for the week. "How about Thursday? We'll catch a quick sandwich, pie, and coffee at Maydene's after we put page one to bed."

"Well, okay, if your editor friends are more important than your brother-in-law."

"Never. But more demanding, for sure," Zak said.

Mick nodded and stood.

"Oh, hold on." He spat donut crumbs and flopped back into the chair. "Sloan asked me for a drawing of a kumquat for an upcoming food section front. What is a kumquat? Some kind of vegetable or something, right?"

"I don't know, Mick. Little orangey things?" Zak shrugged. "Ask Sloan. He's the one who wants it. You want me to Google it for you?"

The sarcasm earned him a glare, which was hard to take serious from a man with powdered sugar on his upper lip. "I'm pretty sure it's a fruit."

"Fruit, vegetable, whatever."

"We're doing a food front on the kumquat? That's hardly a northern Indiana staple."

"Yeah, something about Casey's taking out an ad because they got a special deal on kumquats ... I don't know. Sloan asked for it."

"You want me to talk to him?" Zak hoped not.

"Nope, just wondered if you knew what one was. I don't feel so stupid since you don't either, Mr. Smarty Pants. Later."

As Mick left, Zak lifted the proofs from his desk and started reviewing B1, the sports page, red pencil in hand.

"Oh, hey, one more thing," Mick returned and slumped in the wingback chair. "May 4 is the VFW Family Spring Fling Dance, and Dreama wants to go. She'd like you to, ahem, come with us."

"Hmm. Wednesday? Can't, sorry." Zak knocked twice on his desktop. "Pass."

"Oh, see, ha. That's funny, because it wasn't a request," Mick said. "It's Dreama's birthday, if you don't remember, and, sorry, but I'm afraid she insists on going to the dance."

"So, take her." Zak rubbed his forehead, anticipating where this was going.

"You know I don't dance, Zee. How long have we known each other?"

"And on her birthday, your wife would rather dance with me than with her own husband?"

"Duh. She loves me, but she walks on her feet, you know?"

"Whatever."

"So, I can tell Dreama it's a go?"

"Tell her whatever you want, Mick." Zak gave in to the inevitable. "I'll be there."

"Great. Thanks."

Mick stood and headed for the door, where he paused, turned around, and shifted uncomfortably in place.

"Spill it, Mick. I can see it trying to get out like the alien in that guy's stomach."

"It's just," he stammered. "I know it's early, but ..."

Zak waited. When Mick had something to say, it was best to let him say it in his own time.

"Like I said, it's early, but I want you to know that, well, that if you wanted to bring a date to the dance, I wouldn't think bad of you."

A date? The idea gobsmacked him. Dating was not even knocking on the corners of his mind, at this point.

"Mick, no. I-I, no," Zak sat, feeling like the wind had been knocked out of him. "No, I do not want to bring a date."

Relief flooded his friend's face. "Well, I just wanted you to know you can. I, we ... Dreama and I don't expect you to stay single and in mourning for the rest of your life. Kay wouldn't want that."

Zak snagged a Junior Mint from the bowl on his desk and threw it at Mick's head. "You are the biggest dork ever."

Mick caught the mint, unwrapped it, and popped it in his mouth.

"Thanks, I guess." He spoke around the candy. "I adored my sister and miss her every day. I can't imagine how hard it is for you. But when you do want to, date again, I mean, it's okay."

Tossing his candy wrapper onto the sports page, Mick headed for the door again, before turning back once more.

"Oh, at the dance, make sure you do that thing with Dreama that she likes," he said, hand on the doorknob.

"That 'thing' is called a dip, Mick."

"Yeah? Well, your little 'dip' always makes Micky *incredibly happy*."

"That is so sad—and somewhat sick, I might add."

"I'm a simple man with simple needs, Zak. French silk pie, *Monday Night Football*, and the leftovers of another man's dancing abilities."

He stepped out of the office, then came right back in. "When it's time to move on, you'll know."

Chapter Seven

Jenny Miller was running away. From what, she didn't quite know.

Definitely from Jonas, who couldn't be trusted to keep his marriage vows. But also, maybe, from her marriage, which even before Jonas stumbled—twice—was mediocre.

So, she ran to Aunt Sarah's home in Templeton, Indiana, a small college town three hours south of Chicago. Her options for escape were slim since her parents had died, but Jenny needed space for a while. A place where she could reconnect with herself, her daughter—and her God.

Currently under Sarah's appraising gaze, Jenny wondered if she'd invaded her aunt's solitude long enough.

"Do you remember Maydene Gunderson?" Sarah asked. "She's the one who skipped out of high school for a day, with your mother and me. We drove to Lake Michigan and sunned on the beach."

Jenny nodded. She remembered the story well. Two years younger than Sarah, her mother had enjoyed reliving it often during her final days in the hospital. The three girls chose the same day their pastor and his young family exchanged church duties for the restorative effects of the beach and a picnic basket. The girls had been caught.

But the pastor, they later discovered, had told the church secretary to cancel his appointments because he was going calling. When he saw the girls, he was nearly as shocked as they were, and an unspoken agreement was reached as the three girls nodded and headed farther down the beach.

"Well, I don't see her much these days, but Maydene and her husband own the Main Street Café & Emporium in Oak Hill," Sarah leaned in to look Jenny in the eyes. "I hear through mutual acquaintances that they're in need of a waitress."

"A waitress?" Jenny said. "Wouldn't that be funny?"

"Funny, dear? How?" Sarah asked.

"Oh, nothing. Just thinking of ..." she sighed. Images of Jonas and his waitress flooded her mind. "Just an old acquaintance. It was nothing."

Sarah's pursed lips and raised eyebrows indicated she wasn't buying that. Thankfully, her aunt let it go.

"Well, Maydene needs a waitress, and I'm sure she'd give you every consideration if you're interested, dear. She's a ... a good woman," Sarah said.

Catching the tone of her aunt's reply, Jenny opted to postpone the decision—for a while.

"I'll think about it." She bent to pick up another of Susan's dolls. She wished for the hundredth time that girl could remember to keep her toys in their bedroom. Why was that so difficult?

Susan, her delightful, beautiful, bright-as-a-supernova six-year-old daughter, was a little careless—with her toys and with her affections. Similar in that way to Jonas.

I'm not going to think about him.

As wonderful as Sarah was to allow them to stay with her,

she had never married—let alone had a child—and was not used to having a young child around. Finding another housing solution was moving up on Jenny's list—if she intended to stick around.

Whap. The swinging door from the kitchen slammed open, and Susan ran into the room with a new discovery in her hands —and smelly creek mud clinging to her from head to toe.

"Mommy, Mommy lookit what I found in the backyard." Susan's eyes widened with delight. "It's a frog an' I won't get warts or anything, I promise."

Jenny glanced from her daughter to her aunt—who sighed in resignation—and then back to her daughter. A trail of muddy footprints led from the living room through the dining room. She could probably follow the trail into the kitchen and down to Little Brush Creek.

"Can I keep him, Mommy? Can I?" Susan beamed. "His name is Freddy!"

Sarah reclined in her chair with a wry smile.

"Yes, dear, you may keep Freddy." Jenny had to work hard not to smirk as Sarah nearly fell out of her rocker. "I think I have an extra shoe box in the closet you can use for now until we can find a small terrarium.

"But, first, get yourself back outside and clean up. Then you can go get the box for Freddy and *then* get your little rear end back down here and help me clean up this mess. Next time please remember to wipe your feet."

"Yes, Mommy." Susan whirled toward her great aunt, a sincere sorrow written on her face. "Sorry, Aunt Sarah." Kissing Freddy on his head, Susan twisted around and headed back out the door.

Jenny sighed and looked at her aunt. They both broke up laughing.

"I'll call Maydene tomorrow," Jenny said. "Oak Hill's not

far from here. We probably drove past the restaurant when we came through. Who knows? Maybe waitressing will be my life's calling."

Oak Hill might be just the place to catch her breath.

THE NEXT DAY, Jenny drove to Main Street Café and Emporium to apply for the job. From the look of the place, she expected a woman similar to Flo from Mel's Diner on the TV sitcom *Alice*—big hair and an even bigger attitude. Instead, she found a no-nonsense little twig of a woman who was the queen of her corner of the world.

After Jenny finished the paperwork, she and Maydene sat in one of the booths along the north wall. The process was informal. Following a few minutes of answering questions about herself, Susan, and her experience—which was none— Maydene offered Jenny the job.

"You're hiring me? Today? What about the other applicants?" Jenny's eyes widened. "I've never been a waitress before. You don't even know if I can make coffee, let alone serve it."

"Are ya' trying to talk me out of it, honey?" Maydene released an easy laugh. "At my café, the most important part of waitressing is the ability to talk easily with people—and you did that fine, without once checking your phone. I can teach you the rest, but I can't teach personality."

"Run, child," a male voice shouted from the kitchen. A man who bore a resemblance to Sheriff Woody from the *Toy Story* movies, sans cowboy hat, peered through the pass-through. "Run, and don't look back. The woman's insane."

Maydene pressed her palms to the red-checked tablecloth

and turned around. "Abe, hush, you. Take that trash out, and I mean now. I've seen you ignoring it all morning."

Jenny snickered and raised her hand to cover her mouth.

Maydene laughed, gave Jenny a wink, and hooked her head toward the kitchen. "Ignore the ol' gizzard. Trust me. I've been doing it for forty-five years."

Her expression softening, Maydene sighed. "He's a charmer, my husband, God love 'im. I know I do."

She closed her eyes for a moment, as if lost in memory. When she opened them again, she studied Jenny with an intensity that surprised her.

"I'm a fun-lovin' gal, honey, but God's given me a gift for seeing the measure of a person—and it's not always a pleasant gift. You should have seen Abe back then. My family thought I was insane. But I trust what God shows me, and He's never been proven wrong, in spite of some circumstances."

Maydene softened her gaze.

"Make no mistake. I can tell there's more to you than you're letting on. You're running from something—or someone."

Jenny's mouth gaped, and Maydene chucked her drooping chin.

"But as I said"—and now Queen Maydene was back—"you've a nice personality and carry yourself well. And you're cute as a cucumber. That'll help with the tips, since your hourly's not so hot. When can you start?"

"I, uh, well. I guess I could, uh, tomorrow?" Jenny's composure was slipping. If Maydene knew she was running, what else had she guessed? Jenny didn't want to explain about Jonas. The situation was too complex and painful.

"Well, how about Monday?" Maydene scooted from the booth and walked to the counter. "Will that work?"

"Sure. That will be fine. I'll be here at ... nine o'clock?" She followed Maydene.

"Oh, honey, you'll miss the breakfast rush if you don't meander in here until nine. Abe'll be knackered by then." Maydene reached behind and pulled out an apron and a hairnet. "We open at six thirty. I'll see you at six. You'll need these."

Six o'clock? In the morning? Jenny held the items in her hand, thought to ask if they were the right size, then didn't.

"If you can't find a sitter, the school over on Jackson offers before and after care for the students," Maydene said. "And the woman who heads it up, Dreama Sharp, is a real sweetheart."

"Six will be fine," Jenny heard herself say. "Fine and dandy."

"Finer 'en frog hair," Abe shouted from the back.

Jenny surveyed the diner, remembering her conversation with Maydene, and Abe's quips, and her apprehensions slipped away. Maydene would teach her how to do the job, and the café was such a focal point of the town, she doubted she'd have a spare second to think about Jonas—which would be a good thing.

She smiled, grabbed her purse, and headed for the door.

"Jenny?" Maydene said. "There is one thing I'm worried about."

Her pulse quickened.

"Are you in some kind of trouble?"

She peered out the window facing the street, briefly, before answering. "Why? Do I seem like I am?"

Maydene crossed the dining room and stood next to her. The older woman placed her arm around Jenny's shoulders, her touch calming.

"That little girl you told me about—Susan." They turned away from the kitchen pass through, and Maydene's voice quieted. "She didn't come out of a Cracker-Jack box. Are you running from an abusive husband?"

Jenny paused, considering. "No. Susan's father is not abusive. A bit too friendly with other women, yes. Abusive? No."

A hint of pain flashed in Maydene's eyes but vanished before Jenny could be sure.

"You're sure? It's not a problem either way, but I want to tell Abe if he should keep an eye out for an ex who might show up and cause problems."

Explaining Jonas was not yet her ex was too complicated. The divorce was almost inevitable, but she didn't want to discuss her failed marriage. Not now when things were going so well. "You have nothing to fear from Jonas—unless you don't like Shakespeare."

Maydene's quizzical look made Jenny laugh.

"Jonas loves to quote the bard. That's how we met." She straightened her shoulders. "Is there anything else?"

"No, dear. But if you ever need to talk, I hope you will feel free to confide in me."

Jenny nodded and turned once more for the door.

"Oh, Jenny? Last I heard, there is a nice two-bedroom apartment over on Third Street—top half of a house in the three hundred block. It was available earlier this week. That's just two blocks east of here and one block south. There's a sign on the lawn.

"Templeton's close, but I'm afraid your drive will get longer each day. I can call Yolanda and check on it if you'd like."

"Landlord's name is Dave." Abe stepped out of the kitchen, wiping his hands on a towel. "He's a good man."

"That would be great. Thank you, Maydene—and Abe. I'll check into it."

Maydene stiffened a bit. "Be sure to tell your aunt hello for me. I haven't seen that ol' biddy in a month of Sundays." She turned to look at Abe, who dropped his gaze. "You be sure to tell her exactly that."

Jenny giggled as she walked out the door. Working for Maydene would be a hoot. Anyone who called Aunt Sarah an "ol' biddy" was okay by Jenny.

~

AFTER DRIVING by the apartment to take down the phone number, Jenny stopped in on a whim. The place was too cute not to get a closer peek.

It was perfect. Well, almost.

The tiny eat-in kitchen would take some getting used to, as would the separate entrance up an exterior flight of stairs. But Jenny couldn't wait to sink into a luxurious soak in that tub with claw feet.

The property was well-maintained. And though it didn't include a garage, Susan would love the older playset in the fenced backyard. If it meant her daughter's happiness, Jenny would give up the convenience of a garage.

And she could afford the rent. She wouldn't make much as a waitress, but the savings she'd tucked away when things had been good insured she would be all right if she kept to a budget.

Dave seemed nice, as Abe said. His wife, Yolanda, did as well. With their children grown and gone, they didn't need the upstairs anymore and were looking for the right person to rent the apartment.

"When Maydene called and said she'd hired a new waitress with a little girl and she was sending you over, we were thrilled," Dave said. "It was an answer to prayer."

"Yes, we love having children around," Yolanda chimed in. "And there are no grandchildren in our immediate future—so far as we know."

And, like that, she had a place. With Maydene's reference, Jenny was a shoo-in.

Could this day get any better? Jenny hopped in her car, ready to register Susan for school. The pieces fell together so quickly, it was almost as if her move to Oak Hill was orchestrated from on high.

On her way to Montgomery Elementary, Jenny drove past an office for *The Gazette* and made a mental note to subscribe. Who knew what opportunities might fall into her lap if she kept her eyes open.

Pulling into the school parking lot, Jenny gazed over the playground and smiled. This would be Susan's first school, and she wanted her daughter to have a wonderful experience, particularly with Jonas out of the picture. Susan still missed her father a great deal, which Jenny could understand.

A new school, with new friends, might be just what Susan needs to also move on.

Chapter Eight

"It's a small-town dance, pumpkin. Not an invitation to the White House," Maydene said as the lunch rush wound down. "What's to think about? It's a family thing, and Susan would love it. All the little girls get together and do The Electric Slide line dance. It's just the cutest thing."

Jenny smiled as she imagined Susan learning to line dance. But was *she* ready to attend a city-wide dance at the VFW Hall? She'd only been working at the café for a week, and the dance was in five days.

"We don't really know anyone yet," Jenny said. "And it *is* a school night."

"Honey, you are not listening. I'll speak in sim-pler sen-ten-ces." Maydene grabbed Jenny's head between her hands. "Try to follow, dear. This is a small town. The dance is for fam-i-lies."

Jenny broke away and returned to scrubbing the coffeepot. "I'll think about it."

"You need a refill, Dave?" Maydene turned to her pastor,

who was also Jenny's landlord and one of the café's lunch regulars.

"Not right now, Maydene, but in a few." He smiled at Jenny. "How are you liking the apartment? Everything good so far?"

"Everything is great. Susan and I love that tub."

"See you next time, hon," Maydene called to Emily Serrano as she left with her two kids. "Yikes, what a mess. I think there's more food under their chairs than in their bellies. Abe, bring me the broom and dustpan, will ya, hon?"

Jenny put the filter basket back into the machine. "I'm not ready for a 'small-town fam-i-ly dance,' Maydene. And I need Susan to get to bed on time."

"Other kids will be there, and it's a school night for them too. Do you want Susan to go to class the next day and hear about all the fun she missed because of homework and bedtime?"

Jenny flicked some warm soapy water from her bucket at her boss. "Oh, all right, all right. It sounds like fun. Why not? I'd love to see Susan learn The Electric Skillet, anyway."

Maydene chortled. "It's The Electric Slide. What side of Bumpkinville did you say you grew up on? Abe, where's that broom?"

"You are an evil woman, and I can't stand you." Jenny felt her face heat and unfamiliar giggles rolled out from the bottoms of her feet. "Abe, tell her to stop making fun of me."

Abe entered the dining area with his chef's hat perched cockeyed on his head and his spotted apron hanging loosely on his lanky frame. Instead of the requested broom and dustpan, he carried a skillet.

"I don't know, Maydene. Jenny's from the big city, you know." He waved the skillet in the air as he boogied. "Maybe the dances are different there."

Maydene took that cue and ran with it. Soon they dragged Jenny around the dining room in an impromptu conga line— with Abe's skillet leading the way.

Oh great! It won't be long before the whole town is dancing in the street with skillets—and I'll get the blame.

But she didn't care. She was having fun, and despite the sometimes-exhausting work, the café was the hub of the community. For the first time in months, Jenny wasn't preoccupied with thoughts of Jonas and the life they would never have. Carefree laughter—and fun—had been missing from hers and Susan's lives for too long.

"S'cuse me? Whenever you all finish with your re*vue*, I'll take a re*fill* on this soda," Dave said. "I mean, if it's no trouble."

"What's the matter, Dave?" Maydene called from the kitchen, a twinkle of humor in her voice. "Forget where the soda machine is? One and two and three—*whoo*. One and two and three—*whoo*."

THE VFW HALL was jumping to a local cover band's version of John Mellencamp's classic, *Hurts So Good,* when Jenny walked in with Susan, Maydene, Abe, Dave, and Yolanda. She lifted her eyes long enough to skim a few faces. One man she recognized as a patron of the café. Another looked familiar, but from where?

Mostly, she caught others' gazes as they scoped out the newcomers. She clutched Susan's hand. Maydene, of course, knew everybody.

Beside the dance floor a little man held a video camera and filmed the dancers. Most people gave him a wide berth, but a couple of young kids put on a show for him with their dance moves.

One little girl ran across the room to greet Susan. The two of them squealed with delight.

"Ellen." Susan pried her hand from Jenny's grip. "Mom, this is my friend from school. The one who sits behind me."

"Susan, come dance with us," Ellen said.

When her daughter's eager face turned toward her, Jenny smiled and waved. The girls joined up with a larger group and everyone exchanged hugs. Susan's excitement satisfied Jenny's worry about the night, and she relaxed a little.

As the band switched to a countrified version of *Unchained Melody*, Maydene grabbed Abe's hand and headed for the floor.

"Wait, I didn't bring my skillet," Abe protested.

"You don't need a skillet to cook, old man." Maydene winked at Jenny before she pulled her husband into the throng of people.

Her safety net of friends quickly dwindling, Jenny sat with Yolanda—now where did Dave go?—at a table on the edge of the dance floor. She watched the sea of happy faces around her. How long had it been since she'd laughed and enjoyed a night like this with Jonas? Did he even miss her? Was he alone?

"Have you found a church home yet, Jenny?" Yolanda broke through her haze. "That would help you get more connected, I'm certain."

"Um, not yet," Jenny said. "We're still getting settled and moving in and trying to feel our way around. I haven't given church much consideration—"

How different life is in a small town. In Chicago, few people ever asked her what church she went to.

"Well, there's just about whatever you could want right here in town or nearby," Yolanda said. "Of course, there's our church, Oak Hill Missionary. We'd love for you to visit. Susan would love the Sunday school class, and we've just started a new class for single parents. Some attendees are divorced, others never married, and one is widower."

Jenny feigned interest.

"There's also a Baptist, a Presbyterian, and a Catholic church." Yolanda counted them off on her fingers. "Oh, and of course, a Methodist. They're everywhere. There's a Lutheran church in Templeton and an Episcopalian, but that's a drive for weekly services. The temple's even further, I mean, if you're Jewish."

"Thanks, Yolanda. I want to find a place—for Susan—but it's hard in a new town to feel—well, you know."

"Oh, I understand. My mother always said you don't find a church so much as the church, or rather, Christ finds you."

Jenny smiled politely. She believed, but had other priorities on her mind these days.

"Just visit around a little and when you find a place where you feel at home, that's your church."

Yolanda reached for her purse. "I'm going for a Coke, Jen. Can I call you Jen?"

"Sure, that's what Jonas always ... Yes, Jen is fine."

Yolanda gave her a look she couldn't quite decipher.

"Dave, of course, is off in a corner somewhere talking about this or that theological issue. People always want to debate the pastor—as if he knows it all. I could write a book about what he doesn't know. You want anything?"

"Not just yet, but thank you."

"All righty, then, I'll be back shortly." She patted Jenny's hand. "You'll be fine."

Jenny nodded, disturbed that she was so transparent. She checked her watch and counted the minutes until she could gracefully exit. Just as her energy level reached deflated balloon status, the band kicked into a slamming version of *Addicted to Love.* She had to at least stand.

As soon as she did, every unmarried male in the room turned her way and several edged closer. What had she been thinking?

Needing a rescue, she looked down at the table next to her where a junior high boy sat with his girl. They were busy pretending they weren't interested in each other and Jenny, emboldened by her predicament, spotted her chance.

"Wanna dance?" She grabbed the boy's hand, amused at the "I'm a Winner" gleam that flashed in his eyes.

"Uh, sure." He glanced at the girl before stumbling out of his seat. "Yeah."

Jenny winked at the girl, but the glare she received in return could have cut diamonds.

As the hounds backed off, Jenny sighed and began enjoying the dance—even though her partner was obviously executing his first dance steps. *Glad I'm not wearing sandals.*

"My name's Jenny." She waited for her partner to introduce himself, but he appeared stupefied.

"Jenny," he repeated.

She waited for him to say more, then decided he was old enough to learn a few social niceties. "What's your name?"

"I'm, um ... I'm, um ..."

"Imum?" Jenny smiled. "That's unusual."

"No. No. I'm, um, Gary. Gary Ca-Carlisle."

"And what do you do, Gary Carlisle, when you're not in school?"

"I'm, um, a copy boy at *The Gazette*—and a paper boy too." His shoe smashed her toes—again.

She tried to hide her wince. Her poor feet deserved better, after standing on them all day. "Sounds busy."

"You're gorgeous." A red flush rose all the way up into the roots of his sandy brown hair. "Did I say that out loud?"

Jenny tweaked his cheek. "Yes, you did, buster. Thank you

for the compliment and the dance." She executed a shaky little curtsy and nodded toward his table. "You better go make up with your friend."

The jilted girl bore holes into Gary's back with her eyes.

"Yeah, I guess so." He glanced over his shoulder and stepped back. "Thanks, Jenny."

"Gary?" She motioned him back to her side. "I'm going to get a drink. Maybe you should buy your friend a Coke or something. Girls like it when you surprise them."

He nodded, winked, turned, and tripped over his feet, then fell flat on his face. The girl rushed to his side.

Well, that will do as well.

After getting a Sprite, Jenny returned to the table.

Maydene wagged her finger at Jenny, a glint in her eye. "You just made Gary Carlisle's day. You probably made his week or his month. He'll tell that story into next week down at the paper—and each time, it will get better. Poor Charity Ann. Abandoned at the table for an older woman. Oh, she will make him pay for a long time, you better believe that."

"He's a nice kid—and he saved me from the mob," Jenny said. "He mentioned he worked at the paper as a copyboy. Seems young for that."

"Oh, he's just an errand boy. I'd call him a gofer. He's my paperboy too."

As she sipped her drink, the crowd on the dance floor thinned to make room for the local *Dancing with the Stars*-eligible couple. The band slowed the pace again, picking up the familiar strains of Spandau Ballet's "True."

Jenny sat, mesmerized as the husband and wife moved in perfect harmony. The dance was a beautiful *pas de deux—*

expertly choreographed. But the man seemed detached. His technique was flawless, but he wasn't present in the dance.

"Who is that?" Jenny asked Maydene. "They're fantastic, and she looks familiar."

"Them? Oh, they do this every so often. It's always fun to watch." Maydene leaned in. "That's Zakary Cooper, the editor of the paper. He's my neighbor—lives across the street. And the woman is Dreama Sharp. She's the one in charge of the before and after school program."

"Of course. I knew I recognized her. How long have they been married? They dance so beautifully."

"Oh, honey, they're not married. Not to each other, at least. Dreama's married to Mick." She pointed out a man at another table. "He's the one drawing caricatures."

Jenny had noticed the man and his sketchbook earlier. He was obviously what her father always called "a card." A crowd of people surrounded him as he drew.

"Zak was married," Maydene continued. "Still considers himself married, from what I hear. He's a widower. He was married to Mick's sister. She died this last December. Right before Christmas."

That was about the saddest thing Jenny had ever heard, but it explained his vacant expression. How would she feel if Jonas's wild driving in Chicago ended his life one day?

Zak and Dreama's dance enthralled her. She'd always wanted to dance, but Jonas had claimed he was too busy for lessons. Jenny now knew that "busy" often meant cheating, though to be fair, he also did work a lot of overtime.

The videographer captured the dance on film, much to Mr. Cooper's chagrin. He kept shooing the guy away.

Someone tapped Jenny's arm, and she turned to find Susan at her side.

"Mommy, I'm thirsty. Can I—?"

"Shh. In a minute, sweetie. Watch the dance."

As the song wound to an end, the couple shuffled to the side of the floor closest to Jenny. Dreama's eyes were expectant, but Zak shook his head. What did she want? He hung his head and, as the song's climax wafted from the speakers, dipped Dreama low in the space right next to Jenny.

Jenny gasped, and Zak glanced up.

He cocked his head, smiled at Jenny slightly, and, not so slightly, dropped Dreama squarely on her head.

Chapter Nine

While dancing with Dreama, Zak noticed Mick drawing his caricatures. *He's not even watching, yet he expects to reap the "benefits" from this floorshow.* He decided right then there'd be no dip.

His attention wasn't on the dance, or Mick's drawing, or even the pretty new girl—the one who worked at the café. What did Nancy say her name was? Jessica? Jasmine? Something very eighties.

He was too distracted to enjoy the dance, and while he respected Dreama, dancing was another thing he and Kay had shared.

But thoughts of yesterday's editor's meeting kept pulling him out of the moment. During lunch, Waxman had made it clear that if they couldn't staunch the flow of blood from the bottom line, he'd sell—or close—*The Gazette.*

"If we can't turn it around, then we won't be going forward," Waxman had said. "So, unless you can figure out a way to print the paper in red ink, the end is near."

Zak nearly had a panic attack right then but managed to

hold his countenance. No one understood how much the paper meant to him. With Kay gone, he had nothing else to live for.

"I'd prefer to sell. Keep it open," Waxman continued. "This paper is my family's legacy. But I won't keep throwing money down a rat's hole. I want some realistic suggestions on how to make it work from each of you on my desk within the week." With that pronouncement, he ended the meeting.

The paper couldn't close.

Instead of staying home to work on a solution, Zak was at the VFW dance—preparing not to dip Dreama because her ungrateful and uncoordinated husband didn't even bother to watch her dance.

He had a few ideas about the paper roughed out—including a pay cut for himself—but none of them were sustainable.

His plan was not great to begin with. Lack of sleep always made his head thick. And he sure wasn't sleeping these days, not with Kay making regular appearances.

Last week had been awful. She kept showing up. Since she refused to go to bed with him, and he hated to go without her, they stayed up late talking, laughing, and dancing to their favorite songs.

Zak glared at Sloan and drew his hand across his throat—the universal sign for cut—but the video rolled on. As the band hit the familiar staccato synths of Spandau Ballet's *True*, Zak had enough dancing.

"Dreama, this is the last song," he said. "I need to get back home. I'm exhausted and still have a ton of work to do. Tell Mick I'm sorry there was no dip."

"Mick? What does Mick care about you dipping me? He's not even watching," Dreama said. "And what do you mean by 'no dip'? It's my birthday. Please? Just a little one?"

Judging by Dreama's coquettish pout, if she didn't get her

dip, he'd be stuck in another dance—and another—and this debate would continue all night. *Been there, done that.*

Resigning himself to the inevitable, he hung his head and set up. They had ended up on the opposite side of the dance floor from where they started. Now they were near where Maydene and Abe sat with the new girl.

What had Nancy say her name was? Jocelyn?

Pastor Dave and Yolanda returned to their table. Great. One more sermon illustration from his boring life.

The band began the song's payoff line. He turned Dreama once, twice. Down they dipped, and as they did, the waitress— Jenny. Her name was Jenny!—gasped. He snapped his head up and caught her eyes—robin's egg blue, like Kay's—and his legs gave out.

Mayday. Mayday. We're going down.

As HE AND Dreama hit the floor, one thought filled his mind. *I knew it was Jenny.* He shifted his weight to the side at the last second. He couldn't stop Dreama's fall, but he could keep his 185 pounds from crashing on top of her.

Dreama's head smacked against the floor. It sounded a bit like ... *What? A kumquat? I don't even know what a kumquat looks like, let alone what one sounds like hitting the floor.*

"Ha." Zak guffawed as he hit the floor. He laughed his fool head off, as Gram used to say.

The band stopped playing, and everyone's attention focused on the commotion. Of course, Sloan kept filming—an evil gloat on his face.

Maydene and Yolanda kneeled beside Dreama. Doc Rawlings sprinted over from the other side of the room. Mick dropped his art tablet and rushed over—to glare at Zak. And Zak convulsed in fits of laughter he couldn't control.

"Dreama? Dreama?" Yolanda said. "Honey, wake up."

"There's no blood that I can see." Doc examined her. "But don't move her. Head trauma can be tricky. Let me see if she's responsive."

While Doc flashed a light in her eyes, Mick dropped to the floor next to his wife.

"Babe? Dreama, honey? Can you hear me?" He put his arm under his wife's neck to lift her head.

"Don't move her head," Yolanda, Maydene, Doc Rawlings, and just about everyone else in the hall shouted.

When Zak and Dreama fell, Jenny stood and backed up several steps, taking Susan with her. She wanted to get out of the way—and out of sight—as much as possible. The man who had flawlessly danced convulsed with laughter on the floor. What was wrong with him? She frowned.

"I think Dreama's coming around," someone said from the bevy of concerned friends, neighbors, and others behind her.

"Mick?" Dreama's voice was groggy. "Where am I?"

"Right here, babe. Right here with me," a man Jenny assumed was Mick said. "Are you okay? You took quite a tumble."

"Where are we?"

"At the VFW and you're right here in my arms, as always," Mick said. "You want me to get you anything?"

"Oh, honey," Dreama leaned against Mick's chest. "Not tonight, I have a headache." She giggled.

Then Mick laughed—along with half the crowd—and held his wife close.

"Okay." Doc raised his hands. "Look, folks, this show is over. Make room please. People? The lady's going to be fine if you all would just step back and give her some air."

Jenny turned back toward Zak, who now had started to regain control and was looking appropriately guilty.

"I am sorry." He hiccupped. "That was rude— *hic*—of me. If I could have stopped the fall, I would have."

"Uh-huh. Would you like a hand up?" Jenny held out her right arm. Susan hid behind Jenny. All the while, the video man continued to film.

"Yes, please, that— *hic*—would be great. Thank you."

Jenny gripped his right hand and yanked on it to pull him up. He screamed and she dropped him on his rear end.

The crowd's attention shifted to Zak and Jenny—and there was no getting out of the spotlight this time.

"Is he hurt too?" Doc moved the few steps to Zak's position on the floor and bent down to get a better look.

"I, uh, don't know." She hated all the attention. "I just tried to help him up, then he screamed."

"And she dropped me on my butt." Zak held his right hand against his chest.

"Serves you right," Maydene crowed from the edge of the circle. "At least you've got padding on your backside."

The hall exploded with laughter, and Susan giggled at Jenny's side.

Doc poked and prodded at Zak's hand. "Well, I don't think you broke anything—not even Dreama's head—but you probably ought to get your hand X-rayed to be sure.

"Speaking of Dreama." Doc turned his attention once more to Mick, who had moved Dreama to a chair at one of the tables. "Keep her awake for a good couple of hours and continue to check her eyes. Make sure her pupils are not dilating. When she does go to sleep, wake her up every two hours. Depending on how she feels in the morning, you may want to bring her by too."

"Can I take her home now, Doc?" Mick clasped Dreama's hand. "I mean, if you're up to it, honey."

"I'd rather be at home than here." Dreama stood slowly. "I'm so embarrassed."

"Well, it's certainly not your fault." Mick glared at Zak, who failed to stifle another recalcitrant laugh. "And Sloan, turn off that camera or I'll turn it off permanently."

"Yeah, take her on home," Doc said. "Just be careful and be aware."

Mick and Dreama, along with Maydene and Abe, made their way to the exit.

"Abe, you follow in our car, and I'll ride in the back with Dreama, while Mick *carefully* drives home. None of your hotshot driving tonight, Mitchell Sharp," Maydene said.

"Yes, ma'am," Mick said.

So much for a just a 'small-town fam-i-ly dance,' Jenny thought as they all paraded out.

To JENNY'S RELIEF, most of the crowd had faded away. Even the man with the ever-present video camera was gone. Several people headed for their cars, but a few tried to persuade the band to play another tune to no avail. They'd already packed up their instruments.

Jenny sank to the table to catch her breath and gather her things. Nothing like an injury or two to suck all the fun out of an evening. Zak sat at her table, clearly in pain. She smiled, nodded her head, and was about to escape.

"Are you okay?" Susan reached across the table and gently patted Zak's uninjured hand.

"Yes, darlin', I believe I will be." He grinned. "Thank you for asking."

"My name's Susan."

"Well, good evening, Miss Suzy Q," he said. "My friends, my good friends, call me Zee."

"Pleased to meet you, Zee" Susan bowed a tiny curtsy. "My daddy calls me Suzy Q."

"Well, he must be a very smart man."

"No Mommy says—"

"Hello. I'm Jenny Miller, Susan's mother." She extended her hand between the two.

"Pleased to meet you. I'm Zak Cooper." He held out his left hand, on which he wore a wedding band. "Editor of *The Gazette,* Fred Astaire-never-be, and general, all-purpose doofus."

He managed a slight bow from his seat. "Welcome to Oak Hill."

"Thank you, Mr. Cooper. You certainly know how to make a girl's first night on the town memorable. And lucky Dreama, to be paired with such a ... a ... what was that word you used?"

Zak dropped his head. "That would be doofus."

"Well, yes. I suppose that fit of laughter was uncalled for." What was it about this man that made her want to cut him some slack? "You'll probably be front page news tomorrow if that little man with the bow tie has anything to say about it."

"Well, I think I'll be able to put a stop to that." He sighed. "Although the video will no doubt be shown on an unending loop at the next Christmas party." Zak focused on Susan once more. "So, Suzy-Q, do you like Oak Hill?"

"Yeah." Susan slurped her ice. "My school is fun. My best friend, Ellen, who sits next to me in school, said her daddy is gone, too, and—"

"Zak?" Jenny needed to steer the conversation to safer

ground before Susan spilled their entire life story. Which, for some reason, she did not want Zak to know. "Is that short for Zachariah?"

He met her gaze, and she felt assessed. "Zakary, actually. It's Zakary Bryan Cooper, but, uh, you can call me Zak."

Jenny studied him. Had this man with the insightful green eyes and chestnut brown hair and—were those dimples?—easy smile also taken a hit on the noggin? He was unusual. And a little too cute.

"Well, we've got to go." Jenny nudged Susan toward the door. "It's a school night. Say goodbye to Mr. Cooper, Susan."

"Goodbye, Zee."

"Bye, Suzy-Q." Zak tweaked her nose.

Jenny pulled back. It was one thing to make small talk with someone she'd just met. It's quite another to give out nicknames and tweak noses and ... and make her feel off-kilter, if she would admit it.

"C'mon, Susan." She took her daughter's hand, spun on her heel, and headed for the nearest exit, her heart kathumping in her chest.

She almost reached the door—was almost free—when Zak called her name, and she spun around.

There he stood, running his uninjured hand through his hair. "Um, I think I've been abandoned. Mick and Dreama left me here in their rush to get home. I'm sure they forgot I rode with them."

An uncomfortable silence settled.

"Would it be too much trouble for you to take me home, Jenny? I mean drive me to my home?"

How did she get herself into these situations? Oh yeah, Maydene had practically forced her to attend this stupid fam-i-ly dance. This was all her fault.

"Yes, of course. But you'll have to sit in the back, Mr. Cooper," Jenny said over her shoulder as she left the hall.

"That's fine, but, uh, you *can* call me Zak. And I may need help in and out of the backseat since I'm ... *damaged.*" He wagged his arm like a broken wing.

"Front, then."

"Yay. Zee's gonna ride with us. Zee's gonna ride with us," Susan said in her singsong voice and scampered into the back seat, where she reached for her stuffed rabbit.

"Where to, Mr. Cooper?" Jenny set her business persona firmly in place and cranked the key to start the car. She was only driving the man home. The injured man. The foolish, injured man who, regardless of his charming personality, was a passenger. One who did not require her to look at him. Still, she peeked to her right.

Zak cleared his throat. "I hate to be a problem."

"Nonsense. I said I'd take you. It's not a problem—at least not for me."

"No, that's not what I mean."

She rotated to look at him and her throat tightened as she got caught up in his gaze again.

"The door?" He tilted his head to the right.

"Door?" She snapped out of her reverie. Of course! He could not reach to close the car door—not with his injured arm. He was asking her to help. Nothing else. She read too many romance novels.

"Oh. I'm sorry." She unbuckled her seatbelt. "It's late and I wasn't thinking."

"It's okay." Zak chuckled. "You, uh, you want *me* to drive me home?"

"Certainly not. I only had a Sprite. I'm fine. Just zoned out a little there."

Jenny turned the car off and walked around to the passenger side, determined to keep her composure.

"There." She shut the door with a little too much force and headed back to her side.

She felt his gaze on her again, as she got in and started the car. She refused to look, but she could tell.

"Is there a problem?" She gripped the wheel, her eyes straight ahead.

"Seatbelt? Gram always told me the car wouldn't start without the seatbelts fastened. Isn't that right, Suzy-Q?" he said over the seat.

"Yep," she chirped. "That's what you always say, too, Mommy."

Jenny turned the car off—again—and walked to the other side—again. She opened the door and grabbed the seatbelt to fasten it around Zak. *It's just the same as when I used to put it around Susan when she was little. It's just the same. Just the same.*

As she leaned in across his chest, she breathed him in. No cologne, just a solid, clean, manly aroma.

It was not at all the same. She needed to fasten the belt and get some fresh air. *Click.*

"Okay, then." Her satisfied tone sounded like she'd just solved the problem of world peace. "That should do it." She backed out of his space, determined not to look him in the eye.

"Jenny?" Zak said. "Thank-you."

As his gaze caught her eye, she stepped back. "You're welcome, Zee."

In the back, Susan's head rested against the seat behind her. Even though her mouth hung open and her eyes were closed, she clutched Harry B. to her chest. The long day was catching up with her—with them.

I could kiss him now, and only the two of us would know.

Jenny had never felt so vulnerable. But vulnerability was something she could ill afford. She had to pull herself together. She was married. Legally, if not in her heart.

She rounded the car with determined strides, climbed behind the wheel, turned the key, shifted into gear, and asked, "Where to, Mr. Cooper?" as she pulled out of the lot. She cracked her window and inhaled the fresh air to clear her mind.

~

Zak stared down the street as Jenny, with Susan asleep in the back, drove away. Standing in his driveway, he realized how much he'd enjoyed the playful bantering he'd enjoyed exchanging with Jenny. That testing of the waters. The giving and taking. He smiled. A real one. For the first time in a long time.

Though he was not particularly interested in dating, Jenny was a good-looking woman and could probably be fun. Unless his radar was misfiring from lack of use, she'd felt an attraction to him too. And, silly as it seemed to think about, she also had a silver Honda. Like Kay.

Susan had enchanted him as well. She was about the age Zak and Kay's child would be, if not for the miscarriage. He'd made no secret he had wanted a daughter. But Kay would have been satisfied either way.

Susan had the same deep-set eyes Kay did and, though the girl's hair fell around her face in natural ringlets and Kay's was straight, the rich mahogany color was a perfect match.

"I was always surprised you didn't want a boy to play ball with and spit with and pee on trees in the woods with," Kay said from behind him.

Spinning around, he met her moist gaze.

"I would have taken a boy," he said. "Or a girl. I was never dissatisfied, Kay."

"I'm sorry, Zak." She was on the verge of crying. "I meant to give you the home you always wanted. I really did. I had a plan. Three kids, a dog, a cat, and an aquarium full of fish.

"We'd all ride bikes together. Even the fish. I'd fix massive Sunday dinners. We'd grow old and fat together. It was all planned. All of it, Zee. I'm so sorr—"

"Shh. Quiet now, darling. It's okay. Shh," he said.

"It's not okay, Zak. It's not!" she said. "Being dead sucks. I'd give it all, our house, our cars, our jobs—everything. I'd give it all for one more night in your arms."

He ached to hold her, to comfort her. He too would give it all to have her back, truly back, for even a moment. For one final chat to tell her how much he loved her. To finally say goodbye.

He moved to take her in his arms, but she held up her hands to ward him off. Then she was gone, and Zak was alone, again.

He gazed at the moon and cursed the feeble light it gave— light that illuminated his pain and his tears. Light that revealed how alone he was—and likely to remain. He received no comfort from the heavens and understood all too well the advice Job's wife had given as he sat on his ash heap. "Curse God and die." It was what Zak wished he could do right now.

Zak pointed at the sky. "I hate You."

He trudged inside, the pleasant evening with Susan and Jenny forgotten.

Chapter Ten

S itting at his desk on the fourteenth floor of Clarity Tower in Chicago, Jonas Miller gazed at the city out his window. The black expanse of Lake Michigan rippled further out, and occasional flashes of light from the office buildings twinkled on the waves. His tie loosened and his loafers off, he drummed a pencil against the arm of his chair.

He was distracted and he didn't like it.

His mind raced with thoughts of everything except his job as a backgrounder for media mogul Phillip Esch. Part of his position included finding the weaknesses, the chinks in the armor, of the newspapers Esch and Clarity sought to acquire. His work normally excited him. He enjoyed digging up weaknesses and exploiting them.

But not tonight.

Tonight, he'd stayed late because he had no life. If he went home to an empty house, it would only remind him of that fact, which would lead to trouble. The kind of trouble that had sent Jen running in tears, and towing Susan, six weeks ago.

With his lack of focus, he was falling behind at work—and he couldn't risk losing that as well.

"Jonas, you are a moron. You threw the best parts of your life away." He drummed his fingers on the desktop, the staccato rhythm urging him to focus.

But he couldn't. He could have stopped Jen. Should have. Instead, he'd wasted time waiting for her—expecting her—to come back. She always had before.

Then he'd wasted more time with Erica—the same someone who had gotten him in trouble with Jen in the first place.

After tossing Erica back into the bar where he'd found her, he'd realized what he'd lost. He and Jenny had been married for seven years, the last six with Suzy Q, the first female in his life he'd been completely faithful to.

"Well, that's not even true, is it?" He rubbed his eyes. He couldn't call himself faithful to his child if, instead of spending time with her at home, he chased the next promotion—or worse.

Though he loved Jen like no other woman before or since, he had let the part of him that was never satisfied—his ego—lead. No matter how many women he slept with, or promotions he received, it was never enough. He craved more.

"Honestly, Jonas, you think you're God's gift to women," Jenny had said during one of their first arguments. She'd almost left him then, but she was pregnant. And as a Christian, she didn't believe in divorce. At this point, her belief was his only ace in the hole.

She wasn't wrong. He was a great catch, and women were attracted to him without him doing anything. He knew how to smile. Big deal. His eyes shone with confidence—as long as people didn't look too deep. His rakish attitude appealed to many, until they got to know him better. Jen was the first who had wanted to stay—and he'd run her off.

He'd met Jenny in the library at Lake Forest College.

They were both researching Shakespeare's plays. He was writing a paper comparing the romantic themes of Shakespeare and Nathanial Hawthorne, and she was preparing lesson plans for *Romeo and Juliet*, which she planned to teach the next semester at a local high school.

"But soft! What light through yonder window breaks? It is the East, and Juliet is the sun!" He gave a regal bow.

She lifted her face from her books, peered over her glasses —and smiled. "Excuse me?"

"She speaks, yet she says nothing. What of that? Her eye discourses; I will answer it."

Smiling wider, Jenny closed her book. "Who are you?"

"Jonas Miller, m'lady. All-seeing, all-knowing seer. I am at your service." He bowed again.

Laughing, she stood, curtsied, and extended her hand, stepping into her role. "Jenny Miller, good sir."

"Really? Miller? The both of us? Do you suppose thou art my sister? What a disappointment that would be."

"Nay, good sir. I am but an only child."

"Forsooth," he said, before dropping the courtly manner. "At least you won't need to change your name when we marry."

Her face blushed the deepest, most attractive red Jonas had ever seen. She gasped, grabbed her books, and bolted.

He smiled after her. If his books weren't on a study carrel two rows down, he might have chased after her, even though he'd known, even then, doing so wasn't necessary.

Now, after seven years of marriage and one daughter, he might have to do some chasing.

Jonas gazed again at the city below. In college, he had found Jen again and successfully wooed her. Now she was gone, presumably for good. Her friends weren't talking, and Jen had no parents or siblings. The only relative he'd ever met was her Aunt Sarah, and that was years ago. He barely remembered the woman—didn't even know her last name. Didn't she live somewhere in Indiana? Aunt Sarah. In Indiana. Not a lot to go on.

He slumped in his chair and pressed his fingers to his temples in a vain attempt to staunch the looming headache. It was time to go home.

Jennifer. Jennifer. Wherefore art thou, Jennifer?

After getting Dreama settled in, Maydene and Abe left the Sharps and headed to their home for the evening. Abe turned into the family room to watch TV.

"Who are you foolin,' old man?" Maydene said. "You're going to sit down in that narcolepsy chair of yours and before long, you'll be watching nothing but the inside of your eyelids."

"And what if I do? You got a better idea for what we should do?" Abe said. "You want to come with me and have a little snack on the couch? I think I could be hungry tonight."

"Oh, you. Forty-five years married and you're still wanting your 'snacks on the couch,'" she chided. She touched her finger to his nose. "I would, you know, but I'm feeling called to prayer. I'm going to sit down and pray for Dreama. Try not to fall asleep, you hear?"

"I hear," he said. "I'm hoping you won't have much of a prayer life tonight, 'cause I won't be watching ESPN for long. Go on then, pray for Dreama."

As he walked off to the family room, Maydene almost changed her mind and followed. Even with his droopy old man pants, he was still her idea of perfection. But God called again, and He was not one she wanted to ignore. If the call was this insistent, someone needed prayer—and she would provide it.

Maydene didn't bother flipping on the lights before she settled in the rocker by the front window. She liked to pray in the dark. She could feel the presence of God envelope her without the distractions around her illuminated.

She gathered her Bible and an afghan to cover her legs from the footstool. While she wouldn't be doing any reading, she liked the familiar weight in her hands and often stroked the worn leather when before her Lord.

Closing her eyes, Maydene began her prayer, as always, with a praise chorus. Even an old woman who was bottle-fed the hymns could see the place for worship choruses.

She chose, "I Cast All My Cares Upon You," the song about giving God her cares and burdens. How when she didn't know what to do, she'd give her concerns to Him.

Despite her preparation, the calm of the Spirit's presence didn't fall on her. Something still tugged at her. She assumed it was prayer—that's usually what this prompting involved. But like one of those dolls little girls used to play with, her eyes wouldn't stay shut while she sat upright.

"Okay, then, Lord, Make it plain to this old woman what You want because I'm not getting it."

Maydene looked out the picture window, waiting for her bolt of lightning. She was where God wanted her, the rest was up to Him.

Across the street, a sedan pulled into Zak Cooper's driveway. Didn't Jenny drive a silver Civic?

The driver never got out of the car. Zak edged out of the passenger seat, favoring his right hand, shut the door, and waved goodbye as the car drove away.

Hmm, he must have asked for a ride home. Still, Jenny might be what Zak needs right now. Maybe I'll—

Just then, Zak spun around on the sidewalk in front of his house as if someone called his name. She didn't see anyone else, but it was late, and the streetlight was too far away to provide any assistance.

She leaned forward. Yes, Zak *was* talking to someone. She was sure of it. His mouth moved and he gestured, but she couldn't see who else was there. She scooched to the edge of her seat like a spy—one who was a bit mad.

Zak stepped forward with his arms out, as if to take someone into his embrace. Then he just stopped. His arms fell to his sides.

As he shifted toward his house, he wiped something—tears? —from his face and his steps were labored. He stared at the sky for a moment—said something—and went into his home. No lights came on.

Now, Maydene. The still small voice returned. *Now you can pray.*

And she did.

Chapter Eleven

More to distract himself than to get any work done, Jonas reached for the manila folder he'd left lying on his desk the night before. The papers inside contained his life for the next four months—fewer if he did his job right.

Esch was building a media empire—a chain of newspapers to rival Gannett. Working for Esch and Clarity Communications, even as a lowly backgrounder, would cushion his resume when the next step up the career ladder presented itself.

His journalism degree was fine, but to make the big bucks, he'd skipped working for a paper in favor of moving straight into media acquisition and management. Sometimes he missed the fun and reward of writing. But entry-level pay was not his style.

His work for Clarity was—well, work. Nothing too exciting, but it paid well—and he loved the adrenaline rush he got when he won and forced a target to sell on the cheap. He'd search through every detail about a proposed acquisition and find its weaknesses. Esch and Clarity would use those to their advantage when plotting their takeover.

Who was their next mark? But more importantly, what were they hiding? He opened the folder with a modicum of anticipation.

The top of the dossier read "*The Gazette*, Oak Hill, Ind."

Indiana? Jonas yawned. The center of fly-over country.

The paper had been owned and operated by the Waxman family since its inception in 1904. Charles Waxman, current publisher. He flipped through several pages and came to a photo of a man in his late fifties, strong, strapping, no-nonsense, former Marine type.

Probably pigheaded.

Zakary Cooper, the 40-ish editor, had only been there five years. He was a local boy who had returned home to run the paper.

Good looking in an Opie-all-grown-up sort of way, but darker hair.

The Gazette seemed the epitome of an entrenched good ol' boy, family-owned, until-the-end-of-time situation. Jonas wetted his lips and smiled. His job was more fun when the acquisition was unlikely. He enjoyed the chase.

Jonas scanned through more pages. Assistant editor, Sloan White, had been assistant editor five years and a rising reporter at the paper for five years before that.

That bit of information was useful. White put in his years but had been passed over for the hometown hero at the editor change. Jonas highlighted White's name and made a note in the margin. *Jealous of new editor? Could be swayed.*

The description of Oak Hill painted the picture of a town plopped into the middle of a cornfield. With a circulation of 12,331, the place had to be bigger than he imagined. He hoped a visit wasn't necessary. He hadn't pressed his flannel in ages and didn't own a pair of overalls.

According to the report, nearby cities included Fort Wayne, LaPorte, South Bend, and Templeton.

That last one rang a bell. Why?

The answer hit him like a foul ball in Section 416 of Wrigley Field. He closed the folder.

He was going to Oak Hill. The sooner the better. No-last-name Aunt Sarah lived in Templeton, or at least she had.

"Interesting," Jonas said. "Or as Willie the Shake would say, 'What is past is prologue.'"

Finding his focus, he opened the folder again and began combing through it for pertinent details to help Clarity. He also searched for anything that might lead him to Jen. When he found her, he'd beg her to return home. He'd swear to change—and this time he'd mean it.

Chapter Twelve

"Maydene says apple's the best today, Mick." Jenny wiped her hands on her apron.

"Hmm?" Mick's eyes glassed over as he lingered in front of the pastry case. "Apple? I don't know. I've got my eye on that French Silk in the corner."

Jenny coaxed the pie out of hiding and slid it in front of the man. There was time to entice the customers during the slow period between lunch and dinner.

"How's Dreama doing today? No more problems after last week?" She wiped a rag over the countertop to clean the mess from a previous pie encounter.

Pastor Dave was a great customer and, as far as she could tell from Sunday's service, a solid preacher, but the man was a slob. He couldn't drink a cup of coffee without sloshing half of it on the counter.

"Oh, she's fine. Feisty as ever. I got in trouble for the, uh, dip thing." His face went from pasty to crimson in two seconds flat.

She cocked her head. "Dip thing?"

Somehow, his face went even redder. "Um, it's nothing. I guess I won't be able to foist Dreama off on Zak anymore for her dancing fixes. I'll just have to crush her toes, I guess."

"Or take dancing lessons?" She poured a cup of coffee to go with the pie.

He raised his palms in mock surrender. "Honey, there's not enough money in the world."

When she'd driven Zak home after the dance, Zak had mentioned Mick was both his brother-in-law and best friend.

"I tell him just about everything," Zak had said. "There are only a couple things we don't talk about."

She'd heard the wound of his loss in the words. Had Zak told Mick about his ride home, or was that one of the off-limit topics?

"Where is Zak?" She disinfected the counters in an attempt to appear nonchalant. "Doesn't he usually get pie with you?"

"He'll be along soon. He's making final changes to the front page." He caught her eye and winked. "Miss him already?"

So, Zak *had* mentioned her. A nervous laugh escaped.

"Not at all, Mr. Sharp." She wiped the exterior of the coffee machine with more force than necessary. "I'm a little short on tips today, and he's a sucker for a nice smile, that's all."

"Yes, he is." Mick glanced at her as he downed the last of his pie. "Zak *is* a sucker for a lady's smile."

Why was her mouth going dry? She'd only met the man mere days ago, yet she felt like a silly sixth grader passing notes in the hallway between classes. She wanted to ask if Zak had said anything about her, but thankfully, managed to hold her tongue.

As she continued cleaning, she reminded herself of her marital status—again. Just because Jonas was an idiot, didn't mean she had to be one too.

To change the subject, Jenny unpacked her go-to

conversation starter—innocent newcomer in town—and inquired about local parks where she could take Susan to play.

"Where do you live?" Mick set down his coffee, got up, and walked to the map hanging on the far wall. "There are a couple of small parks in the city, here, here, and here. But the best one by far is the county park—here. It has a huge playground."

He smiled at her as if he'd recognized her ploy. "You know who spends a lot of time at that park? Zak. He'd probably be happy to show you where it is."

Why did his smile remind Jenny of the Cheshire cat from *Alice in Wonderland?*

"I'm sure I can find my way without bothering Mr. Cooper." Jenny wiped down the chairs with ineffective flips of her wrists. "I don't get lost easy."

"Well, if you do, Pastor Dave's your man. He can help you get found again."

Zak had been right. Mick Sharp was a regular card, just not the joker.

"Har-de-har." She snapped her wet towel in his direction.

The door to the café banged open, and Zak entered, deep in an animated discussion with a weasel-faced man. Jenny had never met him, but he was the same man with the video camera at the dance. She wet her lips and smoothed the front of her apron—and tried to ignore the amusement on Mick's face as he returned to his stool. She flicked her wrist at him as she would a persistent mosquito.

"Sloan, I made my decision. Let it go." Zak perched next to Mick at the counter. The two men shared a quick glance, and Mick nodded before Zak gave her a bright smile. "Apple please, Jenny. And thanks again for the ride home the other night."

Mick wriggled his eyebrows as she retrieved the pie.

"It's A-1, not the features section, Zakary." Sloan sniffed, apparently not ready to end the conversation. "People expect to read *news* in their newspaper, not some fluff feature on the 18th Annual Puppy Paw Parade written by a reporter who's not paper-trained herself. And who made 'cutesy' an acceptable journalistic writing style?"

"Not a dog man, Sloan?" Mick eyeballed Zak's pie when Jenny set it down. "Because in six months, the animal shelter will hold the Kitty Kat Korral."

Zak laughed and stole another peek her way. As he did, he moved his pie out of Mick's reach.

She smiled and shook her finger and twisted away from the counter.

"Oh, ha-ha, Mitchell." Sloan raised himself his full five feet, two inches. "But what can one expect from a graphic *artiste* such as yourself? Seriously, Zakary, that story about the expansion of Clarity Communications into the Midwest is of much more import."

At the mention of Clarity, a sudden chill made her skin prickle. Jenny turned her head back toward Zak and strained to listen—glad her back was to the men, making eavesdropping easier.

"Not to our readers." Zak's fork scraped against his plate. "I agree the story is important, but our readers like the Puppy Paw Parade. They expect photos of their children marching around the track with their dogs. If we don't give them that, we'll get letters and—"

"I don't see how—"

"—*and*, as I already told you, the Clarity piece is on A-3 in the national news briefs column for those who are interested. Follow the story for a few days and see if anything develops. If you find proof they're interested in a paper near us, *then* it becomes more newsworthy."

Sloan huffed. "We'll see what Waxman thinks."

Jenny turned back to the counter in time to see Zak and Mick share a bemused look.

"By all means," Zak said. "The paper is in bed already but give Charlie a call if you'd like. I'm sure he won't mind the interruption to his golf game."

Sloan walked to the door. As his hand turned the knob, he looked back, his voice taking on a portentous tone. "Well, Zakary, one day you'll regret not paying more attention to what the world is doing around you. Of course, by then it could be too late."

As the door shut behind him, Jenny made a mental note to read A-3 tonight. What was Clarity doing? And more importantly, was Jonas involved?

Zak spun back to the counter, caught her eye, and massaged the support bandage on his right forearm.

"Arm bothering you?" Mick asked. "I noticed the strap earlier."

"It's okay," Zak said. "These muscles aren't used to working so much. They have to overcompensate for—"

"Uh-huh, fascinating. I was only being polite. Don't need the medical transcription service."

"I could still kick your butt, if that's what you're wondering."

"Boys, boys, boys," Jenny's arms parted the area between the two men. "Do I need to separate you?"

"It's *his* fault," Mick said.

"Nuh-uh," Zak replied.

All three of them giggled like children and Jenny saw a light flicker in Zak's eyes. But the smile that came with the light seemed out of place. How long had it been since Zak had truly laughed—other than that maniacal episode at the dance.

The scrape of the key in the back lock caught Jenny's attention. Maydene and Abe entered from the door to the alley with bags of cleaning supplies. Maydene had exchanged shifts with Jenny today because Susan had a special program at school. Jenny would repay the favor by working for Maydene tomorrow night. To keep their time together, Abe had also switched hours with the evening grill cook.

"Howdy all," Maydene called from the kitchen. "You having a *kaffeeklatsch* without us?"

"Hey, Maydene. Abe." Zak gestured toward Jenny. "Mom's trying to keep us in line out here. We're getting a little rowdy, I guess."

"Well, how is that any different than usual?" Maydene pulled on her apron as she entered the dining room. "You ready for your little one's program, Jenny?"

"I am, but I'm not sure she is. Thanks again for switching with me. I know you prefer working early."

"Honey, it's not a problem for me. I just wish we could all go." She cleared Zak's pie plate on her way back to the kitchen. "I'll keep the coffee pumping into Abe to keep him awake."

The door swung closed behind her.

"Say, Zak, Jenny here asked me a question earlier." Mick grinned at Jenny.

She scowled at him and drew her right hand across her neck as Zak turned toward her.

"You have a question? Just ask. Reporters love questions, and I'm an open book—well, mostly."

Jenny glared daggers at Mick. "Oh, it's nothing really. It's just that—nothing. Never mind. I can manage."

"Well, now I'm curious. I can't leave until I hear the question."

Maydene entered the dining room. Her quizzical gaze took in all three of them, Jenny, Zak, and Mick. "Good gracious glory," she said. "What's going on out here?"

"Jenny asked about parks where she could take Susan to

play." Mick sidled over to Maydene, then raised his eyebrows at Zak. "And I told her that Zak often goes to the county park and he would be happy to show her where it is and walk the two of them around. That's all." He tossed his hands in the air and sat down on the stool next to Maydene—out of Jenny's reach.

Maydene leaned on the counter and made goo-goo eyes.

Zak smiled expectantly at Jenny, then glanced around the restaurant as if looking for someone. Jenny busied herself rearranging the pies in the pie case.

"I would be honored to show you and Suzy Q around the park," Zak said. "It's a great place, with an almost-new swing set and a viewing tower. I go there often to clear my head. When do you get off tomorrow?"

"Oh, I couldn't," Jenny said. "I'm sorry, it's kind of you to offer, and I'd love to, but I couldn't. Really. It's sweet of you. I'm working the night shift tomo—"

"She gets off at four." Maydene stepped around the counter. "You can pick her up here."

Jenny gawped at her. Zak and Mick burst out laughing.

"And, since it's spring, she'll fix a picnic dinner." Maydene said, oblivious to the holes Jenny's eyes drilled in her back.

MAYDENE!

Jenny escaped to the kitchen with the excuse of washing some dishes that weren't a priority. The flush in her face spread. Of course, Maydene didn't know Jenny was married, but she could tell Jenny was attracted to Zak. That was enough of a problem. How was she going to get out of this picnic?

Maydene stayed in the dining room to refill the napkin dispensers while Zak and Mick finished their coffee. As they headed for the door, Jenny watched their progress via the pass-through. Zak turned back, held up a finger to Mick, and walked toward the kitchen. His face soon peered around the doorjamb.

"You don't have to go." His gaze was gentle, holding no expectation. "We railroaded you back there. I'll give you a pass if you like, but it's just two friends and a child enjoying a picnic in a beautiful park. Nothing more."

She kept her hands in the dishwater and swallowed before looking up.

"I understand that," she said. "It's just that, well ..." How could she explain her attraction to him made her nervous because she was married?

She couldn't. Simple as that. They were practically strangers. "It's just that, it's been a while. Let's leave it at that."

She returned to her dishes, arguing with herself. Zak fiddled with a coffee cup beside the sink at the same time she reached for it. Their fingers brushed. She took a deep breath, grabbed the cup, and plopped it into the sink.

"I'd like to go to the park. And Susan would enjoy the outing."

"So, we're on?"

He'd left the decision in her hands, which she appreciated. When she met his gaze, the uncertainty she felt reflected in his eyes. That made her decision easier.

"We'll be here, picnic basket in hand, Mr. Cooper. We'll have a nice dinner between friends. I'll see you at four."

"Okay then. Four it is." He hesitated a moment. "You really can call me Zak."

She nodded, and he rejoined Mick.

With one hand against her abdomen and the other at her mouth, her butterflies had taken flight again.

～

WHEN ZAK STEPPED into the kitchen, Maydene motioned for Mick to join her outside.

"Whew, Maydene, you are a born matchmaker," Mick said as the café door closed behind them. "Between us we'll get him—"

"Hush, Mitchell. and listen. No questions, just listen. He won't be in there long, and we need to talk."

As she relayed the condensed version of what she'd seen—or thought she had—the other night from her window, Mick's congenial smile disappeared.

"Did you know about this?" Maydene asked.

"Did I know? No ..." Mick rubbed his forehead. "But I'm not surprised."

He closed his eyes. "There've been a few times when I've walked into his office and felt like I had interrupted a conversation, even though Zak was the only one there."

"If we're not imagining this, who is he talking to?"

"I do not know." The concern in his eyes belied his words. "But I wonder. Indeed, I do. Pray that I'm wrong."

"Keep your eye on him," Maydene said. "He may need you."

"Maybe Jenny will be a good distraction. Help him forget the past and move on."

Maydene shrugged. "They could help each other. Raising a kid alone must be tough. Jenny's ex, Susan's father, is not in the picture—at least right now."

Mick sighed and hugged Maydene.

"I'll watch Zak. You watch Jenny. Maybe something beautiful will come from this. For both of them"

Chapter Thirteen

After saying goodbye to Mick in *The Gazette's* lot, Zak climbed into his Jeep. Talking to Jenny at the café had been fun. He was grateful he'd joined Mick for pie this afternoon.

He hadn't missed her flinch when they'd discussed Clarity Communications. He had honed the skill of reading body language. Understanding when to ask more questions—dig deeper—and when to back off had made him a better reporter. What about that conversation had provoked her and why?

Zak shrugged the question off as he pulled onto the road. Maybe he'd ask her at the picnic.

"What's for dinner, lover?"

His hand flew to his heart. He'd always had a healthy startle reflex, but distracted by thoughts of Jenny, he'd failed to notice Kay's arrival. Her visits had become more sudden, unexpected.

"Kay." He gripped the steering wheel. "Are you trying to scare me to death?"

"Now, there's an idea." She smiled. "Since I can't join you there, you could join me here."

He glanced at her, not sure how to respond.

"Relax, Zak. It doesn't work that way. Besides, you wouldn't like it here. There's no pie."

Kay rarely used sarcasm, but he heard notes of indignation in her voice. Or was his guilt making him imagine something that wasn't there?

"I'm not sure I follow."

"You're so cute when you lie. Speaking of, isn't that new waitress a cutie patootie? What is she? Thirty? Thirty-two?"

Zak sighed, rubbing the spot in the middle of his forehead where the headaches always started.

"It's not what you think."

"And you're, what? Forty-five? Forty-six?"

"I'm forty-four, which you know full well. I don't know how old Jenny is. I just met her Wednesday."

"Ooo, Jenny. That is such a *sweet* cheerleadery name."

"Knock it off. She's a friend. You don't even know her."

"Neither do you—yet."

For a moment, Kay was silent. They had rarely argued when she was alive. He wondered why certain things provoked her now. It wasn't like he had any lasting interest in Jenny. Did he?

"When will you see her again?" Kay's silence was short-lived.

He pulled into the Kroger parking lot and slid into a spot near the front. "I need milk." But his true intention was to get away from Kay.

"Make it skim, darling," she called after him. "Less fat. That's some middle-aged spread you're sporting. I think you can pinch an inch."

He stormed into the store. Her mean-spirited comments

surprised him. Sarcastic? Jaded? That was *his* territory—came with the job—not Kay's.

Middle-aged? Pinch an inch? She had never said anything so petty. He could write some of it off to the disappointment of being dead, but criminitly, she should be over that after a year.

He headed for the dairy aisle for his milk—maybe he'd pick up some Chunky Monkey ice cream too.

Jenny drained the sink and wiped it down. Maydene slipped into the office, presumably to work on the books but more likely to avoid a lecture from Jenny. She was both excited at the prospect Maydene had engineered and miffed that she'd gotten involved.

Jenny had something else on her mind, and maybe assisting Abe with preparation before the evening rush would allow her to work some of it out.

"I see the crazy woman has got you fixed up with our most eligible bachelor" Abe chuckled as he cut veggies for his salads. "Zak's a nice guy. Respectable and respectful. You'll have a fun time." He set out twenty bowls in four rows of five and began filling each half full of lettuce.

Jenny smiled weakly as she hung up her apron. "Yes, a picnic will be fun." A mixture of apprehension and excitement churned inside her. "Maybe it will be too cold."

Abe chopped carrots, green peppers, and onions, parceling them into each bowl. The fresh cut scents filled the kitchen.

Jenny moved to stand beside him. Could she ask his advice about Jonas? One man might have insights into another.

She followed behind Abe with the bucket of croutons and dropped six in each bowl. In the silence, she recalled how she used to prepare a similar salad for dinner on the rare nights Jonas didn't work late.

The memories of those lonely nights, and the abandonment they'd created, came roaring back. Tears fell yet again, and she angrily brushed them away. She would cry no more for that man and the marriage she'd longed for, but never had.

Men. Why couldn't they be true? Like Abe.

Fueled by her frustration, she blurted out, "Abe? You've never cheated on Maydene, have you?"

Talking to him was almost like talking to her father—before he'd died of a heart attack when she was seventeen. She missed him.

Despite how the question sounded, it hadn't come out of the air, and she already knew the answer. She had watched Abe and Maydene interact and seen the sincerity in Maydene's eyes when she'd claimed her ability to take the measure of a person.

A deep and abiding love thrived between her employers. The kind Jenny wanted.

Abe set down his knife and looked at her. He exhaled long and low and closed his eyes. When he opened them again, they were filled with regret.

When Jenny's question drifted into the office, Maydene set aside her paperwork. She sent up a quick prayer, quietly rose, and stole closer to the door where she could hear and see, but not be seen.

Oh, dear God, here we go.

"Yes, I have," Abe answered.

Though he'd said those same words to Maydene many years ago, they still cut her heart like Abe's favorite knife.

"And it was the dumbest choice I've ever made." His voice thickened and he cleared his throat. "To this day, I wish I could take it back. You would not believe the hurt that one stupid act caused—and continues to cause in some ways."

Jenny didn't reply. Maydene suspected Jenny already understood the pain adultery caused.

"How could you?" Jenny stepped back, anger and indignation in her tone. "You love each other. Anyone can see that."

Abe bowed his head, not in resignation but in contemplation. Possibly prayer.

"I don't think you understand," Abe said. "It was a long time ago, and—"

"A long time ago? That's no excuse."

Jenny burned with a fire kindled much earlier than today.

She leaned forward, her face bulldogging Abe's. "Don't you condescend me. I understand plenty. Jonas is an adulterer too. And me? I'm a fool."

Maydene wanted to step out of the office and put an end to the conversation—for Jenny's sake and Abe's. But she waited.

"You—you, men! It's just another conquest. Another five minutes of your life." Jenny's long-suppressed anger and heartbreak vied for equal time. She turned her back on Abe indignantly. "You don't stop to think. There's no connection between your heart and your ... need."

Maydene gasped and started to leave the office, but her husband's upraised hand stilled her. She was to stay put.

You ol' buzzard. Is it this way, even now?

But she remained where she was. Her heart ached to hold Jenny and offer what little comfort she could.

Jenny crossed her arms around her middle, as if doing so would help her win the battle against her tears and emotions.

Abe walked up behind her and placed his hands on her shoulders.

She jerked at his touch yet didn't shrug him off.

"There are some men like that." Abe spoke to the wound in Jenny. "And there always will be. But not all. For us, it wasn't that way."

He was trying to protect Maydene. Just like before. Only this time she couldn't let him carry the burden.

Oh Lord, help me.

She breathed deep and stepped out of the office, smoothing her apron. Abe caught her movement and shook his head at her.

Maydene kept walking forward.

No, Abe. Not anymore, my darling. Not anymore.

Jenny stood with her back to the office, her hands clenched.

Maydene came up behind her and placed a palm between her shoulders. "Jenny, your anger at Abe is misplaced. I was the unfaithful one. I was the adulterer."

Jenny twisted around and stared at Maydene.

"Wh—? Why would you do that?"

Maydene embraced the young woman who, day by day, was becoming a daughter of her heart. Then she walked to the front, put the "Closed" sign in the door, and pulled down the blind.

Over the next hour, a pot or two of coffee, and some pie, Maydene told her story to someone other than Abe or God for the first time. It was hard but necessary. Release and freedom came in the confessing.

Jenny's question of why she'd done it was valid. But all of these years later, answering was still difficult.

Oh, she'd had a litany of excuses for her unfaithfulness. Disappointment at being unable to conceive with Abe. Restlessness in her heart. Distance from God. An inopportune hiring of a second cook who said all the right words to a wounded woman's heart. All of those things, and none of them, had led to her affair.

"Why? Oh, honey, I can only blame myself, my fallen human nature, my pride—and I even considered myself a Christian. 'Pride goeth before a fall,'" Maydene prayed for wisdom to reach past Jenny's pain.

Jenny rounded on Abe. "So, you lied to protect Maydene when you said you had cheated?"

Abe shook his head and his eyes begged for understanding. "No, I did not lie."

Maydene reached for his hand, but her gaze held Jenny's. "He did sleep with another woman. After I kicked him out of our home and our bed in favor of my new man. I was such a fool."

"That doesn't excuse my behavior." Abe stroked her hand. "I knew right from wrong. I knew what God required, but I closed my heart to His invitation and chose to nurse my wounds at The Whistle Stop with J—a barfly."

"Jean," Maydene said. "Her name was Jean."

How could these people, who were the most "Christian" Christians she'd ever met, have this kind of a past? Jonas's flaws were deeper and more wrapped up in his ego than in the situation. He'd had no problem kissing her goodbye in the morning after they'd shared intimate moments and by the same afternoon, having sex with a secretary in the supply closet.

That kind of behavior made a woman wonder if her husband even valued her.

Jenny shook her head. She refused to wallow in that again.

But if Abe and Maydene could change and pull their lives together, could Jonas? Would he even be willing to try?

"How'd you move past the hurt and stay together?" Jenny asked. "How did you put it behind you?"

Maydene's gaze shifted to Abe—to the depth of the love held in his eyes.

"It was Abe. Abe and God. I was hell-bent on being 'happy'—whatever that meant."

Maydene stroked Abe's face, wiping away the tiniest of tears. He reached for her, placing his large hand at the nape of her neck and drew her in close. Then he swept a delicate kiss on her forehead.

Jenny sighed at the easy physical affection the couple shared. She'd never have that with Jonas.

"Abe wooed me a second time," Maydene said. "He forgave me first, then he set out to win my heart back. One day he asked me to go to church with him, and Joe..." Maydene turned to Abe, who nodded. "That was his name. Joe. Anyway, Abe asked me to church, and Joe was sleeping off a drinking binge, so I went. It was a God appointment."

"After a month or so with ... Jean, I began praying with my pastor about my messed-up life." Abe put his arm around Maydene's shoulders. "One day, after our prayers, God told me to leave Jean and return to my wife. I listened."

Jenny watched the couple strengthen each other.

"I asked Maydene to church because she needed Him again even more than she needed me."

"And He called me back," Maydene said. "During the service, a soft voice kept saying my name." She walked to the coffeemaker and offered the dregs to Abe, who declined.

"I have no recollection what Pastor preached on, but God spoke right into my heart." She scootched into the booth beside Abe. "He told me my life was all wrong, but He loved me and wanted me back. I came, dragging the tattered remains of my life behind me. He rebuilt it—us—stronger and better."

Something new beat in Jenny's heart. Could it be hope?

"When I got back to the house, Joe was gone. He'd left a note, though. 'Sweetcakes' that's what he called me. I hated it then and I still do. 'Sweetcakes: Saw you all dolled up and walking with Abe. Figured you were going back to church and the gig was up. Thanks for the kicks—and the fifty bucks.'"

"He took money from you?" Her voice shook.

"Honey, he took something worth much more than fifty dollars."

"But the fifty was money well spent," Abe said. "Things haven't been hunky-dory, milk and honey, since then, but God has been faithful. He is faithful."

Maydene squeezed his hand and rose again. "Who needs another piece of pie?"

Jenny declined, but Abe grinned.

"What a beautiful—sad, but beautiful—story." Jenny toyed with her coffee cup, swirling the lukewarm drink. "Abe, I'm sorry for the things I said to you earlier. I was out of line."

"Don't give it a second thought. I understood your anger wasn't with me."

"I don't know how to thank you. Both of you." Jenny looked at the two people who had become so much more than friends and released a contented sigh. In this moment of truth-telling, could she reveal her secret? "It's too bad something similar will never happen with Jonas and me."

"Are you so sure it won't?" Maydene said. "I know being divorced is different, but no problem is beyond God's reach."

"We're not..." Jenny pulled back from the truth. "Jonas doesn't believe in God. He believes in himself." Why was she hiding the fact she was still married?

"Doesn't matter what Jonas believes." Maydene paused. "What do you believe?"

The question caught Jenny off guard.

"Do you believe in forgiveness?" Maydene continued. "In restoration? You either believe in grace, or you don't. It's for everyone or no one."

"But—"

"There are no buts in God's eyes. All are invited to the party. Some will choose not to attend. Nothin' you can do about those. But God's grace is available to everyone. Has to be. You're no more worthy of it than Jonas."

Jenny's eyes blazed anew.

"How can you say that when you know what he's done? We had to move out of our apartment complex because he'd slept with every woman in our building." *Well, almost.*

"'For all have sinned and come short of the glory of God.'" Maydene's voice was a touch louder than a whisper. "That includes you as well as Jonas—and Abe and me. If forgiveness is for us, it's for everyone."

Jenny put her head in her hands. A chill swept over her. She needed to face the truth. "Including me."

Curiosity and compassion filled Maydene's eyes.

"Jonas and I are not divorced. I walked out on him after his latest … episode. Just packed up Susan and left."

"Oh, Jenny."

"Here I sit, a married woman, looking forward to my date with Oak Hill's most eligible bachelor tomorrow night. And it's all your fault."

Maydene quirked an eyebrow, then smiled.

MICK ALMOST DROPPED his three gallons of milk when Zak sailed passed him in the grocery store parking lot without notice. If not for Maydene's caution, he might have headed home.

She believed Zak was talking to someone who wasn't there, and Mick was afraid that someone was Kay. So, he retraced his steps.

He walked back into the store, milk jugs in his arms, and gave the cashier who'd checked him out an awkward shrug. The stormy expression on Zak's face as he'd stomped toward the store was out of character.

He spotted Zak's brown hair on the dairy section side and hurried to catch up, cold lead forming in his gut.

"SKIM MILK. THAT BURNS ME UP."

Zak paced the dairy aisle to his regular two percent, then looked down at his waist and reached for the skim. That made his insides boil over again.

"I think you can pinch an inch." Kay's taunt percolated in his mind. "I think you can pinch an inch. I think you can pinch an inch."

Why was she being so mean? Where had her biting sarcasm come from? That was his *modus operandi*, not Kay's. He and Jenny weren't dating. Yet.

Zak plunked the skim back on the shelf and grabbed a roll of cookie dough and a container of onion dip from the refrigerated section and, to top it off, a jumbo bag of potato chips off the end cap. On his way out of the dairy aisle, he snagged a gallon of whole milk—and a pint of Chubby Hubby ice cream.

~

MICK JUGGLED his milk gallons as Zak careened into the dairy section. He'd never seen his friend so mad. Zak grabbed one gallon of milk, only to set it down and pick up another. Then he set that one down, grabbed a roll of cookie dough, a bag of chips, some kind of dip—and another gallon of milk. And ice cream?

Sheesh, is he pregnant?

Adding the chips at least made sense, but what was with the ice cream? And whole milk? He and Dreama hadn't used whole milk since the kids were weaned from breast milk.

The guy can eat whatever he wants. Relax. Maybe he's having friends over for a little ESPN or WWF.

Standing behind a display of mini donuts, Mick set down one gallon of milk and smacked his head. "If Zak was having people over, he would have invited me."

"Check my waist, Kay? Check my waist?" Zak's staccato words reached Mick.

"Well, you can sit there tonight and check it as I eat all of this myself."

Mick dropped another gallon of milk and his jaw at the same time. The milk hit the floor, and the bottom of the plastic ruptured. As white liquid pooled at his feet, he stared after his friend as he stormed up to the cashier, oblivious of anything around him.

Chapter Fourteen

The next day, Zak left the office early to get ready for his not-a-date with Jenny. Sloan could finish the layout for A-1 without him. Only Mick knew why Zak was leaving, and that was the way he wanted to keep it.

It was a picnic between two friends. No biggie. So why didn't he want anyone to discover his plans?

He drove home for a quick change of clothes—and a chance to catch his breath. Kay had been absent since the big blowup, but he wanted to give her every chance to show up again. He didn't want her to wait until the last minute and ruin his good mood before his date—or whatever this was.

He peeled off his work clothes, glad to lose the tie and button-down shirt. He was not a tie man, but for the editor meeting today, the formality lent credence to his proposals to staunch the bleeding bottom-line.

Waxman had accepted all proposals for consideration but appeared distracted. Either the situation was worse than he'd let on, or Waxman's mistress was making noise again.

Shucking his twills, Zak considered a pair of shorts. The

plan was a picnic, after all, and he'd likely play with Susan. He decided against them and pulled out a pair of jeans. Before he allowed himself to think too much about it, Zak stepped out of his boxers and slipped on a clean pair. He followed with the jeans, sweat socks, his tennis shoes, fresh deodorant, and a madras shirt with a jaunty stripe.

In front of the mirror, Zak ran his hands through his hair and over his face. Should he shave? Nah, the five o'clock shadow look worked.

He appraised the man in the mirror. "You look like you're going on a date. Are you?"

Despite his insistence this wasn't a date, he wanted it to be one. Or at least a trial for an eventual date.

He sat on the bed, his hands sinking into the comforter he still pulled up each morning out of habit. His final morning with Kay replayed in his brain. It was a seductive memory. One that had waylaid him many times in the past. Today, it had the power to distract but not cripple.

He laughed freely, his breathing shallow and heartbeat at a salsa tempo.

Standing again, Zak inhaled deeply in front of the mirror in a futile attempt to calm himself, snagged his wallet and keys from the top of the dresser, and walked out of the room.

On impulse, Zak pulled into the grocery store parking lot. His nerves danced in his stomach like some manic scene from *Fantasia*. He was light-headed and giddy.

He walked into the store with one intention—to buy Jenny and Susan flowers. Daisies, if he could find them. Maybe he'd visit the candy aisle too.

Thirteen years ago, he'd married Kay. They'd dated since

junior high, so he had not had a first date since, well, ever. He and Kay had always been together. Friends, then more. Their transition to couple was natural. He didn't regret a single moment of their time together. How could he?

Today's date was truly a first, and he enjoyed the adrenaline rush.

At the checkout, Patti Simkins, one of the strategic stops on Oak Hill's information highway, saw Zak's daisies and chocolates. Her mouth formed a perfect O of surprise.

He winked. "Patti? Heard the latest?"

Shaking her head, Patti stepped into her cashier's alcove, eyes wide and leaned in conspiratorially. Zak imagined she was already mentally dialing the phone number of her gal pal to share the news, whatever it was.

"This is between you and me." Zak drew Patti into his confidence. "I would hate for this to get around, so you can't tell a soul."

Patti nodded her reassurance.

She was nearly salivating, so he moved in for the kill. "Patti?"

"Yes?"

After scanning the area in mock seriousness, Zak dropped his bomb.

"I. Am going. On a date." He pulled a daisy from his bouquet and handed it to her. "A date with a lovely young lady. We're going to the *park*. And having a *picnic*. The flowers? They're for her."

"And the chocolates?" Patti raised her eyebrows, rabid for more details.

"The chocolates?" Zak picked up the box as if he'd forgotten them. "Oh, those are for me."

He tore off the cellophane, opened the box, and popped a chocolate in his mouth as he sauntered out of the store.

"Delish."

~

Jenny had told Susan about the park and picnic over breakfast that morning. Her daughter's face had lit up with excitement, and she danced around the kitchen as if she were a high school freshman who'd been asked to prom by the captain of the football team.

Susan was so excited, Jenny had to convince her *not* to change clothes right then and put on her "for special" dress. The picnic wasn't until after school. To placate her, Jenny added a yellow ribbon to her hair for the school day.

Amusement and concern battled within Jenny at Susan's excitement. It illustrated how much her daughter needed a Daddy. If Jonas wasn't in her life, she would welcome her new friend, Zee, with open arms.

After her talk with Maydene and Abe last night, Jenny woke up determined to tell Zak everything and make sure they stayed on a friendship level—for her own sake as well as Susan's. Jenny had to believe things could work out with Jonas if he wanted them to. If he didn't? Well, she'd worry about that possibility when—*if*—it arose.

By the end of her shift, Jenny was exhausted and wished she could cancel the date—even at the expense of Susan's disappointment. All she wanted to do was put her feet up—or better yet, soak in her tub with lavender bath oils.

But the picnic basket was packed, and in spite of her cautions, shivers of excitement ran up and down her spine. She kept reminding herself that even though Zak was nice—and handsome—she was married and needed to respect that covenant. Protect it.

So, why did her heart go pit-a-pat when Zak walked up the street? With daisies.

Chapter Fifteen

Jenny and Zak walked along the paths of the park, enjoying the cool spring afternoon while Susan dashed here and there, picking up rocks, chasing down bugs, and racing ahead making new discoveries each minute. All the while sporting the daisy chain headdress Jenny had made with the flowers from Zak.

They had left Jenny's car at the café and ridden together in Zak's Jeep for the short drive to the county park.

After half an hour at the playground, during which Susan and Zak tested every slide, every swing—everything except the teeter-totter—Zak picked up the picnic basket and suggested a special place by the river for dinner.

As they approached a small grove of blue spruce trees, Zak stopped Jenny with a hand on her shoulder. "I found this nook of the park years ago when I needed it." He leaned in and his breath warmed her cheek. "My mother died when I was eight and my father disappeared shortly after her funeral."

She had no idea of the misfortunes that had shaped Zak's life, though Maydene had alluded to some trauma.

"I had my Gram, my mother's mother. I wasn't Little Orphan Zee." He widened his eyes into saucers.

Jenny shook her head and pushed him away, smiling as he came back. "I was in junior high, feeling ... unmoored. Typical junior higher. Nothing belonged to me, and I didn't belong. Yada yada yada."

During her junior high days, Jenny had been the ugly duckling. What had Zak looked like at that age? Boys were cuter, in her experience.

"So, I came to the park to be alone—even though I was always alone—but that day I walked farther through the brush until ..."

He paused and brushed several branches of a large blue spruce aside, then motioned for Jenny and Susan to enter.

Jenny bent and peered through the branches, but Susan dashed past, eager to explore. He continued holding the branches, so Jenny followed her daughter in.

Susan's delighted squeals filled Jenny's ears. An outdoor sanctuary stretched in front of her. "It's beautiful. Like a little park within a park."

He nodded. "I know. I love it." He entered behind her, his hand on her elbow guiding her forward.

"I've never brought anyone here," he said. "Except Kay."

As a comfortable silence built, Jenny remembered what Maydene had told her about Zak and Kay. To her ears, their marriage had sounded like everything hers and Jonas's was not. Close, intimate, reverential.

After a time, when Zak reached for her hand, she gave it to him without hesitation—only to pull it back a moment later as Susan returned from her grand exploration. She crowded between them and took both of their hands in hers.

"There's a lake. With a little island in the middle," Susan tugged them forward. "Let's go wading."

Zak bent over to untie his shoes.

"No wading." Jenny bent to stop Susan from taking off her shoes. "We'll be eating soon."

Zak stooped to Susan's level as her pout threatened. Taking her hands in his, he folded his legs under him and sat on the ground. Susan slid into his lap as if she belonged there.

"It's a river, not a lake," Zak said. "An incredibly special, magical, river. Would you like to know why?"

Susan nodded, her daisy crown sliding down over one ear.

"I've not seen them lately, but a beautiful family of swans lives here." Zak spread his hands to take in the area. "They don't come out often, but I think they live right out there in that bramble."

As her daughter's eyes grew wide with delight, Zak mirrored her.

He's not afraid to play with her. Even knowing it wasn't fair, she compared Zak's interactions with Susan to Jonas's.

"Can we go see them?" Susan leaped off Zac's lap and danced in an eager circle. "Please? Can we? Can we? Can we?"

He took her hand. "Perhaps we can"—he looked up to Jenny—"Ask Mom, uh, your mother."

"Can we, Mom? Can we?" Susan folded her hands beneath her chin.

Jenny smiled at her daughter. "Maybe after dinner. We'll see."

Content with the answer, Susan bounded off in exploration.

"Thank you for sharing this spot with us." Jenny gave Zak a hand as he stood. "We would have never found it on our own."

"It's a great place to think. It's become my home away from home. My escape when the newsroom doesn't cut it."

His refuge was a bend in the river. A gentle ripple of water provided the background music as he spread the blanket and waved a hand for her to sit.

She settled on the ground and stretched her legs in front of her. Her resolve to keep this friendship as only that slipped away with the river's current.

His every move, every laugh, every smile, every freely shared word or emotion, intoxicated her. If she dared, she could grasp the fulfillment of every fantasy she had entertained about marriage and family.

She sighed and scanned the area. Where was Susan?

Her daughter hunkered down on the riverbank with a stick, splashing in the water and singing one of her made-up songs. Her joy made Jenny smile, and her eyes welled with moisture.

"Zak, why don't you go down by the river and play with Susan." Jenny opened the picnic basket. "I can handle the food prep and her over on the bank is making me nervous."

He sprung up so fast, she was half afraid she'd scared him away. "I really wanted to help with the prep, but if you insist." He was off without a backward glance.

Jonas would have discounted her concerns about Susan and remained with Jenny. He loved his daughter, but preferred Jenny's affirmation and affection.

Comparisons continued to leap to mind as she set out their dinner. Her conflicted heart was as full as the picnic Maydene had packed. For each item she removed from the basket, she unpacked arguments to God about why she should be free to pursue a relationship with Zak. Jonas wasn't interested and had turned her down.

Potato salad. Susan hungered for attention from a man—a daddy. She would flower with Zak.

I will be her Father. Her Abba.

Fried chicken. I could be so happy. You want me to be happy, don't You?

Be happy with Me, beloved. Rest in Me.

Deviled eggs. He makes me feel safe, protected, secure.

Find your security in Me.

Plates and forks. Jonas doesn't love me. You've seen how he treats me.

I love you—and I love Jonas.

Napkins. I deserve this. I need this. I've put up with so much.

I know the plans I have for you.

When Maydene's homemade apple pie was the last thing in the basket, Jenny ran out of arguments.

She shifted toward the river to check on Susan, but her gaze landed on Zak. He stood several feet from Susan and had moved to the edge of the river, hands in his pockets as he stared down the river at something she could not see. With his right hand, he wiped a tear away, and water pooled in her eyes.

Not wanting to intrude on his private moment any longer, she returned her focus to the food spread out beside her.

The crackle of twigs and leaves under his feet announced his approach. She bent over the blanket, pretending to arrange the plates. The soft caress of his hand on the back of her neck made her shiver as she turned toward him. When he held out his hand, she took it and stood on shaky ground.

He took her face in both of his hands and lifted it to meet his. The fulfillment of her desires reflected in his eyes, and she made her choice. As his mouth touched hers, gently, tentatively at first and then more hungrily, she closed her eyes and opened her heart to him—and the fantasy he represented.

Susan looked up from her play by the river to see if the food was ready. She was hungry. Mom was still setting things on the blanket, but where was Zee?

She twisted around until she found him behind her looking at the river. He wiped his face with his hand. She liked Zee. He played with her and made her laugh.

She missed Daddy. When would he be home? Sometimes she cried because she wanted to see him. Was that why Zak was crying? Did he want to see his daddy too?

Zee spun away from the river and walked back to the picnic blanket with a little smile. She followed him, ready to eat.

When he touched Mommy's neck, Susan stopped and scrunched down behind a tree, peeking around it like in hide and seek.

Mommy stood up and he gave her a kiss. A little one like the ones Mommy gave Susan when she tucked her in at night. Then he kissed Mommy again. It was different. It reminded her of Daddy, and she started to cry, but Mommy didn't hear. Zee didn't hear. Daddy didn't hear.

She felt someone hugging her—and she knew Who it was. He'd heard her cry. She sat behind the tree in Jesus' arms and cried out all the hurt inside her.

Chapter Sixteen

Jonas parked his Lexus and stepped onto the sidewalk in downtown Oak Hill. He gazed south down Main Street. A sign for *The Gazette* on the west side of the road and down one block caught his attention. He wasn't ready to make his presence known to the folks at the paper, but after the long drive from Chicago, he needed a bathroom and some serious caffeine. In that order.

He stretched, shaking the car cramps out of his shoulders, and locked the car.

He spotted the Main Street Café & Emporium—one of *The Gazette's* advertisers—and headed there at a trot, certain to meet both needs.

Shinola, no Starbucks.

With a coffee shop in the lobby of his office building, he'd developed a taste for the Cinnamon Dolce Latte, with an extra shot of cinnamon and espresso. As a result, regular coffee seemed, well, regular. Jonas had avoided regular since graduating fourth in his high school class, a defeat his father had made certain he never lived down.

"Jonas, you didn't even show, for crying out loud," his father had railed. "Fourth is no better than last. You settled. I didn't raise a loser. Prove me wrong."

While he couldn't change his fourth place standing, Jonas had decided he'd never settle for less than the best as he set off on his quest for more. More impressive grades. A more powerful car. An extraordinary house and the prettiest wife.

He worked more hours than anyone else and enjoyed more encounters with more women than any man he knew who *wasn't* lying. So, yeah, Starbucks cost more, but more was worth every penny. And if he occasionally used a credit card to get what he wanted, so what? In his plan, he'd be making big money—more money—in three to five years and would catch up. *Live like a loser, become a loser. Live like a winner, become a winner.* The philosophy of more drove him.

Which is why Jen leaving was not an option. Losers' wives walked out on them. Winners' wives stayed—even if only for the money or the prestige—and he was not a loser. Would never be one.

At the corner, Jonas eyed the flashing "Don't Walk" sign. The nearest car was two blocks away and turning into the lot next to *The Gazette*. After taking his life into his hands every day as a pedestrian in Chicago, crossing against the light here seemed like a vacation.

His hunch was that Jen was nearby, and his hunches usually played out. Soon he would visit Templeton, find Aunt Sarah, and convince her to tell him where Jen and Susan were. Then he'd buy some roses, maybe chocolates, and convince Jen to return. All would be right in his world again. He'd change his ways if necessary. He could do it. He wouldn't be careless again. He'd learned his lesson. The cost of a hotel room was worth it. Losers got caught at home.

He burst through the café door, waved at a dowdy old woman behind the counter, and headed for the john.

"Coffee. Black, extra caffeine," he hollered behind him as the door slammed against the bathroom wall. "And a paper."

Maydene made a mental note to check the men's room. This man wouldn't take the time to lift the seat, let alone remember his target practice. She poured his coffee and set it on the counter, then grabbed today's edition of *The Gazette* and laid it next to the cup.

The young man was much relieved as he exited the bathroom, hiking up his pants. He was handsome if a trifle rough around the edges. A heartbreaker, she guessed. Fun-loving but careless.

He carried himself with a bravado she was sure he viewed as authority. She nodded at his coffee, and he smiled big as he lifted the cup and drained most of it in one gulp. She refilled before he could think to point to the cup.

"There's your paper. Fresh off the press." Maydene set the coffeepot back on the warmer and retrieved her order pad. "How about dinner? Or a piece of pie? We've got all kinds."

"Banana crème?"

Maydene smiled and opened the pie case. He wasn't much out of college, but he sure tried hard to act important. The hope behind the banana crème request gave him away as a young boy wearing a man's power suit. She plated the slice and slid it in front of him.

The man tore into the pie with his fork as if starved. Did mothers not teach their children not to snarf their food anymore?

He didn't seem to mind her watching him. Despite her

reservations, the dopey grin on his face made her like him. He exuded charisma; tempered by the fact he knew it. By her assessment, he was single, likely in sales, and he'd not spend the night alone.

"Passing through?" Maydene asked with a practiced nonchalance that allowed a customer to engage, as he or she chose.

"No, ma'am. I am not." He took another bite of the pie and chased it down with more coffee. "I expect to be here a couple of days at least. Could you hit me with that java again?"

"Good thing the restroom's free," she murmured.

The customer laughed easily, and Maydene chuckled.

"Won't be needing it, ma'am," he said. "I've got a good-sized tank on me. It's just that Chicago's a long way away, and I didn't stop at all."

"Please, too much information." She held one hand up and refilled his cup with the other. "Holler if you need anything else."

She started to walk away but the man's hand on her arm stopped her.

"Do you have any cinnamon creamer, by chance?"

"We've got half and half and the powdered stuff. Sorry, we aren't Starbucks."

He nodded. "Powdered stuff it is, then. And could I have a large to-go cup?" He placed a $20 bill on the counter and stood. At the door he looked back.

"Is there a hotel nearby? I forgot to check. I could drive to Templeton and get a place if I need to, but my business is in Oak Hill."

"The Starlight's out on the highway," Maydene said. "You probably passed it coming in."

The Starlight was close to The Whistle Stop. Though she

didn't know him at all, Maydene wanted to give this man the benefit of doubt.

"But there's also a nice bed-and-breakfast a few blocks east of here called The Tuck Inn." Maydene pointed up the street. "I understand they have flavored creamers." She smiled as she leveled the little jab.

"Maybe," the man replied, "but I'll lay even odds they don't have a banana crème pie as good—or a waitress as feisty. I'll let you know for sure in the morning, assuming they have an available room."

"I am neither feisty nor a waitress, young man," Maydene's feathers were not the least bit ruffled. "I am high-spirited. And the proprietor of this eatery." She stuck out her hand. "Maydene Gunderson. Do you have a name?"

The man returned to the counter, took her hand, bowed over it, and kissed the back. "'By a name I know not how to tell thee who I am: My name, dear saint, is hateful to myself, because it is an enemy to thee.'"

Maydene sucked in a sharp breath and sank onto a stool. She wasn't a college educated woman, but she knew Shakespeare. As a besotted teenager, she had swooned to *Romeo and Juliet* many times. What kind of man went around quoting the bard to little old ladies he'd just met?

And why had he bowed his head to the floor and kissed her hand?"

From a tightened throat and through dry lips, she asked the question again. "Do you have a name?" Her voice sounded like a rusty nail being pulled out of a two-by-four.

The young man smiled that darned disarming smile and bowed once more. "Jonas, ma'am. Jonas Miller, at your service."

As he walked out the door, her hand flew to her chest.

"Oh, Dear God, help."

Chapter Seventeen

Jenny regretted the kiss, but reached for another. Zak's lips trembled against hers, and the fact he was scared, too, excited her. However, his arms had no hesitation as he pulled her closer and held her there.

In his embrace, she surrendered to his clean scent in the same way her resolve gave in to fresh-baked apple pie. She appreciated that he wore none of the cloying, Madison Avenue cologne she associated with Jonas.

Her thoughts of Jonas drew her into the real world, where Susan ... She jerked away from Zak and whirled around, heart pounding as she searched for her daughter. Had she seen Jenny kissing Zak?

Where was Susan?

Before panic settled in, her gaze snagged on Susan's tennis shoe sticking out from behind a nearby tree, bobbing in rhythm to the song she sang as she drew pictures in the dirt.

"Jesus loves me, this I know. For the Bible tells me so. Little ones to Him belong. They are weak, but He is strong."

Though charmingly off key, her daughter's clear, angelic

tones and the words in the song gave Jenny some necessary distance.

What had she been thinking? After berating Abe? After Maydene's challenge about grace for Jonas?

Jenny turned back to Zak, embarrassed and needing to apologize. Before she said anything, the fear on his face made her tremor. He looked *at* her and *through* her at the same time.

"I—um, I'm—I didn't see you there," he said. "How long ...?"

Jenny stared at him, fighting the unreasonable urge to see who was behind her. She reached to touch his arm.

"It's not what you think." His raised voice made her jump back.

Was he talking to her?

"It's a picnic, nothing more."

Relieved to know Zak was thinking the same, even if he got there in a strange way, she calmed. "I'm glad to hear you say that, because I agree that we were carri—"

"It was one kiss."

What was going on? Was he talking to her or someone else? "Right," she said. "We both just got a little carried away—"

"Well, yes, one *series* of kisses." He paced. "Nothing more."

For several seconds, the ripples of the river and rustling leaves filled the air. "No. There wouldn't have been more. No, I wouldn't have."

Jenny spun around, certain someone was behind her, but she saw no one. Her eyes darted to the tree, where she still saw her daughter's shoes. When she turned back, Zak had bowed his head, as if shamed.

"Zak?" His name was hesitant.

"Yes, of course. I *said* yes, didn't I?" He was quieter now.

Feeling like a fool, Jenny stepped closer to Zak and snapped her fingers in his face. The tactic worked.

He focused on her again, but his demeanor was different from moments ago when he'd pulled her into his embrace. Where he'd previously stood tall with the self-assurance of a man who'd found a new truth, he now bent over from an unseen burden.

"Are you okay?" She wasn't sure he heard at first, or that he was going to reply.

His eyes cleared, and he blinked at her as if coming out of a dream. "Jenny." He sighed. "I'm sorry."

"Who...? What...?" She took three steps back, putting some distance between them and keeping Susan in sight.

"I should never have let things get so out of control." He massaged his forehead and covered his eyes with his hands.

She fought to move the conversation onto more solid ground. "Well, yes. Um, of course. You weren't the only one involved, you know."

She bent to pack up the uneaten food. She re-boxed the chicken, put the lid on the potato salad, and covered the deviled eggs. "I should have been more careful too."

When she looked up again, his eyebrows scrunched together.

"I really think its best, for all three—four?—of us to pretend this afternoon never happened," she said. She certainly couldn't imagine explaining it to Susan. She didn't comprehend herself.

He nodded and helped her pull things together.

In the heavy silence, Jenny remembered her argument with God. If she weren't anchored in Him, she, too, could leave behind her marriage vows without a second glance. Had she believed she was above sin?

She had only kissed Zak.

This time.

This time? She was shading her sin. She'd kissed Zak but

she hadn't slept with him—and she certainly hadn't slept with multiple "hims" throughout the years. But the standard was purity of the heart and mind.

"Jenny?" Zak interrupted her thoughts. "You're the first woman I've kissed since Kay died. The first I've *wanted* to kiss."

She said nothing.

"I shouldn't have done it, shouldn't have allowed it, because ... I'm clearly not ready for a relationship but,"–he folded the blanket as his face turned an endearing shade of pink—"it was really nice. Special, you know?"

This was the Zak she was familiar with. But, because she didn't want to add lying to her sins of the day, tears pooled in her eyes. "It was the same for me."

Susan came over from her drawing board in the ground and hugged her. "Aren't we going to eat, Mommy? I'm hungry."

Jenny hugged her daughter close and nodded as she wiped her tears away on the sleeve of her blouse.

"I am too, honey." She sniffed and tweaked Susan's nose. "But it's getting ... a little cold. We can take the food home and eat it there. Is that okay?"

"I guess, but I'm not cold," Susan said. "Can Zee come eat with us?"

Jenny peeked at Zak.

He squatted to Susan's level and took her hands in his. "You know, Suzy Q, I'd like to because I had a lot of fun with you today. But I can't tonight. I have too much homework."

Susan's giggles lightened the situation, and the knots in Jenny's shoulders loosened a bit.

"You don't have homework," Susan said. "You're a 'dult. Only kids have homework. I got mine all done, didn't I, Mommy?"

"Yes, you did." Jenny picked up the picnic basket. "Maybe

Mr. Cooper can come over for dinner another time. Would you like that, Suze?"

"Tomorrow?"

"No, not tomorrow—but soon." Jenny smiled at Zak and squeezed his hand. "I promise."

She paused. "Maybe we could invite Miss Dreama and her husband too."

"Yay." Susan ran off again and explored the woods along the path.

"Good idea. That should help keep things ... safe." His shoulders rose and fell. "Although, they would like to see me date again."

Jenny picked up the picnic basket. She almost told Zak that she was married. She knew he'd assumed she was divorced—and that it didn't bother him.

Why couldn't she tell him the truth? She sighed.

As they walked to the parking lot, her thoughts turned to Jonas. She would have to connect with him again—soon. He'd try to convince her to come home. But she couldn't do that—wasn't sure she wanted to. She needed Jonas to commit to their marriage. But how would she tell if his pledge to do so was the truth or more empty promises?

Reading Jonas was always a challenge. Would he try harder if he found out she had other ... opportunities?

"Jenny?" Zak sounded far away. "Earth to Jenny. What solar system are you in right now?"

She punched him in the arm. "You should talk. I'm not the one who's here one minute and gone the next." As soon as the words were out, she wanted to bite them back.

A cloud settled over Zak's eyes again. "No, of course not." He nodded. "How could you be here one moment and gone the next. You're not a ghost."

They finally reached the parking lot. Susan sat on one end

of the teeter-totter, eyes alight with the possibility of one more ride. Zak smiled at her, but pain etched his face.

"Not tonight, Suze."

Jenny waved her daughter over. "We've got to head home. Zak's going to take us back to the cafe to get our car, and then he's going home to do his homework."

"You got it." Life returned to his face as he swept Susan onto his shoulders. "Last one there doesn't get ice cream."

He took off across the playground, with Susan's laughter echoing across the park.

Jenny trailed behind them.

God? Can I trust You? Help me. Help me do what's right; what You want. Not what's easy.

Maydene pulled onto Pastor Dave's street and parked across from his house. She needed to warn Jenny about Jonas.

She got out and walked to the back yard, but Jenny's Civic was not on the parking pad next to the garage. Pastor Dave and Yolanda were gone, as well. Maydene returned to her car, opened the door, and slid inside again. She started the car for some music and drummed her fingers on the steering wheel while she formulated a plan.

Maybe she was meddling, as Abe had suggested. Maybe she should leave well enough alone and wait to learn why Jonas was in town. Maybe pigs flew and chocolate was calorie-free.

Did Jonas even know Jenny was here? His arrival could be a "coinkydink," as Abe liked to say. But her God did not operate by coincidence, he moved with intent.

She fiddled with the radio dial, moving between a Southern Gospel station and the Classical music station out of Templeton. No plan came.

Maydene shut off the car and got out. Walking up to the front door, she admired Yolanda's beautiful front garden. It was gorgeous. The lilac bushes and forsythias were full and astounding. Her peony garden was the envy of all the women at church. The tiger grasses, which would form a nice backdrop for the daffodils and tulips, were well on their way.

On closer examination, Maydene surmised that Yolanda was a little busier than normal. The garden needed weeding.

She stepped onto the porch, debated whether to knock on the door, then decided to leave a note for Jenny in her mailbox. She walked back to her car, her mind already writing the note, and grabbed a pen and an old grocery receipt she found on the floor of the car. For once she was glad Abe didn't keep a clean car.

Heading back to the mailbox, the garden again caught her eye.

"You know, it wouldn't take but a minute or two to set this plot to rights." She rested her hands on her hips and took inventory of the weeds. "It's not as bad as it appeared—and what a nice surprise for Yolanda."

The note forgotten, Maydene got down on her knees and her joints popped, as they always did when she worked in her own gardens. Tending nature was never work. It was more like a treat—or therapy. Over the years, she had often weeded when she needed to think through something important. It was a great place to be alone.

Abe didn't bother her in her gardens because he was afraid she'd put him to work. But she could always count on time with God while weeding. He never failed to show up—sometimes He bothered her, sometimes He just listened.

Soon, her hands worked their magic, pulling a weed here, straightening a plant there, moving the mulch around to cover bare spots. Before long, half an hour had passed, and she was beyond weeding the front bed. She'd made her way to the side of the house and was elbow deep in dirt and in her conversation with God.

A car door slammed, and Susan spoke. Maydene froze, and not only because the voice had startled her—since she wasn't paying attention.

"Mommy, will we ever see Daddy again?" Susan asked.

"Of course we will, honey. Soon, I think. Do you miss him?" The conversation grew louder as the two moved toward the house.

"All the time, but I didn't think I'd get to see him again."

Maydene remained still, not sure whether she should interrupt the moment. If she tried to get up, the pops from her knees would announce her presence for sure.

"Come sit with me on the swing, sweetie," Jenny said. "Why would you think we'd never see him again?" Jenny's attempt at light-hearted tone wasn't sincere. The porch swing squeaked as the mother and daughter sat.

"I saw you kissing Zee," Susan said. "I thought he was going to be my new daddy."

If Maydene's knees didn't give her away, the kathumping of her heart would. Why was Jenny taking so long to answer?

"Would you like that?" Jenny asked. "Would you like it if Zak was your daddy?"

Maydene's heart nearly quit working all together.

"I guess," Susan said. "But I love the daddy I already have."

Would Jenny answer this time?

"I do, too, honey." Jenny's voice quivered on the verge of tears. "I do too, but—."

"I like Zee, Mommy. He plays with me."

"I like Zee, too, honey."

"Is that why you kissed him?"

Jenny sighed. "Yes, I think so. No, no it wasn't. Well,

maybe." She groaned. "I really don't know why I kissed him. But I can tell you this for sure. I shouldn't have."

"Why not?"

Maydene strained to hear Jenny's answer.

"Why not ... Well, honey, because—Because it was wrong, and I knew that. Mommy's a little confused right now."

"I love you, Mommy."

"I love you, too, Suzy-Q. Let's go upstairs and get something to eat. Maybe pigs-in-a-blanket?"

"Yeah!"

The swing squeaked again as they got up. The shoes hit the steps as they left the porch, and Susan continued talking as they moved to the far side of the house where the entrance to their apartment was.

Maydene tried to rise, then decided to stay a moment or two longer.

"Father, You need to be with this young mother as she tries to sort this out. Help Jenny to keep You in her mind. You and her wedding vows. If she lets go of either, she's going to be sorry. And please protect Susan through everything that comes."

As she stood, her knees gave their customary pops.

"And, Father, help me know what to say and do—if anything. Help me keep my mouth shut if that's the right thing and not if it's not." She brushed dirt from her knees. Telling Jenny about Jonas would have to wait.

Chapter Eighteen

Even though he should be working on his plans to address *The Gazette's* finances, Zak's mind was occupied by his kiss with Jenny. How could he focus on eliminating positions, restructuring beats, or downsizing coverage when all his mind could conjure was Jenny, Susan, and the disastrous ending to their night?

He'd arrived home after dropping Jenny and Susan off, half expecting to find Kay charging around the house like a bull in a china shop. But she wasn't here. She'd been plenty angry at the park, though.

By the time he changed his clothes, he was certain he'd made a fool of himself with Jenny. More than that, he debated whether to avoid the café for the rest of his life. That plan had one flaw—he could not forget the glorious feelings that had risen in him during their kiss. What must Jenny think of him?

Afraid to move forward and unable to let go, Zak sat in his living room in his skanky gym shorts and lime green T-shirt with the holes in it that read "Zak's Diner – Eat Here and Get

Gas." Saving the paper seemed more achievable than straightening out his life.

Instead of setting goals for reviving paper, the little, out-of-the-way diner he and Kay had stumbled upon during their first trip together as a married couple came to mind. Kay had laughed uproariously at the lime green shirt and purchased it. In the early days, he'd worn it often, but it was so ugly that, even while laughing, Kay chased him around their apartment and tried to tear it off him. That was the real reason he'd worn the shirt at all.

When she died, he'd packed the shirt in a box along with other pieces of their life he couldn't bear to keep around. Their wedding pictures. The movie *The Princess Bride.*

Kay's blue polka-dot dress and his ugly green shirt. Packed, sealed, and stored in the back of the storage room. But he had wanted the shirt tonight for reasons he didn't even try to understand and unpacked it.

He got up from his desk and padded into the kitchen, the coolness of the ceramic tile against his feet. Though the weather was nice during the days, summer and the heavy humidity would soon arrive—and with it, the solitude that nearly suffocated him.

Still, summer was better than the run-up to winter and he was grateful. He could handle the ridiculous Christmas in July sales, but he was dreading the fall, when the radio would begin playing Christmas carols and the stores would start luring people in with "pre-Christmas" sales. Commercials on television would tout smiling families sharing cups of eggnog and plates of Christmas cookies, if you just bought this or that insurance.

And he'd sit desolate, watching them on his throne as King of the Dead.

~

No MATTER how hard he tried, Mick could not come to any other conclusion. Zak was talking to a dead woman. So far as he knew, no other Kays lived in Oak Hill, and Zak had been angry at a Kay—when no one had been within sight. *Check my waist, Kay? Check my waist? Well, you can just sit there tonight and check it as I eat all of this myself.* When put together with Maydene's observation, the words Zak had muttered in the grocery store led to no other conclusion.

Zak was talking to his dead wife—Mick's dead sister. This was far outside his scope of experience. He needed to do something, but what?

He sat in front of his computer, trying to work on an illustration, but distraction set in. He toyed with what he saw were his options: Report Zak's issues to Waxman and request he put Zak on administrative leave, gather Zak's friends and stage an intervention, confront Zak himself, or do nothing and hope it all passed. In each scenario, something could go wrong.

Worse, Mick was certain he was missing something important. He needed to sort out his facts. He had never written a news story, but he understood the basics. Who, what, where, when, why, and how—Zak had taught him that. He opened a new file and typed in those questions and the answers he either had or suspected.

Who? *Zakary Cooper, best friend and widowed brother-in-law.*

What? *Appears to be talking to Kay. Was also seen from afar (Maydene) having a conversation with no one around.*

Where? *In the grocery store and in front of his house.*

When? *Two days ago at his house; yesterday at the grocery store.*

Why? *Too scary to speculate.*

How? *I have no idea.*

Those were the facts—sort of. Mental illness was a possibility, but Zak functioned in public well, so far.

"Honey?" Dreama yelled from the top of the stairs. "What are you doing down there? I could use some help with baths up here."

He didn't answer.

"What happened to doing your work at work and doing your family at home?"

Mick smiled at the peevishness in her voice. Dreama was a great mother, but when she got a bee in her bonnet, the only options were killing that bee or tossing out the bonnet. He rather liked the bonnet. "Coming, dear. Give me just a moment."

"Don't you 'dear' me, Mitchell."

He rolled his eyes, took one last look at his list, hit print, and closed the file. He'd have to come back to it later. He had squealing children to tease, taunt, and bathe. He could already feel the backache coming on.

"Mitchell," Dreama called again from above.

He glanced up the stairs. His almost two-year-old daughter, Jazz, peeked around the basement door in her pink pajamas. At least her bath was done.

"Beware of the dreaded Daddy Shark. Chomp. Chomp. Chomp."

The stars in his daughter's eyes assured him all would be okay—if he'd chase her to bed. Giggling uncontrollably, Jazz took off on her newly minted running legs.

He could work on the Zak thing tomorrow. Maybe go into the office earlier than normal. Dreama was right, some things, such as Daddy-sharking, had to take priority.

~

Settled in his room at The Tuck Inn, Jonas sat in front of the TV bored—and lonely. His room was nice, homey even. It had shutters instead of curtains, an en-suite bathroom, snacks, a forty-two-inch TV with satellite, and a queen bed—but no queen.

The owners of the bed-and-breakfast were friendly. He felt a kinship with Steve Tucker right away—despite that incident after dinner.

While sitting on the porch sipping iced tea, he'd made gentle inquiries about where a young man could go to mingle and share a drink or two with a new friend of the female persuasion. Steve had examined him for a moment with a probing smile. But he'd quickly covered that with a tight the-customer-is-always-right grin and suggested that many of the younger adults hung out at The Whistle Stop. Jonas nodded but remained seated and finished his drink. He was in no hurry to leave.

After chatting another half hour or so, Jonas thanked his hosts for their hospitality and excused himself to watch television and unwind. He'd turned a show on but spent the past two hours going through his information on *The Gazette*

All the information he'd dug up was spread on the lace bedspread before him. Jonas couldn't find anything, other than the one disgruntled employee, he could use to force Waxman's hand. The place was clean. No delinquent payments. No employee grievances. High standing in the community.

Frustrated and weary from the long day, he gathered up the papers, opened his attaché, and put them away. The contents in the other pocket of his case caught his eye. Photos of smiling women who offered more. More excitement. More pleasure. More ... That quickly, Jonas was ravenous and wide awake. Maybe he would visit The Whistle Stop. What could it hurt? No one here knew him.

~

Long after midnight, Jenny lay in her bed reliving her afternoon with Zak and her time with Susan. Confusion ruled. While she was attracted to Zak and wanted Susan to have a father figure in her life, his incident at the park had scared her. Being free of Jonas and his infidelity had restored some pieces of her heart, but she still cared for her husband.

Why was life so ... so puzzling? There should be an instruction manual.

In the past, she'd always moved forward with easy confidence, believing the decisions she made were in her best interests and within the will of God. Now? She held no such confidence. What was different?

She already had the answer. She had moved away from God. Not intentionally. The separation was so gradual, she had not even realized the distance. Slacking off on church attendance. Catch-as-catch-can Bible reading. Table prayers and life laments were the highlights of her formerly frequent chats with God. But her life was good.

Although, with no husband, a confused daughter, and a potential boyfriend who talked to ghosts, maybe good was not correct. At the same time, she'd had joy-filled moments of blessing—a new start, new job, new friends, new town.

So why did she feel so disconnected?

For the first time since leaving Jonas, she breathed easy. At least when she wasn't crying. Clearly, she wasn't going to sleep tonight. She may as well get up.

Jenny threw her legs over the side of the bed, toes whispering above the floor. She was not as close to God as she'd been in the past. But why?

An image of Jonas popped into her mind. With Jonas out of her life, had she stopped leaning on Him?

While living in Chicago, church had been vital. The women's group supported her when Jonas went prowling. When he worked late and stopped for drinks on the way home, she'd prayed God would keep him safe. When he was home as Susan's dad and her husband, but not their spiritual leader, she'd turned to God, through his Word, to be her spiritual husband.

Here she had nothing in her life she couldn't handle on her own and didn't need God.

"Oh, dear God." Jenny shot off the bed, her hand flying to her mouth. *Didn't need God?*

She fell to her knees beside her bed, her heart breaking. "Forgive me, Father, for being so full of pride. For using You for my convenience."

She confessed her wrong thinking. Opened her broken heart and set it before Christ, asking Him to place his finger on each wound, pointing out each broken spot. Allowing Him to examine her life, touch each area of selfishness, was to invite healing in.

"Father, a wound can't heal, until it's cleaned. Lord, clean me. Help me make things right. Stay with me. Strengthen me." She laid her head on the bed and imagined herself crawling into her heavenly Daddy's arms.

After several more minutes, Jenny got up from the floor, exhausted but renewed. She examined the debris of her life. Saw how her actions, intended to encourage Jonas to explore God, had turned him away from God—and from her. She had insisted he meet *her* expectations of an ideal husband and father instead of providing love and support while he found his way.

He'd made his choices. She didn't make them for him and would not own them.

Jonas's violation of their marriage vows wasn't her fault.

She had never denied him in that area—had never wanted to. But she had tried to change her husband instead of asking God to work in him.

Jenny sat on the bed, sleepy at last. Before dozing off, she made a mental list. Contact Jonas and apologize for running away. Talk to Zak and make her intentions—and unavailability—clear. Read her Bible, pray, and seek accountability. Commit to a church.

As she drifted off, she wondered if Jonas would even want her back. What if he wouldn't accept her apology?

Chapter Nineteen

Zak stumbled into *The Gazette*. After an unproductive night, he'd given up on trying to salvage the paper and fallen into bed, exhausted and spent. But sleep would not come. Jenny and Kay invaded his rest. If he was awake, he may as well use the distraction of work to keep his addled mind occupied.

"No calls. No interruptions, Nancy," Zak mumbled to his administrative assistant as he lurched into his office. She wasn't there. It was 4:00 a.m. Nancy didn't start until 8:30. But with his eyes three quarters shut and his mind three-quarters fuzzy, he moved on muscle memory.

He laid his folder of cost-cutting ideas on his desk and headed to the breakroom to start a pot of coffee. He needed caffeine. As the coffee percolated, he scanned the pages of yesterday's paper.

"You're a little, well, ragged after your date yesterday."

Zak froze at Kay's icy tone. *One more thing I don't need today.* He poured himself a half-cup of coffee from the barely started pot. Now what?

"How about some cinnamon? I hear it's good for your cholesterol and will help you live longer."

"Kay, I really don't ..." Remembering their last morning together, he hung his head. "No, thank you. It's fine."

"As you wish. Just want you to live for a long time, now that you have such a wonderful young girlfriend."

"Jenny's not—"

"Of course not, sweetie." She leaned against the counter as Zak gripped his mug with both hands and avoided her eyes. "The lip-lock and groping at the park last night were *completely* accidental, I'm sure."

"I told you I was sorry, and it won't happen again," Zak said. "I, uh, I was, uh, I wanted—"

"You *wanted* to have sex with her."

He winced at the sharpness in her voice—and the truth of her words. His body, his mind, and his emotions were at war with each other, each wanting something different.

She wasn't wrong, exactly. Just not completely right. He missed sex, but he missed the intimacy of being married more. A casual hand caressing his neck. A look shared from across the room. A warm body to pull close during the nights when an oppressive loneliness enveloped him.

He and Kay used to have the best conversations. They'd talk about anything—from the weather to politics to whether the Cubs would get another chance at the World Series to why evil thrived in a world created by a loving, all-knowing God. In the give and take, a marriage was cemented—*his* marriage had been cemented.

Emotionally, he wanted Kay. The woman who had stood by him, and periodically stood up to him, for the majority of his life. He wanted the comfort that came when he called her during the day and heard the joy in her voice when she answered.

That is what he missed and that is the Kay whose death had left a hole in his life, his home, and his heart.

But the woman standing before him? This cold, cruel Kay? She was not his.

"Dead doesn't mean gone," she said. "I'll never be gone, Zakary."

Never.

He could take no more.

"Enough!" He threw his coffee cup against the wall. It shattered and left a brown stain. He directed his anger at God as much as Kay, if not more. "Where's my happiness? My joy? Where's my love?"

The faces of all of those he'd love paraded through his mind. His mother. His Dad, who if still alive was as good as dead. Gram, who'd tried to raise him the best she could. His precious daughter, Rachel, whom he hadn't even gotten to hold. And Kay. The one who had stayed the longest and been the most precious to him. He'd given her everything—and she'd left him.

If he cared for Jenny, would she die too?

He turned toward Kay again. Tears filled her eyes, and he recognized the agony of his life. Like so many times before, they were in sync. How he loved her—and always would.

"You did promise me forever," she said.

Yes, he had. Even though he'd spoken the words five years ago, he recalled the promise with crystal clarity.

The miscarriage had devastated Kay, and he found her lying on the bed weeping.

"She's gone. I didn't even get to hold her."

He caressed her back and neck, hoping his love would reach through the emotional distance between them.

"I know. I'm sorry, love."

"I loved her." The anguish in Kay's voice brought tears to his eyes.

Because he could think of nothing else to say, he said what was on his mind. "I love you."

"I love you too." Kay took his hands, a mixture of relief and fear on her face. "Stay with me, please."

"Of course." He had no intention of going anywhere.

"No, I mean stay with me. Forever."

"I'm not going anywhere."

"Promise?"

"I promise." He'd meant it with every beat of his heart. But did that give her the right to haunt his life now?

"I know, baby. I know I promised." He stepped closer. "I'm sorry. But you ..." He searched for the right words, but there weren't any. "You *died*."

"My love for you could never die, Zee. Never. Whether you fall in love again or not, I'll always love you. 'For love is as strong as death,' remember?"

How could he forget? The cross-stitch Kay had given him on their first anniversary. "Place me like a seal over your heart, like a seal on your arm; for love is as strong as death, its jealousy unyielding as the grave." Song of Solomon 8:6.

They'd recited the verse at their wedding. "It burns like a blazing fire, like a mighty flame," the verse continued.

He took half a step back and looked at his wife. The need in her eyes mirrored his. He reached out to caress her face— only this time he didn't pull back from the nothingness where her cheek should have been.

Instead, he moved in, wanting to touch what was left of her. Wanting to comfort. To soothe. And be soothed.

He saw her lean into his hand and saw her frustration when she came up empty.

But Zak was determined. He walked toward her, encircling her trembling body with his arms, and though there was nothing there, she filled the void in his life. He inhaled the familiar scent of her hair and heard her soft sobs. Pulling away slightly, he put his finger under her chin to lift her face and stepped into that mighty flame.

"I'll always love you, Katharine Renee. Always." He searched her eyes. His right hand dropped to her waist, pulling her toward him. The King of the Dead found his queen.

~

MICK WATCHED from his office as Zak embraced nothing. He would not allow himself to believe it. His mind scrambled for a semi-plausible explanation, but his heart shot down each attempt. His friend was losing touch with reality.

After Daddy-Sharking both kids into bed, Mick had been unable to sleep and decided to come to work early. A well-placed support column hid his office from the coffee pot across the newsroom.

He'd been working on a stained-glass illustration for the next Religion section front while praying for Zak. Since the incident at the grocery store, Mick's concern had increased. When he'd climbed into bed with Dreama last night, he had shared his fears, and they prayed for Zak. He'd been praying some more when a crash like a dropped coffee mug startled him.

He rose from his desk and looked into the newsroom. Although no one but Zak was in the room, Mick did not doubt he was conversing with Kay—or at least that was what Zak thought he was doing. Not only had he called her by name, he'd held her with tenderness. He watched, thunderstruck, as Zak walked out of the newsroom holding hands with the air.

What was he going to do? What should he do?

Because of his own grief over the loss of his sister, he understood Zak's pain. He and Kay had been close. How many times since her death had he wished her back?

Once he thought he'd seen Kay shopping in the grocery, but it had been a woman who resembled Kay. He and Dreama called it a visual echo. The desire to see what the heart wants to see.

Zak's situation was different, worse.

Mick returned to his desk to think some more and pray for help. As he sat, he remembered talking to Kay on the eve of her wedding.

"Am I happy? You can't tell, Micky? You can't see it on my face? Can't hear it in my voice?"

"I can and I do," he'd said. "But I want you to say it. I love Zak like a brother, but I'll kick his butt and tell him to move on if you say so."

"Little Micky." She used the nickname he tolerated only from her. "You always did like to act like my older brother."

Kay sighed. The contentment and ease in her eyes told him everything he needed to know.

"He's my life," she said. "He's the reason I'm on this earth, and he's everything I could ever want. He's not perfect. He's a little moody, sometimes too needy. But Micky... he loves me. God brought him to me, and I'm not about to let him go. Not now, not ever."

Mick had smiled and given her a hug.

Overwhelmed, he put his head in his hands and cried again for his sister, whose life was too short. Ah, Kay. Why'd you have to go? Why'd you leave us behind to fight over your memory?

Then he opened his heart and his mind to God and shared

his grief. He asked God for direction—for help in getting Zak the assistance he needed.

You're the one. Help him. Whatever the cost.

SLOAN WHITE CHUCKLED under his breath as he filmed Zakary "Golden Boy" Cooper walking out of the newsroom with his arm around the waist of a woman who wasn't there.

The early bird catches the worm.

If he'd only known Zak's implosion was imminent, he could have eased up on his efforts to assist Clarity in absorbing *The Gazette.* Errors in the articles and ads—ones he'd inserted—made the paper, and thereby Zak, appear careless. Key advertisers had pulled out.

Whisper campaigns about Zak's incompetence, couched in fake concern for his well-being following Kay's death, were working within the staff and key town leaders.

Using Zak's name during his absence, he'd denied time off requests from loyal staffers. As the second in command, he'd demanded unpaid overtime under the guise of helping to keep the paper afloat and created a disgruntled newsroom.

Why? Because the young pup from Clarity had suggested it would force Waxman's hand. Clarity's advance man had also made carefully shaded intimations of rewards, promotions, and power, which he would share with those sensitive to Clarity's needs. Even without those nebulous promises, Sloan had been happy to do what he could. He'd been ignored and unappreciated long enough.

"I guess I can go home, now." He patted his phone. "This'll do fine."

The meeting between Waxman and Jonas was today.

Afterward, the sale of the paper—and perhaps his elevation to editor—would be announced.

Answering the call of nature had given him a close-up view of Zak's downfall. And he had video proof on his phone. "Film at eleven, Jane."

Today was one of reckoning. Debts would be collected and promises fulfilled. He couldn't wait.

Chapter Twenty

Exhausted, Jenny reported for her six o'clock breakfast shift. Her time with God last night had filled her with more hope than she'd had in a long time. Talking to Jonas moved to the top of her priority list.

Thankfully, she could call him and learn what she needed to know. Did he want their marriage to work? And if so, what was he willing to do to make it happen? Using the phone to communicate with him would keep her focused.

Yesterday, with his lips on hers and his body trembling, Zak had made her feel desirable again.

If Jonas was not interested, what did her future hold? Breathing deeply, she pushed the what-ifs from her mind and focused on work.

As she took orders and served her customers, Maydene glanced her way several times. The older woman clucked around the kitchen with more energy than normal, and her gaze darted toward the front door every few minutes. Even Abe was on guard, as if expecting something to happen.

What was up? The regulars filled the café for the breakfast rush.

As she wiped down a table and collected her tip, she pushed her concerns aside and recalled her morning with Susan.

"Janene and I are going to eat breakfast together before school. Then we'll have story time with Miss Dreama and Miss Michelle." She'd been full of plans for her day. "Can I tell Miss Dreama about dinner? You said we could invite her."

"No, honey, Mommy will take care of that."

"Can I tell her about the park?"

"Of course. Make sure you tell her about everything you saw while we were walking on the path—the bugs, leaves, that little toad. You could draw her a picture of the toad."

"No, I'm going to draw a picture of Zee."

Jenny frowned. The connection Susan was building with Zak concerned her. In fact, if things with Jonas went well, a connection between Susan and Zak could cause problems.

In her distracted state, Jenny delivered Faye Schultz's fruit plate to "Big Eddie" McClain instead of his Triple Threat Special of three scrambled eggs, three bacon slices, and three pancakes. And she didn't even notice until the other guys from the road crew guffawed in laughter.

"Oh, sorry Eddie." She stifled a little laugh. "That's not yours."

"Well, it sure better not be. I can't support this physique with a little dib-dab of fruit."

Laughing again at her mistake, she took the fruit plate, which did look tiny in front of Eddie, and gave it to Faye one table over.

"Oh, shoot," Faye said. "I was looking forward to a real breakfast for a change. I'll probably live longer, Eddie."

"Maybe," he said with a mischievous smile. "But what for if all you're going to do is eat fruit?"

"To attend your funeral, of course."

Big Eddie's table exploded with laughter. Jenny filled their coffee cups and headed for the kitchen. She needed a cup of her own.

Maydene met her at the door. "We need to talk."

"It was just a little mix-up," Jenny explained. "No one really minded."

From the look on Maydene's face, she didn't want to discuss Big Eddie's fruit plate.

"I met Jonas yesterday." Maydene closed the door to the kitchen behind them.

Hearing Jonas's name right after her decision to talk to him about their marriage, knocked Jenny off kilter.

"Jonas? How?" Jenny said. "You don't even know him. And what were you doing in Chicago? You were here last night for the dinner shift before I left for the picnic. Which, since you haven't asked, went well—sort of."

"Jonas is in town." Maydene steamrolled over Jenny's picnic info dump. "Stopped in here yesterday for some coffee and a piece of pie—and a paper. I don't know why he's here, but I don't think he knows *you're* here."

"Jonas is in Oak Hill? Why would he ..."

Then Jenny remembered the conversation between Sloan and Zak about Clarity's Midwest expansion plans a few days ago. If Jonas is in town, Clarity was after *The Gazette*. She needed to warn Zak.

"I believe Jonas is staying at The Tuck Inn, and I think you should go see him."

Maydene held up her hand when Jenny opened her mouth to protest. "It's slow this morning. We'll be okay. Jonas will likely stop in for breakfast before his business, whatever that is.

Seeing you then, when he's not expecting you and in public, could be trouble."

Jonas. In Oak Hill. Did he know she was here? Was he after *The Gazette*? Did Zak know? She should warn Zak. She needed to find Jonas. She had to figure out what to do. She needed to ...

I need to pray.

There was no time. She needed a plan, and she only had three blocks to come up with one.

As she tore off her apron and hairnet, panic set in. Her conversation with herself this morning outlining what she would say to Jonas when she called him evaporated. Disappeared like mist.

She'd planned that conversation for the phone—with distance as her ally. Since he was here, she would have to talk to him in person, and distance, or lack thereof, had become a foe.

Then there was the probability Jonas was here to scope out *The Gazette* for a takeover. That meant he'd talk to Zak soon— and Zak didn't know she was married. Her life had become incredibly complicated. She'd prayed last night for the right words to say to Jonas to discover his intent, but she hadn't planned on having to say them this quickly or in person. How could she warn Zak about the takeover and explain how she knew how Clarity functioned.

Oh, dear Lord, help me make the right decisions—and do the right things.

She flew through the café and out the back door, her life— and her table rag—in her hands. She hopped in her car and headed up the street to an unknown future.

~

Jenny stood in front of The Tuck Inn, debating her next move.

She hadn't quite believed Jonas was in town until she saw his champagne-colored Lexus parked on the street. She trembled, nervous as a cat. Would he be glad to see her? Would he look at her in disbelief, relief flooding his eyes at having found her once again? Or would he laugh at the hope he saw in her eyes? Was she old news?

She'd served the Tucks, Steve and Betty, once or twice at the café and shared the church smile with them as they'd passed each other in the hallways before or after service. Steve led the Men's Accountability Network on Wednesday evenings, and Betty helped with the junior high program.

How would they react when she told them she wanted to see one of their guests? She sucked in a great breath of air and headed for the inn's door. Better to have the reunion, whatever the outcome, in private.

Steve Tuck stepped into the driveway, a bag of trash in one hand and coffee cup in the other, as she walked up.

"Good morning, Steve." She extended her hand. The one holding the forgotten dishrag. "Oops. Silly me." She switched the rag to her left hand, trying to ignore the puzzled expression on Steve's face.

He set down his trash bag, wiped his hands on his jeans, and grasped her hand lightly, but firmly. "Jenny? Jenny Miller from church, right?"

"Yes, that's right. I usually sit in the third pew from the back, on the outside aisle seat."

"Right. I remember you. You must get there pretty early to snag a prime seat like that. Most people gravitate to the back."

"Just lucky I guess."

They stood in the driveway for several seconds, Jenny fumbling in the awkward silence.

"Well, what can I do for you Ms. Miller—or are you here to help with the cleaning?"

She giggled and tucked her rag into the pocket of her apron.

"No, afraid not—and it's *Mrs.* Miller. Mrs. *Jonas* Miller. I believe my husband is a guest of yours." She smiled. "He came into town unexpectedly."

Steve stepped back a pace and folded his arms across his chest. His initial welcome ebbed, though his polite smile remained. "Jonas didn't mention he was married when we talked last night," Steve said. "But he did say he lives in Chicago."

Steve studied her, as if appraising her honesty. Did he think she was a crazy stalker?

"We've had a bit of a rough year and are separated. Jonas doesn't know I live in Oak Hill, but when I heard he was in town, it was a sign of sorts. You know, that maybe we could work things out." She tried to keep the emotion out of her voice, but the hope peeking out from behind her scarred heart was overwhelming.

"What I'd really like to do, Steve, if it can be arranged, is head up to Jonas's room and surprise him."

As she spoke the words, she realized that had been her hope all along. Surprise was the trump card that would bring Jonas's real intentions to the surface, even if only for a minute. She had convinced herself he would be glad, no ecstatic, to see her if she caught him off guard.

Steve eyed her. Was he trying to discern her motive? Debating whether she was trustworthy or a maniacal wife bent on revenge?

"Well, technically, Mrs. Miller—"

"Jenny, please."

"Well, Jenny, no offense, but my guest hasn't mentioned

any relationship with you. Let alone that he's married. I'm afraid I can't let you go to his room. You understand?"

Steve stepped more fully in front of the steps to the inn's front door.

"You could leave him a note, or perhaps I could have him call you? You're welcome to sit in the library and wait until he comes down for breakfast, but I have no idea how long he will be."

She bit her lip to try to keep from crying. Of course she understood Steve's position and rising emotions would not help her. Her mind raced. How could she prove she was who she said? Jonas was a good actor, and surprise was vital to discern his true desires where she was concerned.

Wait. She had a photo of them and Susan on her spare keyring—the one that included a key to the Lexus. It was three years old, and she'd had longer hair then, but it ought to do. Jonas hadn't really changed, and she didn't look that different.

She held up her finger and fished around in her purse, knowing her extra set of keys she kept was in there somewhere. Her fingers brushed against a jagged edge, and she pulled the keys from the bottom of her bag. She walked to the Lexus and put the key in the lock.

A screeching alarm wailed, and Jenny screamed. She'd forgotten about the car alarm.

Steve rushed over and tried to figure out how to turn the thing off to no avail. She pushed buttons on her keyless remote, trying to get the right combination. Embarrassed panic rose as Betty ran out the front door.

"Hey, what are you doing to my car?"

Jenny looked up at Jonas's sleepy face glowering down on the scene from the second floor. He wasn't pleased by the rude awakening. His gaze landed on her, and his eyes popped open as a huge smile filled his face. "Jen? What are you doing here?"

Her heart sang at the true joy and excitement that filled his face. He *had* missed her.

She started to raise her hand to wave at her husband and blow him a kiss, but froze in midair.

Another hand, another *female* hand, snaked across Jonas's bare chest and stomach, then caressed his hair before trying to pull him back into the room. Jonas brushed the hand away as he hit the combination of buttons on his remote from upstairs. The alarm silenced, and all sound was sucked out of her world, along with the air in her lungs—and her hope.

"What happened, uh, hon?" The woman stuck her head out the window from behind his shoulder. Jonas's latest anonymous blonde. "Did the maid try to take your car?"

His face fell, and he turned from the window, pulling the blonde with him.

Jenny didn't even consider the woman's accusation over the voice in her head screaming, "Fool. Fool. Fool!" She threw her key ring against the car's windshield, hoping to hear a satisfying shatter of the glass. Nothing happened. She raced back to her car, yanked open the door, and threw herself in.

As the tears came, she cranked the engine and sped down the road, heading anywhere else. She was so intent on escaping yet another betrayal that when she saw Jonas run out of the house in his boxers in her rearview mirror, she hit the accelerator.

Chapter Twenty-One

Jonas stood in the middle of the street and, though he could feel it's ragged rhythm beating in his chest, watched his heart drive away in a Honda Civic. He'd been alone much of his life—abandoned, unloved—but this was different.

Jen was gone, for good this time, and he was to blame. The pain of that knowledge burned in him like an eternal flame in a graveyard. If Steve hadn't put an arm around his shoulders and pulled him out of the street, Jonas might have remained there for eternity, willing time to rewind.

"Let's get some clothes on you," Steve said. "Then, I think, we need to talk."

Jonas stared at him, nodded, and allowed Steve to lead him to the curb, where Betty waited with a bathrobe. They exchanged glances before Steve shooed her off. None of it mattered. Not the neighbors who'd been awakened by the car alarm and stayed for the show. Not the nameless woman he'd spent the night with. The one Betty was currently shushing and leading away. None of it. Once again, he'd ruined everything.

His Father's voice echoed in his brain. "Not good enough, Jonas. Not by a long shot."

How had he gotten here? Jen was everything to him—yet, he'd thrown her away like extra baggage.

He sighed, dropped his head, and pulled the robe tighter around him. Seeing Jen reminded him of why he'd been attracted to her in the first place. He'd loved her because she'd loved him, just as he was. She was worth more than hundreds of the anonymous women he wasted his time with, but he wasn't worthy of her. Or the faith she'd placed in him. He wasn't worthy of her love. And now she was gone and had taken what little shred of love she'd yet held for him with her.

He peered down the street once more, unable or unwilling to give up. The cool morning breeze blew against his face, but it couldn't dry the tears running down his cheeks. Nor would the robe warm the coldness of the solitude he'd brought upon himself—solitude no pretty pictures could penetrate.

"How could I have been so stupid?" Jenny thumped her hand on the steering wheel as she sat on the side of the road. "How could I have been so stupid, *again*?"

Because hiding her tears and anger from her daughter would have been impossible, Jenny was grateful she'd dropped Susan at the school before going to work. With her hands clenching the wheel, she'd driven until her tears had so blinded her she had to pull over. She didn't know where she was going, other than away from Jonas.

Now that she'd cried a while, her breathing and heart rate slowed down, but when she inhaled she still breathed along a jagged edge. Oh, her heart ached. She had loved Jonas. Even after discovering his cache of pornography. Even after his first affair—and his second. Even now, after everything, she carried the bud of her love like a rose waiting to bloom.

She hadn't realized how much she'd expected Jonas's joy at seeing her again. He'd been happy. His eyes had lit up with the same delight they'd had when he'd first approached her in the library. He'd missed her. Of that she was certain.

So, why had that woman been stroking his chest? Stroking her husband?

"No, I will not think of that. I will not allow it." Jenny shut down the memory track. In order to move on, she had to put Jonas behind her—and the sooner the better. She'd had unreasonable expectations and had romanticized her meeting with Jonas. He'd proven over and over what kind of man he was.

Jenny stared at the landscape around her. She was on Templeton Highway. The road to Aunt Sarah's place. Sarah, who always said just the right thing and had such good advice, was who she needed.

Jenny turned the key to start the Civic, but a small cross decorated with plastic flowers and a small sign at the side of the road caught her attention. *Kay, I'll always love you.* That had to be Zak's Kay—and his sign. Jenny snorted at the word *always*.

"I thought Jonas would always love me too." She hit the accelerator of the Civic, and it climbed the hill. "Doesn't happen that way."

Sara would see things her way and assure Jenny she was making the right decision.

~

"KAY?" Zak rolled over in bed. His head ached, and miniature ballpeen hammers rang against the inside of his skull. Rising on his elbow, he scanned the room and groaned. He rubbed his eyes, trying to force reality to take hold. His hand fumbled on the headboard in search of his glasses, but they were not there.

"Kay? Do you know where my glasses are?" His voice croaked. "Kay?" He squinted, trying to read the clock on his dresser. No luck. Why was he awake so early? It couldn't be later than 6:00 a.m.

"Kay? Honey? Where are you? Do you know what time it is?"

No one answered. Groaning, he slid out from under the covers and padded into the hallway, headed for the bathroom. As he passed Kay's bureau, he grabbed his glasses from the top and carried them with him.

"No cinnamon in the coffee. Okay?"

Where was she and why wasn't she answering? She'd probably fallen asleep on the couch reading again. No one got as caught up in a book as Kay.

After flushing the toilet, he stepped over to the shower, turned the water on and adjusted the temperature so the steam would quickly fill the bathroom. He did his best thinking in a hot shower, and today he needed a plan to present to Waxman.

Stepping into the shower, he pulled back from the nearly scalding water and eased under the spray while inhaling little puffs of breath until he adjusted to the temperature. He exhaled, then stuck his head under the cascading water.

Before long, water rained down his back as he kneeled on the floor of the shower, weeping as the truth swirled in his mind. Kay hadn't fallen asleep in the living room. She was dead. Almost eight months. Grief swept over him like a tidal wave. Would he ever get over losing her?

He looked up. Something else was wrong. It nagged at his mind like an eighties music earworm, circling round and round. He turned off the shower, grabbed a towel and his glasses, and stumbled into the kitchen.

Dripping all over Kay's Pergo flooring, he stared at the clock on the microwave. Nine thirty-seven. How had he slept so late? He should probably call Nancy and tell her. And Sloan too. He dried off as he walked to his office to find his phone. He wrapped the towel around his waist and noticed a pile of notes on the desk.

I was working late last night on the financial plan. But...

But what? But what? What was missing?

I must have fallen asleep here and woke up long enough to go to bed.

That sequence didn't seem to match the facts. Zak was a reporter and dealt in facts. A piece of the puzzle was missing.

He sat at his desk and perused his notes. Something had distracted him last night, but what?

Jenny.

Yes, her, the park, and their kiss. But what else? He tapped his red, fine-point marker on his desk pad. He stood from his chair and walked to the window.

When he closed his eyes, the memories came easy. Holding out his hands to Jenny. Her rising into his arms. Her eyes open with excitement, then closing as their lips came together. It was wonderful ... until ...

The aftermath flooded his mind. Kay watching him kiss Jenny. Him breaking away from Jenny to yell at Kay. Leaving with Jenny and Susan. Exhaustion swamping him as he strove to figure out how to save the paper.

Embracing his dead wife in the middle of the newsroom.

Zak froze. His marker fell from his hand and rolled across the floor. He shuddered, chilled to his core. He and Kay had left the newsroom hand in hand and come home.

What is happening to me?

His stomach churned, and with his hand covering his mouth, he raced for the bathroom. As he kneeled before the toilet, expelling what little was in his stomach, one trepidation raced round and round his mind like Dale Earnhart, Jr. at the Brickyard 400.

I'm losing my mind.

~

MICK WOKE FROM AN EXHAUSTED SLEEP, aware he'd developed a serious crick in his neck from his unfortunate choice of falling asleep on his desktop. But he felt rested, and his mind was clear. He knew what he had to do, but first a phone call to Dreama—he needed all the prayer support he could find first.

As he picked up his phone, he glanced into the newsroom. Sloan White whistled—*whistled?—as* he walked around among the desks and handed out assignment sheets like a first-grade teacher overseeing his charges. Glancing Mick's way, Sloan grinned and mouthed a cheerful "Hi."

Mick raised his right hand and wiggled his fingers in a wave. He rolled his eyes at the ridiculous gesture, but Sloan moved on with his tasks.

There was no time to figure out what new torture Sloan planned to inflict on the staff. Mick grabbed his phone and pressed Dreama's number. She was his anchor, his sanity, and he needed to hear her voice.

"Hello?"

"Hey, baby." He set down his pen and leaned back in his chair. "How're things going this morning?"

"You mean other than Jazz snatching Satchel's lunch and him being hot-wired about it?"

Despite his concern over Zak, Mick smiled. At seven, his eldest got peeved by his little sister's impetuousness.

"Do you need me to talk to anyone?" He held his breath, hoping he didn't have to referee.

"Nah, we'll be copacetic here in a few minutes. Everyone is taking some breathing room. What do you need?"

He sighed. "Prayer, babe. I need your prayers."

He told Dreama everything about Zak's encounter in the newsroom, Mick's subsequent prayer and nap, and his plans for confronting Zak about his behavior. Dreama listened patiently, asking clarifying questions here and there, but mostly, she let him talk and decompress. It was a welcome relief.

"Have you thought about asking Pastor Dave to be there with you?" Dreama asked.

"Actually, I have," Mick said. "But I want to keep this as quiet as possible for Zak's sake. He might get defensive if he thinks we're ganging up on him."

"Mmm." Her silence reached across the line, speaking louder than any words.

"You don't think that's a good idea?" He switched the phone to his other ear.

"I don't know, hon. Zak's always confided in you, but if what you suspect is true, he may not be the same person you're used to."

"What do you mean?"

"It's just ... Hold on a sec." She left him hanging.

To Mick's ear, she found Satchel's lunch and picked up Jazz. He marveled at her ability to multi-task.

"Okay, I'm back. You're probably right, Mick. I just ... I want you to be careful, that's all. Zak's in a precarious place. If you confront him, you will be too."

She was overreacting, but he also understood her concern. "I'll be all right, Dream Baby."

"Jazz, put that back. I gotta go, hon. Be careful. I love you. I'll pray."

"Love you too." He imagined the glee on Jazz's face as she made off with her brother's lunch again.

How should he approach Zak about what had happened earlier? How did he ask his best friend if he'd lost his mind?

Mick glanced at the clock. Nine fifteen. Zak's office was dark.

After waking his computer, Mick opened Zak's calendar for the day. The editorial meeting at 8, which he'd missed. A lunch meeting labeled "finances" with Waxman and Sloan that would last the entire afternoon.

Guess it'll have to be before lunch. If he makes it in by then.

Mick sent a private meeting request with a subject line of "Catching up." With a sigh, he returned to his stained-glass illustration.

Chapter Twenty-Two

Within half an hour of the episode in the bathroom, Zak's panic subsided as his rational brain took over. He wasn't losing his mind, couldn't be. Insane people didn't question whether they were insane. Did they? He attributed the incidents to vivid dreams, no doubt intensified by the emotional roller coaster his new relationship with Jenny had put him on.

Talking to Kay and seeing her is one thing. Well, technically two. But embracing her? How is that possible? That seems beyond Harley's "bereavement hallucination" suggestion. Had to be a dream.

He picked up his pen. Pushed the clicker and exposed the point. Pushed again and watched it recede. Expose. Recede. Expose. Recede.

Click-click. Click-click.

The whole situation was beyond impossible, preposterous even.

He called Nancy with a phony excuse for oversleeping more than three hours.

"Are you sure you're okay?" Nancy asked. "You could take a sick day if you need to. Sloan has everything going."

"That sounds like trouble."

"No, he's doing fine. He's even smiling—and whistling."

He couldn't picture Sloan whistling. Zak was a reporter, not a fiction writer.

Click-click. Click-click.

"Whistling? That doesn't sound good. I'll come in." Zak stood. "I have that meeting all afternoon and some small projects I need to finish up. If Sloan's on top of things, I can wrap those up before the meeting."

"Suit yourself. The mess is all cleaned up, but you'll need a new mug. Oh, gotta run. The other line's ringing. See you soon."

"What mess?" *Click-click. Click-click.*

She hung up.

He set his cell phone on his desk.

By the time Jenny pulled into Aunt Sarah's driveway, she'd convinced herself the encounter with Jonas was a good thing. It had hurt, but sometimes, she needed to experience pain before healing could start. And she was more than ready for some healing.

Yes, she thought she was healing. It had begun with Zak's kiss. Pain at the end of a relationship was natural, according to her girlfriends and women's magazines. She should have seen the end coming. Instead, she'd put faith in Jonas loving her, which had left her helpless. Blindsided.

Take charge of your life. Chart your own destiny. Ten ways to heal.

She could imagine the magazine front, with those

headlines. She peeked out her car window. Aunt Sarah peered through the living room window.

Jenny took several deep breaths, then eased the car door open. She needed Aunt Sarah's unconditional love and acceptance. Those, too, would aid her healing. She stepped from the car and waved to Sarah, who now stood in the door.

She inhaled a deep breath and walked up the stairs of the porch.

~

"I KNOW I'M MARRIED. You hardly need to remind me." Jenny turned her back on her aunt. "I'm the one who lived with him and his infidelities, remember? Susan and I are the ones he left at home, preferring his little hotties. We didn't leave him."

"Didn't you, dear?" Sarah asked. "You left Chicago in the dead of night with your daughter—without leaving Jonas word —and showed up in my living room? Or am I remembering someone else who lived with me for a month?"

Jenny wanted to scream. How had things gone so terribly wrong? When she'd entered the living room, her aunt had greeted her warmly and offered her a cold drink—which she hadn't taken a single sip of. She'd babbled about Jonas, divorce, Zak, the future, and more—trying on new ideas and possibilities.

"But ... You don't understand."

Sarah's lips pressed together as if she were holding something back. "Well, let me recap. Eight years ago, you and Jonas vowed before God and others to love each other as man and wife. He broke those vows with another woman twice—"

"Three times—that I know of."

"Three then, that you know of. Then nine months ago you left."

Jenny tried to interrupt, but Sarah silenced her objections with a look that discouraged further interruptions.

"You left your husband and your life together, moved to Oak Hill with your daughter, and started a new life. Now you're telling me your marriage is over, counseling won't help, and you may even have a new love. Have I missed anything?"

"Well, yes. You've conveniently *missed* Jonas's continuing —and ongoing, I might add—contribution to the dissolution of this marriage."

"I didn't miss that, dear." Sarah touched Jenny's shoulder. "But Jonas is not the one standing before me making what I believe is a terrible mistake based on emotion."

Sarah moved from her chair to sit on the couch next to Jenny. "Jonas hurt you. Repeatedly. I don't deny that."

The tension in Jenny's neck relaxed a little.

"But I remember you saying 'I do' in a wedding ceremony where you pledged 'for better or for worse, till death do us part' before God and the congregation."

Jenny stood and spun toward her aunt, her mouth a big O of shock. The woman standing before her looked like and sounded like Aunt Sarah, but couldn't possibly be her.

"Jonas said those words too. Were you at the same wedding I was?" Jenny walked to the living room window—the same one Sarah had been at when she arrived. Why was Sarah making this so difficult? Jonas had been unfaithful. Divorce was allowed—even Biblical—in that circumstance.

Sarah came up behind Jenny and laid her hand on her shoulder.

She stiffened at the touch.

"Do you think you're the first woman whose husband watered another's garden?" Sarah's voice was just above a whisper.

Jenny rounded on her, rage set to spill out. The compassion in Sarah's eyes stilled her.

"I'm not saying you are wrong. Nor am I suggesting Jonas is right, and his affairs should be ignored or forgotten. I'm asking you to slow this train you're riding and search your heart. Consider Susan's heart. Is divorcing Jonas what you want? Allowed or not, is it what you *want?*"

Jenny swallowed the lump of anger, frustration, and betrayal. She'd fed on the distrust born in her heart and had enjoyed the taste. Sarah's words hurt because there was truth in them.

Truth Jenny willfully pushed aside.

"You don't understand. You've never been married. Never known the intimacy of a husband and wife." Her voice was controlled and as cold as ice. "Never known the betrayal of that intimacy—or the jagged cut of the knife when you discover your husband is sleeping in another woman's arms."

Catching Sarah's reaction to her words made Jenny regret spewing them. The pain in her aunt's eyes had her on the edge of apology.

"Jenny, my darling child." The pain in her expression turned to pity. "I have always thought of you as the daughter I never had, but sometimes ..."

Sarah shook her head and crossed the room to head upstairs. As her aunt stepped on the first stair, she exhaled heavily. From behind, Jenny noticed for the first time the effort climbing the stairs took. Her aunt, always so strong and assured, now carried her age in each step. Jenny wished, madly, she could hit the *Undo* button and erase her attack. Return to the point where their lives were comfortable.

Then Sarah's carriage on the stairs stiffened and her shoulders raised in determination. When she pivoted on the stairs and descended, the resolve in her eyes made Jenny's heartbeat accelerate.

Her aunt stood in front of her, holding her hands together at waist level. Though her hands shook, Sarah's resolve held.

"My dear, other people have needs. Other people have problems." When Sarah spoke, her quiet words reverberated in Jenny's ears. "You are right, but you are also woefully wrong. It's true I never married, but I *have* known the betrayal of an affair."

Jenny was losing her footing.

"Did you never wonder why I didn't marry?" Sarah stepped further into the living room and closer to Jenny. "I can understand why you may not have given it any thought as a child. But you're thirty-two now, and we've been more like friends than aunt and niece since your mother died. It wasn't *all* my choice—depending upon how you look at it."

Jenny could not think of a single thing to say, so she sat on the couch and waited for Sarah to go on. To her surprise, Sarah began to sing. Her voice a dusky, but pleasing alto, and Jenny recognized the song from a movie musical she used to watch with Sarah on overnight visits. She sang about a secret love that lived within her heart.

Sarah sighed, settled beside Jenny, and took her hands. "I was once the other woman. Did you know that?"

She glanced at Jenny and laughed lightly. "I can see you did not. Your mother guarded my secret well. But it's true. I have changed a lot since then."

Her stomach churned. Should she respond? How could she? Sarah, the woman who had loved and cared for her after her parents died, had an affair. Had she destroyed someone's marriage? "Jenny, did you wonder why I was watching for your today?" Sarah looked over her glasses.

Wait. Sarah *had* been watching for her out the front window. "You already knew. You were expecting me."

Sarah glanced toward the window. Jenny scooted to the edge of the couch, finally ready to listen.

"Maydene called me. Betty Tuck phoned her after you sped away, and Maydene thought—hoped—you'd end up here."

She closed her eyes and breathed deeply. "*She* wanted me to send you home."

Jenny stared at her aunt, confusion swirling in her mind with comprehension out of reach.

Her aunt leaned back. "Maydene said she'd already told you about the time she and Abe had their problems ... I assumed—"

Jenny's hand flew to her mouth. "Sarah *Jean*. Your middle name is Jean."

"Yes, it is."

"You're not ..."

"Yes, I am. I was the woman Abe turned to when Maydene took up with Joe."

Jonas sat on the patio with Steve Tuck, feeling like he'd somehow let the man down. The umbrella above him kept the morning sun out of his eyes, which was fitting since the true light of his life had driven away.

"Coffee, gentlemen." Betty Tuck wove around the other tables until she reached theirs. "Are you hungry? Would you prefer a full breakfast or some pastries and fruit? This is a bed-and-breakfast, after all. You've paid for the bed alrea—"

Steve cut her a quick look.

Jonas sighed and gave her a weak smile. "It's okay, ma'am. I understood what you meant." He fell back in his chair, his arms hanging listlessly at his side.

Betty left the coffee mugs on the table, then placed a hand on Jonas's shoulder and squeezed.

When she returned to the house, the men sat in a lull. Jonas had already peppered Steve with questions about where Jen might have gone. Who she'd go to? Steve said he'd seen her at church and at the café where she worked, but he'd properly met her just this morning.

If she'd been working yesterday when Jonas arrived in town, would his wife be with him right now? Would she have forgiven him and returned home?

The warmth in his fingers from holding his coffee mug wasn't making its way to his heart. He stared across the Tucks' backyard. Colorful flower beds carpeted the expanse. The gurgle of water features and a flowing stream sang mournfully. The gardens along the winding path were plotted to enhance relaxation.

But today, they only reminded him that his garden—his life —was filled with the weeds he'd nurtured.

Steve remained silent, but Jonas caught him stealing glances at the gardens. Was he appraising what he needed to do to keep them flourishing?

"You the gardener too?" he asked. "They're beautiful."

"Thank you," Steve took a long sip of his coffee. "I needed something to keep my mind occupied, if you know what I mean."

Jonas did—it was one of the reasons he worked so much. He nodded and took another deep draw from his mug. The hot liquid slid down his throat and began to abate the chill inside.

The back door opened again. Betty carried a tray loaded with pastries and a bowl of fruit salad toward them. The care and attentiveness she showed her guests, and her husband, reminded him of Jen.

She had catered to his every need those first years—happily, unconditionally. She'd given all of herself to him.

And what had he done? He'd ripped the rug out from underneath her and not bothered to help her up. The hollowness inside him deepened.

Betty set her tray on the glass tabletop and set a plate and napkin in front of Jonas. "I brought a variety of pastries."

While her smile didn't appear forced, it was undeserved. She shook a finger at her husband with a raised eyebrow. "You remember you're supposed to be watching your cholesterol."

"Yes, ma'am," Steve said when she was almost to the door.

"Seems you're on a pretty short leash." Jonas forced the good humor into his tone.

Steve smiled. "Seems that way. But leashes can be liberating if you're wise enough to recognize what, or even better, who you're leashed to."

"Hey, now. That wasn't a criticism." Jonas raised his palms.

He glommed onto a gooey chocolate éclair while Steve bit into a blueberry muffin. Silence surrounded them like a cloud while they ate.

When they'd both finished eating, Steve lifted the carafe Betty had left behind and filled Jonas' mug. "It is possible for men like us to be faithful to one woman—in case you're wondering." Steve stood and walked toward his garden. "I can tell you how it works for me."

Chapter Twenty-Three

All nerves and jitters, Zak burst into the newsroom. This morning had shaken him, and his afternoon meeting with Waxman and Sloan had kept the day on edge since it had shown up on his schedule. Thankfully, he had a blessed hour to decompress in his office before noon.

He breezed past Nancy, concentrating on reaching his office and shutting the door before anyone could buttonhole him with problems or excuses for missing a deadline. On most days, that stuff didn't bother him, but one complaint today would send him screaming into the street.

He slowed at the coffee station where a half pot sat. Who knew how long it'd been frying on the warmer, but that didn't matter. He needed a transfusion. He glanced around the countertop, but didn't see his mug.

That's odd. Must have left it in my office.

He crossed to his door and gripped the knob.

"Zakary?" Sloan's voice was congenial. Gone was the normal irritation. "Are you ill? It's not like you to come in this late."

"Yeah, sorry Sloan. I should have called. Sorry. I'm fine. Had a long night working on the plan for the meeting today, you know. Just overslept. No problems."

"Yes, that's what Nancy told me. You overslept." He shuffled a stack of papers from one hand to the other. "Well, with the busy night you had ... I mean, like you said, of course."

Zak stared at Sloan's pasted on smile.

"See you at the meeting."

He nodded, hesitated, and said, "Thanks for taking charge this morning. I heard you did a decent—a good—job of handling everything."

"Oh, no problem, Zakary. That's what an assistant editor is for. Tomorrow's budget is on your desk."

Sloan paused for a second. "I know we haven't always gotten along." His eyes were wide with compassion and his lips ... Were they pouting? "But if there's anything I can do for you ..."

Zak hesitated. "I'll let you know." Sloan spun on his heel and headed for his desk.

Shaking his head to clear the cobwebs, Zak sighed and entered his office. His head throbbed in the bright sunlight, so he closed the blinds. He sat at his desk, booted up his computer, and set Sloan's budget aside. He grabbed his pen.

Click-click. Click-click.

When his calendar loaded on his screen, an alarm box opened. *Meeting, 11:00 a.m., Mick Sharp, "Catching up."* He glanced at the clock in the corner of his screen. His hour had just shrunk to ten minutes. He considered calling Mick and begging off the meeting since he had a legitimate reason for postponing. But maybe some time with Mick's good nature would settle his nerves.

~

OVERWHELMED, nervous, and frightened, Mick rubbed his eyes and bowed his head in his hands. Zak had entered the newsroom five minutes ago.

"Father, I don't know what You expect of me. I'm not over her death myself. But Zak needs me. Help me, Lord. Help my friend."

He sat and listened for an answer. Preferably one that was something like, "Aw, forget it. I'll handle this." Instead, he got a confirmation. *Help him.*

Sighing, he ran his hands through his hair, laced his fingers together behind his head, and rotated his shoulder to relieve the tension. He took a deep breath, stood, and walked around his office. Opened the door. Looked out. Stepping across the threshold was like stepping off a cliff.

Gazing across the newsroom of six reporters, a photographer, and three ad sales reps, Mick caught Sloan's eye. Standing at his door and surveying his kingdom, Sloan's lips curled into his smarmy little smile that held more venom than glee.

Father, are You sure?

The thought of Sloan White in charge of the newsroom was harrowing. The entire staff disliked the little weasel—for good reason. If Sloan took over, all bets were off. Surely Waxman was aware of the assistant editor's maneuverings. He wouldn't let Sloan assume Zak's position, would he?

Mick was getting ahead of himself. He hadn't even talked to Zak yet.

Another deep breath. Another silent plea for guidance.

Help him.

Another surrender as he stepped across the threshold.

~

CLICK-CLICK. *Click-click.*

Zak stared blankly at the page proofs for the local news section as he waited for Mick. Someone knocked at his door, and he jerked his head up. He forced a smile and motioned Mick inside.

"C'mon in." He stood, walked around the desk, and gave Mick a slap-hug.

His friend didn't flop into Zak's spare chair as usual. Mick remained in the doorway, looking as if someone had shot his dog. "You ... want to sit?"

But Mick remained in the doorway, shifting from one foot to another and cracking his knuckles.

"What's up, bro?" Zak leaned against the front of his desk. "You don't look so good." Had something happened to Dreama or the kids? What else would have Mick so on edge?

Click-click. Click-click.

Mick's chest expanded and he finally stepped in the room. "Zak, we need to talk." His voice shook.

But Zak had no desire to talk with anyone—even Mick. "Whatever, whenever, my friend." The sooner he could get this conversation over, the sooner he could get through this day. "There are no secrets between us."

A tear slid down Mick's right cheek, and Zak's guard rose higher.

Mick was an emotional guy—had wept even harder than Zak during Kay's funeral—but a single tear? Not good.

Zak circled his desk and plopped into his chair. A barrier, something to hide behind, seemed necessary right now.

"No secrets, Zak?" Mick's voice quavered. "You're seeing someone you have no business in this world seeing and you're claiming we have no secrets?"

Horror momentarily stripped Zak bare.

Click-click. Click-click.

His mind searched for a logical explanation and found one —latched on to it with tenacity. Mick must have seen him kissing Jenny in the park. Must have. *He thinks I'm seeing Jenny and forgetting about Kay.*

"Mick, Mick, Mick. Jenny and I are not dating." He straightened some papers as he fought to keep panic out of his voice. "That kiss you saw was just me caught unaware by long unused hormones. It was just biological—"

"Zak, I—"

"What was it Tina sang? Something about the thrill of boy meets girl? " He barreled on, striving to prove to himself—and Mick—Jenny was the only person he was seeing. "I've already decided to tell Jenny I was wrong and—"

"We're not talking about Jenny, Zak. I wish we were. That I could understand. I would encourage. I'd even stand, whistle, and applaud." Mick still stood ramrod stiff.

Why wasn't he moving? Sitting? Something. Anything.

Zak's defenses flared. How had Mick found out about Kay? *Click-click. Click-click.*

"My life is mine to do with as I please." Zak opened his top desk drawer and placed the pen inside. A shroud of coldness dropped over him as he pretended to read Sloan's budget, hoping Mick would leave.

"Was there more?" He peered over the top of the budget.

Mick finally sat on the edge of the chair. Placing his hands on his knees, he looked Zak in the eyes. "You're talking to and interacting with a woman who's been dead since December, so yes, there's more, Zak."

"Do you want to be faithful to your wife?" Steve sat again and raised his eyebrows at Jonas.

"Of course I do." Jonas shifted in his chair and raked a hand through his hair. "Are we confessing our faults now...? If that's the plan, I'll pass."

Steve didn't respond just kept looking at him. Jonas knew this technique. Wait for the other guy to fill the uncomfortable silence. He hated that it was working.

"I've messed up pretty royally—no pun intended—but I'm going to pass on the Dr. Phil session."

While Jonas preferred espresso, he was grateful for the coffee as he lifted the mug to hide his face. He'd never been one for sharing his faults with others. It reeked of weakness.

Steve leaned across the table, getting too close to Jonas's personal space. "Are you saying you don't have a problem? If that's the case, I have my answer. You can go." Jonas scooted his chair back. He liked Steve, and his wife, but he was in no mood for a self-examination this morning. "What I'm saying is that it's none of your business. I'm checking out." He plunked his cup on the table and scrambled to his feet.

"So, you don't have a problem with infidelity? You don't engage in dangerous sexual practices?" Steve fired out questions like a machine gun. "How about pornography? No problems with that?"

Jonas turned back to Steve, restraining an urge to lash out. "I said—"

"Have you ever paid for sex, Jonas? Ever had anonymous sex? Can you tell me the name of that woman you spent last night with?"

Jonas had had enough. Stuffing down his anger, he stomped to the house.

"You don't have to continue this way." Steve's voice rose. "There's a way out."

Jonas stopped. His chest rose and fell.

"Jesus, Jonas."

He spun around to stare at Steve. "What?"

"Jesus is the answer you need."

"That's your solution? 'Let go and let God?' That's the best you've got?" Fighting a compulsion to flee, Jonas detoured toward the Lexus. He had to get out of there.

When Steve followed him to the driveway, Jonas fumbled the alarm code, and for the second time that morning, the neighborhood rang with an obnoxious *whoop-whoop-whoop*. He ignored it and threw himself into the car. Once the door was closed—and locked—he silenced the alarm.

"Do you want her back, Jonas? Do you want Jenny back?"

His head snapped up. Steve stood outside his window. He hadn't spoken the words loudly, yet they reverberated through the car.

"Do you want her back?" Steve asked again. "If so, you need Him."

Yes, he wanted her back. How could he not? Jenny was the only good thing in his life. But Jesus? Did adults still believe in that?

He shifted into gear and pulled out of the drive, thoughts consumed with Jen—and Jesus.

Chapter Twenty-Four

Sloan White hummed a happy tune as his new favorite video ended. This was no Hollywood blockbuster. Oh no. This was homemade and only five and a half minutes long. But it was a real potboiler. He'd already watched if four times.

The film had intrigue. Danger. Romance. And it foreshadowed a major conflict on the horizon, but that scene hadn't been recorded yet.

He had, however, played Zak like a Stradivarius. "Oh, and if you need any help." Sloan mocked his solicitous tone. He laughed like a rusty gate banging in a windstorm.

He sipped his tea and fast forwarded to that unfinished scene. It was a little early, but he longed to shout "Action" and watch the plot play out.

Patience, Sloan. Patience.

With retribution so long in coming, patience was difficult. But he would be editor soon.

He bit his lip and held on.

∽

Although he didn't want to hear what Mick had to say, Zak waited for him to continue. He didn't want solutions. Didn't want to face reality.

When Kay died, Zak had stopped praying. His single prayer had always been to find someone who loved him. Kay had answered that prayer, because with her absence now, God had certainly not answered it.

God was out there somewhere. He knew that in the same way he knew his father was out there. But like Pete Cooper, God had simply disappeared.

He and Kay had walked the path of life together, with God in the middle. But when the road dropped off on the left, God had not prevented or protected Kay from falling over the side. Then He'd left Zak behind as well. Just walked away.

Zak stole another peek at Mick over the top of the pages. The guy was fighting tears and about to lose the battle.

"I have a meeting in five minutes," Zak said. "We can continue this later, but if there's—"

"I saw you last night. In the newsroom embracing a woman who wasn't there. You called her Kay. I saw everything, Zak." Mick choked on his last words. "And the other night at the grocery store too."

Zak stared at the papers he held.

His memories from last night were, well, real-ish. They hadn't been vivid dreams. He glanced out the window, which looked out at Main Street. Kay smiled at him from beside the plant she'd bought. He rose from his chair and crossed the room.

If Kay was really back—somehow—he didn't want to lose her again. Mick would have to understand.

"Yes, I know." He turned back to his desk.

Mick's eyebrows knit together. "You know what? That I saw you last night?"

"No. I mean, I didn't know then, but I know now." Zak sighed, returned to his desk, retrieved his pen from the drawer, and picked up the budget.

Click-click. Click-click.

"Zak, I'm glad you're willing to listen to reason." Mick wiped a hand over his eyes. "I was afraid that you ...Well, that you ..."

"That I was crazy?" He swung his chair around until his back was to Mick and his eyes were on Kay. "I just might be." His voice was no louder than a whisper.

He couldn't afford Mick's concern right now. He'd lost Kay—his whole life. Apart from his job, nothing of his life remained. He wasn't about to risk losing the one thing he still had.

Click-click. Click-click.

"So, you'll get help? I'll go with you if you want. Anything you need. Zak?"

Zak had to get rid of Mick. Keep his brother-in-law from ruining the last good thing he had. He blinked. Again. Would his conscience leave him alone if he fired his best friend?

WHEN ZAK slowly rotated his chair around to face Mick, his eyes would not look directly at him. Mick did not like that at all. Zak looked like a mouse cornered, eyes darting left and right to find a way out.

"I never told you—apparently, I should have—but I didn't. I was ashamed, I guess." Mick fumbled to reestablish a connection. *Stop rambling and get to the point.* "I, uh, well, I had a few sessions with Harl— "

Zak held up one finger, and Mick's chest constricted. His

friend's eyes were closed to him. That had not happened before. Not even after the unfortunate prank in the cemetery.

Zak picked up his phone and dialed. "Yeah, it's me. Could you come in here for a minute? Yeah, right away. Okay, thanks." Zak looked across the desk. "I hope you understand. I have to do this. I'm not—"

Someone knocked on the door. Mick twisted around as Sloan popped his head in.

Zak motioned him in and pulled him to the far corner.

Mick tried to listen, but with Zak's back to him and blocking Sloan's short stature, he couldn't pick up what was being said. When they parted and Zak returned to his desk, the self-satisfied smirk on Sloan's face did not bode well.

"The *Gazette* is no longer in need of your services, Mitchell." The corners of Sloan's mouth may be turned down and his lips pursed, but the glitter in his eyes betrayed his glee. "I'll take you to collect your personal things from your office and escort you out. Follow me."

Mick stood on wobbly legs and staggered to Zak's desk. "Why are you doing this? I'm trying to help you."

Zak studied those darned papers on his desk, but a bead of sweat dripped from his hairline toward his cheekbone.

"You can't be serious." He pounded a fist on the desk to get his friend's attention. "Zak?"

Sloan gripped his arm and tugged him toward the door, but Mick jerked away and stepped to the other side of the desk. "You need help. I'm sorry I didn't see it before."

"I have all the help I need." Zak's gaze shifted toward his window. "You know that."

Zak's voice was so soft, Mick had to lean in. When he spoke, his voice wavered with grief. "She's here now, isn't she?"

Zak nodded at Sloan, who again attempted to grab Mick's

arm. Mick glared at him, and he raised his hands before taking a step backward.

"Don't make me call security, Mitchell," Sloan said.

"If you're firing me, I want you to say it yourself. Don't hide behind Sloan." He held his place. "I deserve that much."

Silence, and another bead of sweat, was all he got from Zak. He nodded and moved to the door.

Sloan opened the door for him, still trying to take charge.

"I know the way out. I don't need a viper like you to show me." After another glance at Zak, he shook his head, sighed, and walked away.

As Sarah relived her old pains and frustrations, Jenny remembered something her mother had told her when she was involved in the drama of her teen years.

"Some people move on from hurts but they never really leave them behind."

Had her mother been talking about her sister?

"Maydene and I both fancied Abe in high school," Sarah said. "But it was clear he always preferred her. I believed if I could just show him how much he meant to me, he'd be mine."

She sighed.

"When they married, I tried to go on as best I could." Her delicate finger circled the rim of her teacup. "As hard as I tried, though, I couldn't. I could not give up my dream. Every time I saw them around town so obviously happy, I cried. My love for Abe, my obsession with him, was destroying me.

"So, I moved. I thought Templeton was far enough that I wouldn't see them sashaying around. And maybe I could move on."

Jenny sat stunned as the image she'd always held in her

mind of her aunt tilted. Imagining Sarah in those settings, with those intense feelings, was, well, unimaginable. What other truths about people she loved had she overlooked?

"It didn't work, did it? Moving away from Oak Hill?"

Sarah hesitated. Was the memory causing her aunt so much distress that Sarah wanted to back away from it, instead of embracing it and finding healing?

Wasn't she doing the same thing? Trying to put Jonas's infidelities behind her, instead of dealing with them upfront?

"It would have worked." Sarah looked down into her lap where her hands fiddled with a tissue. "If only I hadn't been so weak."

When Sarah looked up again, Jenny saw the familiar steel in her aunt's eyes had returned.

"I grew up in a home where church was an important part of our lives and considered myself a Christian. But I hadn't yet learned what yielding sovereignty to Christ meant."

Jenny nodded her head, understanding too well what her aunt meant. There were places in her life where she still kept a tight hold on ownership. Certainly, her marriage.

"So, yes, it would have worked had I been strong enough to remove myself from the situation," Sarah continued. "But I wasn't."

She stood and paced.

"I stayed connected, through a mutual friend. Even if I didn't admit it, even to myself, I harbored a hope for a future that wasn't mine." She stepped into and out of each memory as she walked from one end of the living room to the other. "And each argument I heard whispers about, every little bump in their road, fed that hope."

"Years passed. I never sought romantic involvement with others, even when doctors or orderlies I worked with at the hospital expressed interest." She stopped and pinched the bridge of her nose. "I declined everyone so often, I got a reputation and men stopped asking."

"And all of that time, I prayed God would open a way for me to be with Abe." Her pacing became more strident. "I was praying for my will, not God's.

"Then Joe came to town and Abe hired him to help out at the café. My friend told me the sparks between Joe and Maydene were hotter than the grill."

When Sarah looked at Jenny again, determination filled her face. "I'm ashamed to say this, even today, but I prayed Maydene would fall in love with Joe. In my arrogance, I believed—made myself believe—she had married Abe outside of God's will. When you refuse to acknowledge God's sovereignty, you think any foolish thing is His will."

"I was certain of one thing. God wanted Abe and me together. I was a Christian, and I couldn't want something so deeply that God didn't want for me, could I? After all, didn't God promise to give us the desires of our hearts in the Psalms?"

Jenny thought of her own prayers about Jonas and her desire for a divorce.

Sarah reached over and put her hand on Jenny's shoulder. "I skipped right over the 'delight yourself in the Lord' portion of that verse. I chased after Abe—a flawed man who could never give me everything I wished for."

Sarah smiled at Jenny and took her hands.

"Sometimes our prayers must sound so foolish, so selfish, to God's ears."

"Like my prayers," Jenny said. "I wanted Him to approve of what I wanted." She searched for the words to express her reasoning. "But there's a difference between what's *allowed* and what's right."

"Tell me, dear."

"I'm not sure I can." She stood and put her hands on her head. "My head's all full of stuffing."

Sarah sat beside her and gave her a small smile, encouraging Jenny to push on.

"First Corinthians seven says that if a woman marries an unbelieving husband who is willing to live with her, she should not divorce him," Jenny began.

Now it was her turn to pace as she tried to untangle what the Bible taught about divorce.

"But there's a verse in Matthew which suggests divorce for marital unfaithfulness is allowed."

She made another circuit.

"God also says He hates divorce."

"Yes, in Malachi," Sarah said.

"And Jesus told the Pharisees that Moses *allowed* for divorce because of their hardened hearts, *not* because it was part of God's plan. I just don't know what is right." Jenny plopped on the couch, and Sarah encircled her in a hug.

"Jenny, all of that is true. It's not one or the other. God does hate divorce, but He allows it for reasons of abuse or marital infidelity—and our hard hearts," Sarah said. "Your confusion isn't with what's written in the Bible."

"What do you mean?"

Sarah took Jenny's hand and placed it over her heart.

"Your heart is not hard toward Jonas, but your mind is closed to him. Your mind and your heart both understand how you've been wronged. They're in agreement on that point."

Jenny's heart beat in a solid, if a bit elevated, rhythm as her aunt's words cut through the stuffing in her head.

"What you have to ask yourself, my dear, is d—"

"Do I still love Jonas?"

"Yes, that, of course, but also, does he love you? And if so, is your love, your life, together worth fighting for? Worth giving up what's *allowed* to pursue healing and wholeness as a couple?"

Jenny remembered the look of delight on Jonas's face when he popped his head out of the window and saw her this morning. And she remembered the joy that warmed her at seeing his smile.

"Would you like a cup of tea, dear?" Sarah asked. "I have Sweet Dreams or Earl Gray, and I think one Raspberry Zinger —which, if you don't mind, I'm going to drink."

Jenny looked at her aunt with new eyes. It took a tremendous amount of guts—and love—to share her painful story. That her aunt trusted her with it touched Jenny.

"How about a Diet Coke?"

"Well, I have one, but it's caffeine free."

"That'll do. Over ice, please."

Sarah walked around the stairway toward the kitchen. Jenny closed her eyes and rubbed her forehead with the tips of her fingers.

She rose and walked around her aunt's living room again, running her fingers across the shelves filled with Sarah's books and other knick-knacks. There was no dust. The house was meticulous in ways Jenny could never keep up with, especially with Susan. A grandfather clock, complete with a revolving moon dial and a big chamber case where the weights and pendulum glowed, stood in the corner of the living room.

The clock was about to strike noon, and Jenny remembered Zak's meeting. She wished he could hold on to his paper, but if Jonas followed Clarity's normal procedure, Zak was out. What would another loss do to him?

Chapter Twenty-Five

Mick stood on the street in front of *The Gazette*. Unemployed and friendless. Could his day get any worse?

Dreama would say, "Best not to think of that, Mick. Don't tempt fate."

He stared down the street he'd walked all his life. Today, Main Street appeared different, muted. Even though the downtown area had changed little since he'd first walked its cracked sidewalks, it had always been vibrant, active. Now tinged in grey, the day plodded like a Monday on steroids.

Mick's appetite took over. While not yet in survival mode, tough choices lay ahead for him and his family. But right now, he'd eat lunch at the café, one place he could expect a solid footing.

He could go home, but Dreama would have too many questions about why he was home early. He couldn't give her the news that Zak had fired him. Not yet. She'd storm down to the paper and whup Zak's posterior.

No, not home to Dreama just yet. First a piece of French

silk pie. With pie in mind, Mick marched toward the café, his hunger quickening with each step.

Zak stood at his window and watched Mick walk toward the cafe.

What had he done? He'd betrayed his best friend. For what? Exhaling loudly, Zak turned to Kay.

Why was she so vindictive in death? The pinch an inch line. The accusations at the park. Encouraging him to fire her brother. None of that was like the Kay he'd married and loved. None of it made sense. The sarcasm, the meanness, the vindictiveness—those were his faults, not hers

As Kay moved toward him—did she want to make amends? —Zak backed away. What had become of the woman he once adored? Death did not become her. That much was clear. But did it matter if he had her with him?

Of course, it mattered. But Zak could not figure out how to make things right again or if he even could. His time was running out.

"I have a meeting to get to." He grabbed his planner and the folder of notes, scribbles, and ideas and walked out the door, leaving Kay behind.

He reached up to massage his left temple. A headache that could fell an elephant was coming on.

In the hall, he met up with Sloan.

"Afternoon, Zakary." Sloan's eyes sparkled. "Did the budget meet with your approval?"

Sloan's good humor knocked Zak off balance. "Uh, sure. It was fine. Thanks."

"I thought it had a nice balance between local and national

news, with a sweet feature on the local front about the end-of-school Field Day over at the elementary school." He chuckled. "The photos are precious—lots of little kids competing for ribbons and hugging each other. But you probably didn't have time to review those since you came in so late, not feeling well and all."

"Yeah. And all."

They reached the conference room and walked inside. Zak was glad to arrive at the meeting before Sloan's incessant chirping drove him the rest of the way out of his mind. He smiled politely at Sloan and made for the far side of the table, where a man around ten years his junior sat.

If Zak could just get through this meeting, he'd sort out the mess he'd made.

Sloan took the seat to Waxman's right. The editor's chair. Zak set down his notes and eyed the stranger, who was playing a game on his laptop.

"Zak Cooper." He extended his hand. "Don't believe we've met."

"Jonas Miller. Pleased to meet you, Mr. Cooper."

Jonas exuded calm and confidence, but the man's hand was sweaty. And his left leg kept up a constant nervous bounce under the table, as if it couldn't wait to be on the way to somewhere else.

Another Miller? Well, this is the Midwest. Millers were a dime a dozen.

Without giving Zak any more information, Jonas returned to his game.

"Mr. Miller, I don't mean to be rude, but this meeting is for the editorial staff of *The Gazette*. Why are you here?"

At the head of the table, Waxman stood and commanded the room's attention. He was agitated but gave a curt nod to Jonas. Okay, Waxman expected him. Across the table, Sloan beamed at Jonas. Why was Zak the only one surprised by Jonas's presence?

He wished Mick were here. Though he wasn't editorial, Waxman had invited Mick to the meeting as a nod to his longevity at the paper. The paper's daily columnist and the distribution manager had also received invites.

The three of them were key influencers in-house and, when necessary, on the street. Mouth pursed in a grim line, Kathe Siler sat across the table from Zak. Next to her, Stan Becker nursed a Diet Coke.

"Is Mick coming?" Waxman looked at Zak. "He's late."

Zak sighed. "About Mick –"

"I think we should just go on." Sloan tipped his head at Zak. "Mick had an emergency to take care of and he probably won't be back." He flashed a conspiratorial smile in Zak's direction.

Zak's stomach churned.

"I hope it's nothing serious," Waxman said. "But Sloan makes a good point, we ought to get on with it."

Waxman sank into his chair like a much older man. Half-moons of darkness covered the bags under his eyes. He spread some papers in front of him and traded the positions of a few of them like in a shell game.

"As you all know, we've struggled to keep the paper open the past two years. The bottom line has been in the red for at least six months—this time. The increasing costs of paper, ink, and staff placed a heavy burden on our financials. Add to that the steady decline in our subscription saturation, and..."

Never strong in the human relations department, Waxman struggled to find the right words.

Zak's stomach clenched. *He's selling. We're going chain. That explains video game man and why I wasn't given a heads-up.*

A tangle of emotions passed over Waxman's face until the mask of pragmatism won out.

Zak's mouth moved, but he was unable to speak. It was as if he'd eaten one of those sports antiperspirants he'd seen advertised. *Extra strong for when you need it most.*

He giggled and caught himself. *Get a grip.*

What was Waxman saying? Zak had dropped the plot. He couldn't lose his job.

"... then I realized staff cuts weren't the answer," Waxman said. "Not if I could find another way. We're family here, and we don't turn our backs on each other."

No staff cuts? That, at least, was something. Zak's plan had included some pruning of the staff. The room was sweltering, and his equilibrium wobbled.

"I've decided to sell the paper to Clarity Communications," Waxman said.

Breathing became a struggle. Chains replaced existing editors to make their presence visible. Keeping his job wasn't likely, which could explain Sloan's cheerfulness. He likely assumed—wrongly—he'd be elevated.

Zak eyed the others. Everyone watched him. Expected him to say something—to give some kind of rebuttal. But he had nothing.

Silence overwhelmed the group. It moved in and set up shop in the center of the table.

Waxman nodded at Zak, encouraging him to speak, to take the leadership that was his as the editor and team captain.

"Well," Zak said, the word tasting like moldy bread in his mouth. "I guess we should all be grateful we still have a place to work."

The words were lame to his ears.

When he looked at Waxman, Kay stood behind him, shaking her head.

"What?" Zak shouted at her. "What is it you want from me now?"

Kathe Siler's eyes darted to Stan, and both then looked at Waxman, before returning to Zak. Kathe clasped her hands and looked at the packet of information in front of her. Stan took a chug of his drink and discovered a fascinating message in the design of the can.

Jonas and Sloan looked at each other and Sloan smirked.

Zak missed the easy humor Mick would have brought to the moment.

Waxman stood and pushed his chair back from the table. "I was hoping that, as the editor of this paper, you'd have something more encouraging to say to the rest of us. Some indication you're interested in our future."

Zak opened and closed his mouth. What had he done?

His face red with anger, Waxman set his chin and turned to Sloan, who was the picture of restraint. "Do you have anything, Sloan?"

He nodded and stood, buttoning his suit coat as he did so. "Of course, Charles. Happy to fill in where needed. Always have been."

Jenny took the soda and downed half of it in a single drink before setting the glass on a coaster atop the coffee table. "Thank you. That is exactly what I needed. Caffeine or no, nothing like a little phosphoric acid to clear the throat—and mind."

Sarah cradled her tea in both hands, smiling over the rim of her cup. While her aunt's hands were small and the skin over them thinning, they were also lithe and strong. They had not spent much time wringing themselves in despair. Instead,

Sarah had used them to minister healing and comfort to the patients she'd nursed back to health in much the same way she'd nursed Jenny this morning.

She took Sarah's teacup—a delicate, lilac-patterned china with a matching saucer—and set it aside. She grasped her aunt's hands, brought them up and kissed them before placing them on her own cheeks.

"So warm." The gentle heat from Sarah's palms flowed from Jenny's face through her whole being.

"Are you all right, dear?" Sarah brushed her fingers through Jenny's hair.

"Yes, I am. And yes, I will be."

With effort, Jenny left her aunt's side and picked up her glass. She downed the rest of the pop and returned the glass to the coaster. "I will be all right. But I need to ask a favor of you."

"Anything you need, Jenny."

Jenny drew in her breath and placed a hand over her mouth. "I need you to pray for me. For me and—Jonas. And Susan." Her heart protested, from fear instead of rebellion. She'd made the right decision.

Her eyes filled with tears of fear, relief, and sorrow. She bowed her head and grasped her aunt's hands again. "I need to be faithful to God. I could leave Jonas, and a part of me insists I should, but another part—a bigger one—isn't sure she wants to."

A strength that was not her own filled her. "Until I know for sure, you're right, I need to hold on. I'm scared to be hurt again, but ... I'm going to give it another try."

"It won't be easy," Sarah said.

Jenny lifted her head and gazed out the window at the world outside the comfort of her aunt's home. Her hands trembled and tears threatened, but she'd made her decision. "No. It won't."

More was on her heart than Jonas and her troubled

marriage. She turned and caught her aunt dabbing at her eyes with a tissue. "Sarah?"

"Yes, dear?" She folded the tissue into her waistband.

"Please pray for Zak too. He's suffering and needs someone to help him find his way home." She blinked back tears of her own. "And it can't be me."

"I love you, child. And I will pray. For all of you."

Chapter Twenty-Six

A frigid wind snaked around his legs, threatening to upend him as he stood along the highway, trying to force him to turn back. For twenty-five years, he'd run from this town and all it represented. Turning back would be easy.

But for the last three years, since the night that now seemed a lifetime ago, his steps—both real and symbolic—had all been leading him here. Yet, he'd pulled the car to the side of the road when he'd seen the ten miles to Oak Hill sign shaking in the wind.

Why?

That question haunted his life. Kept him awake at night. The question mocked him and berated him.

"Why?" Every time he picked up the phone to call his son to try and explain.

"Why?" As he set the handset down each time before the ring could be answered.

It was also the question he asked God almost every day until finally God had thundered down His own unanswerable question. *Why not?*

Why not his wife? Why not his family?

He spoke the words, again, to the night sky. "He makes his sun rise on the evil and on the good and sends rain on the just and on the unjust."

That was when he had collapsed with weeping. How did he dare demand accountability? From God! The Great God of the Universe. Immortal. Invisible. God Only Wise.

The words from the old hymn, which had once mocked him, comforted him.

Yet, to this day, "Why?" remained. Probing him. Haunting him. His thorn in the flesh.

Twenty-eight years ago, he'd been content in his Christian life. He'd had a loving, healthy wife and a young son. His life had been close to perfect.

But then the lump on Carol's left breast. She prayed. He prayed. The whole church and most of the town prayed. The lump grew. He gave more and prayed more. He had her anointed. Paid for every treatment he could find. The lump spread.

Why?

He promised continued service. He pledged fealty for life and beyond. He begged to take her place. He believed; he was sure of it. He believed and claimed her health—until the day she died.

Why?

Carol's death had been his Nebuchadnezzar, his fiery furnace. Only, he'd been burned, nearly consumed, before coming to the point of knowing that God *could.* But even when he didn't, he was still God.

Had he learned? Was he still pretending? This trip back to Oak Hill would reveal those answers. By God's grace, he faced another fiery furnace.

The wind howled and whipped his hair back from his face.

He smiled and returned to the driver's seat. The time had come to face his past. He pointed the car toward Oak Hill and ... what?

Home, of course. Pete "Bud" Cooper was heading home.

~

"WHY?" Zak glared at Kay. "Why did it have to be this way?"

The people around the conference table stared at Zak, uncomprehending. They couldn't see her as he could, he knew that. Kay was his secret. His guilty pleasure.

She shrugged her shoulders. "It didn't have to be."

Zak recognized the truth. He had chosen to keep his wife alive in his mind because the alternative—that she was dead and gone—had been too much to bear. He couldn't survive another desertion.

First his mother, then his father, Rachel, Gram—and now Kay. One after another those most important in his life had abandoned him, including, it seemed, God. His life had been nothing without Kay, so he'd brought her back. A sort of romantic Dr. Frankenstein.

Harley Culp had been correct about the bereavement hallucinations, but Zak discounted his warnings and would pay the price. Things were going to get worse, and he could not endure them anymore. The King of the Dead wanted to abdicate.

Movement in his peripheral caught his attention.

Sloan reached into his suitcoat and produced a remote control. He smiled at him with a beneficent malevolence. "It had to be this way, Zakary, because you would not seek help." Sloan answered the question no one asked. "Help you're not getting here."

Zak closed his eyes for a second. When he opened them,

everyone around the table, except for Video Game Guy—was it Jonas?—gaped at him like he was some crazy drunk preaching hell, damnation, and the end of the world from a pulpit of Jack Daniels. The Clarity rep stared unabashedly.

"This video was taken here at the paper early this morning," Sloan said. "I was here, as I frequently am, taking care of details our editor couldn't be bothered with—or was incapable of dealing with. It matters not."

He circled his hand in the air. "I was here, and nature called." He twittered. "As I exited the men's room, I heard someone talking and—well, you'll see the rest."

He pressed a couple of buttons, and the television screen on the wall came to life, broadcasting Zak's late-night fight with no one.

A carnival barker shouted in Zak's mind.

See the maniac throw his coffee cup against the wall. Watch the lunatic rail against the losses in his life. Swoon as the nutcase caresses the cheek of a woman only he sees. Gasp as the crazy man embraces nothing.

As Freak Show Zak moved out of the frame, a low chuckle escaped Sloan's mouth before he masked it with a cough and a clearing of the throat.

Zak massaged the back of his neck with his hand as the brain trust of *The Gazette* fidgeted, wondering what he would do next.

"What do you want, Sloan?" His fingers kneaded the center of his forehead. "What was the purpose of this?"

Sloan licked his lips, and the gleam in his eyes revealed his glee.

"It's not what I want, Zakary. I have no say in the matter. I only want you to face your problem and get help. Katharine died. You do know that, don't you?"

He shut off the TV.

"Better to ask Charles what he wants, Zakary. Or maybe Mr. Miller, who is here to represent our new owner. As long as the paper's needs are met and our reputation is not damaged, and you get some ... help, I want nothing else."

Zak attempted to meet each person's eyes. Kathe glanced down. Stan met his gaze with genuine concern. The usually unflappable Charles Waxman stared at the table. Zak refused to shift any attention to Sloan. Kay was gone.

How appropriate.

Silence screamed as Zak pushed back his chair, placed his hands on his knees, and stood. His troubles would soon be over.

"Charles?" He waited for the man who had once believed in him enough to leave his legacy in Zak's hands to acknowledge him. His stomach sank as the seconds stretched. When he finally raised his head, his eyes were rimmed with red.

His boss opened his mouth, but Zak held up his palm.

"I resign, Charles. I resign as editor of *The Gazette*, effective today." The words came from a voice he didn't recognize and echoed off the walls. "You'll receive written verification of my intent by the end of the day."

He whirled and trudged out the door into a vast, lonely emptiness.

Jonas's mouth dropped open as he watched the video, but not for the reasons that weasel Sloan probably imagined.

What most interested Jonas was that the behavior didn't seem all that strange. The whole scene could have come from one of those romance movies Jen liked. Odd, yes. Crazy, maybe. In fact, as usual, the Bard, this time "As You Like It," came to mind. *Love is merely a madness.*

He loved her. Sure, he had some issues, but that kind of love, devotion? Jonas wanted that. He wanted a love that lasted beyond death.

Since Jen had walked out, Jonas's world had been breaking apart. Nothing worked right. He was off-kilter, out of place, and shipwrecked. Only his obsessions—his work and his ladies—had kept him from wallowing in pain. But they were pale replacements and brought their own pain.

He wanted Jen back. How could he convince her of that? He was getting ahead of himself. First, he had to find her before she bolted for good.

Around him, the business and opinion leaders of *The Gazette* sat in stunned silence. Their paper was gone, sold to a national chain. Their editor was gone too—in more ways than one.

Jonas should be celebrating. Taking charge of the situation, passing out the new operating procedures, and naming an interim editor. There were plans to make and execute, reports to file, personnel evaluations to begin. He had the outline in his briefcase. But he could not make himself take it out.

He had to find Jen.

He'd start at the café. Didn't Steve mention Jen went to his church? Maybe he or Betty had heard something through the church grapevine. Maybe someone at Susan's school?

Someone tapped on his shoulder, and Jonas blinked back to the present.

"Mr. Miller?" Sloan's slimy voice repelled him.

"Was, uh, was there more?" Sloan tried too hard to oil his way into Jonas's good graces.

"Look, Sloan—Mr. White." He was done wasting time. "I'm, uh. Yeah, I'm—I'm thinking. Give me a minute."

"We need to tear up the front page and get a story about Clarity's acquisition of *The Gazette* – and, the new editor being named?" Sloan refused to be deterred. "In fact, in anticipation of that, I prepared a few headlines and nut graphs, if you'd like—"

Jonas held up his hand to halt Sloan's freight train mouth. He forced the thoughts of Jen and Susan from his mind, but itched to get out of the room—and on the road to Jen.

"Let's hold off on those, Sloan. Can we do that?" The words just tumbled out of his mouth. What in the world was he saying? "There's been enough change for one day, and the trouble and expense of tearing up the front page isn't wise. Let's, uh, let's just hold off."

He expanded his focus to the rest of the staff in the room.

"I also want to be sensitive to Mr. Cooper's situation. Let's go forward with today's budget as is. We—we'll put things on *hold*, sort of."

Sloan's eyes narrowed, and Jonas guessed he was calculating his next move.

Jonas surveyed these people he'd just bought—Clarity had bought. In a normal acquisition, their eyes would show hatred or fear. At the least, they'd be mentally updating their resumes. But, with one notable exception, everyone smiled at him with unexpected respect. That was new. His chest expanded.

"Certainly, Mr. Miller," Sloan said through gritted teeth as he gathered his papers together. "I will carry on."

That was the venom he was used to. "Yes, I'm sure you will, Sloan." Jonas chuckled.

He shut down his laptop, stowed his papers, and looked about. "Goodbye."

He exited the room with an air of hopeful expectation.

Maydene glanced down the counter again. Something was up. Silence wasn't the first—or the twentieth—thing that came to mind when describing Mick.

He'd ordered his normal French silk pie and a cup of java, but this was three hours too early. And despite her best efforts, he refused to talk.

Entertaining Susan hadn't given Maydene much time to pry him with questions. When school had let out, Susan walked the four blocks to the café instead of going to aftercare. Which would have been fine—if Jenny was back from Sarah's. And that situation was weighing on Maydene's mind too.

Maydene laid down her table rag and lifted her gaze to the ceiling. *When it rains it pours, Lord.*

She looked toward Mick again. Even her comment about it being a slow news day had netted nothing more than a quiet "Guess so."

He dragged his fork through his whipped crème topping and played with the chocolate curls she had painstakingly laid on the top.

That's it—the man had not eaten more than two bites of pie. She was going in. The other patrons were all served and she'd just need to watch for a signal or a new arrival.

Wiping down the counter as she went, she moved into his space and touched his arm.

"Mitchell Thaddeus Sharp, either your dog died, Doc Rawlings put you on a diet, or you've lost your best friend, because I *know* it's not my pie."

A small smile sputtered onto his face, until whatever trouble he was facing wiped it away before the humor had a chance to move to his eyes.

"I failed him, Maydene." Mick set down his fork and looked into her face. Tears shimmered at the bottom edge of his eyes. "I watched him like you said but couldn't do anything to help."

Her hand flew to her mouth and her eyes bulged. "Charles Waxman fired him?"

Waxman had thought himself better than the whole town since they'd been in grade school together, but this was too much. Zak was the best thing to happen to *The Gazette* since—as long as she could remember, which was a mighty long time.

She tossed her rag on the counter and untied her apron. "I'm going over there right now." She headed for the door.

Mick laughed, and to Maydene's ears it sounded like the winning song on Dick Clark's *American Bandstand* competition—it had a nice beat, and she could dance to it.

"No, Maydene, Charles didn't fire Zak, but I do suspect Zak has lost his job by now." Mick placed his hand on her arm. "I'm the one who got fired. He fired me."

"Charles fired you?"

"No. Charles hasn't fired anyone as far as I know."

He rubbed his eyes and cracked his knuckles, then drew in a long breath. "Zak fired me."

Maydene flopped onto the stool next to Mick. "Mitchell, what are you talking about? Zak wouldn't fire you." From the way Mick's shoulders hunched before he picked up his fork and drew it through the pie, she knew the truth. "Oh, my."

Chapter Twenty-Seven

When Jenny pulled into the cafe's parking lot, she hesitated to get out of the car. Too many uncertainties bounced around in her head. Her decision to try again with Jonas wasn't one of those, but how much should she let him back into her life? Could she allow him in a little at a time? Or should she fully commit?

She turned the car off.

Lord, it's me again. If Jonas is willing to come home and work things out, he'll want to come home as my husband—and all that involves. I'm not sure I can ... let him ...

She blushed. Talking to God about sex was certainly new. If her girlfriends could see her now.

But why not? Why shouldn't she? God knew her completely. Knew her before time and in the secret places. Isn't that what Psalm 129 talked about? God created sex. He had blessed and sanctified it between her and Jonas on their wedding day.

She rested her head on her steering wheel. She was afraid

of making herself that vulnerable to him again. And what about disease?

Her mind raced with possibilities. No, probabilities.

Place Me like a seal over your heart. God whispered between her worries.

Her heart fluttered, and she forced her mind to quiet. Had God spoken to her?

Place Me like a seal over your heart.

She'd heard that line before, but what did it mean? To seal something meant to close it tightly so that nothing could get in or out. Like a Tupperware lid?

Like a seal over your arm.

A different kind of seal, then. More like an insignia. Or the wax seals people used in the past as a mark of authority on correspondence. The King's signet, his seal, meant the bearer was in service to the King and under the King's protection.

"God will take care of me."

Well, that was fine, but sin had consequences. God could protect her. Could heal her. But there were no guarantees. Plenty of good Christians had died from disease. Plenty had also trusted God. Her heart peeked open to possibility.

Beloved, love burns like blazing fire, like a mighty flame.

On her wedding day, she'd been so nervous, so happy, so scared that she hadn't paid much attention to the ceremony, other than concentrating on getting her vows right and saying "I do" when asked.

But the words God spoke to her soul now rang with authenticity.

A chilly breeze crossed her heart. What if the flame had burned out? What if Jonas ...

She choked back her tears and her fears. If she didn't say it, maybe it wouldn't come true. Yet, the moment demanded honesty. She was talking with God. He already knew her fears.

What if ... Jonas didn't want her anymore? No longer loved her.

Many waters cannot quench love; rivers cannot wash it away.

Jenny hesitated again. Did God mean Jonas did still love her? Or was He saying Jonas *could* love her again? *Might* love her again. Might wasn't certain. Jonas had free will, and even if he still loved her, he could choose not to acknowledge that because of what it would cost him.

If the reconciliation were to be successful, a price would be required. It would cost him his women on the side. His pornography. His pride.

But it would also cost her. She was the one who'd been wronged. If she wanted reconciliation, taking Jonas back would cost her the right to retribution. To a justified payback.

If one were to give all the wealth of his house for love, it would be utterly scorned.

She had never had a season of prayer like this. Part woodshed, part reassurance, all covered in love. Her time was ending, and she dreaded the closing of the connection. But this was the first in a series of reconnections.

"It doesn't have to end," Jenny said to her steering wheel. "It's up to me to stay close. God is always there."

She lifted her head as Abe came out the café's back door with a bag of trash. His whole body lit up when he saw her, and the smile on his face was part joy and part relief.

"She's back! Jenny's here," he hollered back into the kitchen.

She opened the car door and stepped out. "I am back, and happy to be."

"So, I can see. That's a peaceful smile."

As she hugged Abe, she noted the concern on his face.

Before she could allay his fears, Maydene appeared, dabbing at her eyes with a handkerchief.

As the older woman enveloped her in an embrace, Jenny felt at home.

"You'll have to excuse my tears, I was cutting onions," Maydene said.

Jenny laughed. "I talked with Aunt Sarah."

Maydene pulled back, and her eyes probed for the answer to an unasked question, but she held her tongue. The back door banged open, and Susan ran full tilt into Jenny's arms.

"Mommy, Mommy! Maydene let me help her cook. And I washed dishes. And I took Pastor Dave's order—and got it right, didn't I Maydene?"

"Yes dear." Maydene placed her hand on Susan's head but held her gaze on Jenny. "Yes, you got it right?"

Jenny nodded and then kneeled on one knee in front of her daughter.

"Guess what, munchkin?" She poked Susan's nose. "I have great news. It will make you happy."

"Is Zak coming to dinner? Zak and Miss Dreama?"

"No, honey. Even better." She pulled her daughter in close for a hug as she said words a year ago she'd have sworn she'd never say. "Daddy's here and I'm going to ask him to dinner."

Susan eyes flew wide, and a grin lit her face. With her arms spread wide, she twirled in a dance of joy. Jenny's laugh sparkled as she watched her daughter with delight. When she looked toward Abe and Maydene, she nearly cried to see the lovebirds locked in an embrace, eyes igniting between kisses.

"Like a blazing fire, indeed," Jenny murmured.

She gazed upward and watched the clouds float across the sky. Her unhappiness sailed away with them. *Thank you for this. And for a new future. Now, if I can only find Jonas.*

She hugged Susan again, her mind racing with possibilities and her gut knotting with anticipation.

"Maydene? May I use your office to make a phone call?" She'd start with a call to The Tuck Inn and ask if Jonas had checked out.

∼

JONAS RACED out of *The Gazette*. In his excitement, he fumbled his keys out of his pocket. They crashed to the ground and slid under the Lexus's frame. As he kneeled to retrieve them, he considered praying—then froze.

Where'd that come from? He hadn't prayed since his wedding. In his rush to find Jen, he pushed the thought from his mind with a practiced disregard.

He'd embraced Christianity when it suited him—or when it was expected. It was in his life, always had been, but it was not a part of his life. He had his church clothes paired with his church smile. Both had helped convince Jen of his faith. Shortly after their wedding, work commitments kept him from church, and the ruse eventually no longer mattered.

He grabbed his keys, stood, and unlocked the car. As he turned the key in the ignition, the engine roared to life. He was ready to roll.

From the choices at hand, his best chance of finding Jen with minimum embarrassment and trouble lay with Steve Tuck, even if the man was a meddler. Maydene likely knew more, but trying to pump information out of her at the café was too risky—and too public. Besides, that woman was no pushover. The school was a last resort.

He put on his game face and calmed the pistons pumping in his gut. It would not do, not do at all, to publicize his eagerness to Steve. When people saw how much he wanted something, they would make him pay for it. And Jonas knew Steve's price.

"Do you want her back?" He'd asked. "Then you need Him."

"I don't think so. Not today, my man."

Jonas gunned down the street, his goal ahead.

❧

Pete "Bud" Cooper looked around Oak Hill's downtown and saw reminder after reminder that time had indeed moved on. The former State Theater on Main was now the home of Faith Mission, where signs in the windows advertised services for women and children.

In his time, a man down on his luck in Oak Hill had to hump his buns over to Templeton and the Salvation Army for a warm place to sleep. Homelessness had come home.

Though there was no movie theater, *The Gazette* remained in the same place, but Murphy's Five-and-Dime was gone. The Main Street Café & Emporium sat across the street from the paper. Was Maydene Gunderson still slinging hash inside? Pete stared at the café, remembering his last meal in Oak Hill. Blueberry pie, coffee, and a lecture.

Maydene had tried to force him to pull it together and quit mooning around. For his sake, but more importantly, for Zak. She urged him to move on with life. Instead, life had moved on without him.

Getting on with what little life he'd had left at the time had not seemed a good option. It was better to make a clean break. Geneva, his long-suffering mother-in-law, would take care of Zak. His decision to leave hadn't been right, but neither had it been completely wrong.

Geneva Crump was a strong woman, but she'd only

tolerated Pete. Had told Carol not to marry him because he couldn't be trusted. The old bitty had been right. But she loved Zak.

Pete shook the memories from his mind and, though there were no cars in sight, looked both ways before stepping into the street. Was he here for redemption? No, he'd settled that score three years ago, and it had set him on this quest.

His old life? Doubtful. Carol was long gone, and the only people in Oak Hill who had any chance at being alive would likely not remember him. Or would not remember him fondly.

What then? Forgiveness? A new life? *Any* life? Yes, to all, but mostly forgiveness from Zak, the one he'd hurt the most. If he could get that, the others would likely follow.

However, forgiveness from his son was not something Pete allowed himself the luxury of considering. Simple abandonment? Perhaps. But abandoning your kid in the wake of his mother's death? Impossible. Unthinkable. Still, he meant to try.

He stood outside the café —his first stop—and stared at his reflection in the window. A man much older than his years stared back at him. A man who had lived hard but never well. If Maydene didn't recognize him, it would be a blessing.

He would make general inquiries about Zak and decide what to do based on the information he gleaned. Maydene would know where he could find Zak ... if she was still alive. If she wasn't? Well, he would have to deal with that.

He breathed in deeply, shot an arrow prayer to heaven, opened the café door, and took his place at the counter—third stool from the end—for the first time in twenty-five years.

Chapter Twenty-Eight

"**B**ud Cooper! Oh glory, of all the lousy times for you to finally show up."

Pete shifted on his stool under the woman's glare. So much for hoping Maydene wouldn't recognize him. He was grateful for the other man at the counter. Maybe his presence would serve as a shield from the fire bound to come out of her mouth.

"Maydene."

She pursed her lips and shook her head. Then she stepped back from the counter, folded her arms across her chest, and studied him.

He glanced toward his would-be savior, but he also looked at him with more than a passing interest.

Pete caught Maydene's eyes, neither smiling nor frowning. He would not grovel. Yes, he'd made poor choices, but he was forgiven where it counted. His task would be easier with Maydene's help, but her assistance was not required.

"You need to leave." She walked around the counter and grabbed his elbow. "I want you to walk right out that door, just like you did twenty-five years ago. I'll even throw another handful of change at you as you go. Now, git."

Pete stood and faced her, hands clasped in front of him. He considered compliance, noting the set of her jaw, but then remembered why he'd returned.

"Now, Maydene, don't you think—"

"Don't you tell me what to think, you ... you ... skunk. You're to blame for all of this. All of it, you hear me? And I want you out. Now go, or I'll call the police."

I'm to blame?

She could be talking about any of several things—and she'd be right about all of them. Her eyes filled with tears, but Pete would never see them fall.

"Maydene, I want to find—"

"Out." Maydene stood as a sentinel, arm pointing to the entrance.

"Maydene, I have the right—"

"Out I said and out I mean. You have no rights here. You gave them up when you walked out on your son. Don't talk to me about rights. What about Zak's rights?"

The man at the end of the counter stood and stepped toward them.

Maydene motioned for him to sit back down, but he kept coming.

"I watched him grow up without you. Struggle at school—and with his faith. Even when he was happy, the sadness never left." One disobedient tear fell on her cheek.

Pete lowered his eyes.

"His mother died, and his father deserted him. What do you suppose that does to a young boy?"

Before Pete could answer, the man from the end of the bar was in his face. "You're Zak Cooper's father?"

Pete stepped back. "I am."

"You hopped a westbound train when he was eight and never looked back?"

"Yes ... and no."

Maydene's hands flew up in the air and she turned from the little reunion, then whirled sharply back.

"Mitchell Sharp."

Little Mickey?

Maydene's holler saved Pete from the full impact of Mick's flying right hook. He leaned out of range as the fist sailed by and grazed his chin. The sudden movement, coupled with the surprise of the attack, made Pete lose his footing and crash to the ground.

Pete's flailing legs tottered Mick as well, and the younger man went down onto one of the tables, upending it and sending it crashing into the table and chairs next to it. Glasses, ceramic plates, and tableware hit the floor at the same time as Mick, showering the men in debris.

Mick took his feet full steam and grabbed Pete's collar. "Stand up, you slime, so I can knock you back down!"

And Mick would have, but Abe rushed from the back room. He stepped between them, placing one hand on each man's chest.

"Now hang on here, gentlemen. Mick, what in the name of ..."

As Abe caught sight of Pete, recognition flashed in his eyes. "Pete Cooper? Is that you, Bud?"

Pete focused on Maydene. "Where's Joe?"

Mick, Abe, and Maydene stared at him.

"Joe was the guy protecting you last time I was here. You booted Abe before Carol died and took up with Joe. Now, Abe's back? Where'd Joe go?"

Maydene glanced toward the kitchen, her hand pushing a loose strand of hair from her face. She smoothed her apron and faced Pete. "That mistake is in the past. We've moved on."

Pete nodded and bent to pick up the overturned table and chairs. "The past." The words escaped his mouth like a prayer. "That's a good place to leave mistakes, providing you learn from them."

After righting the furniture, he stooped to pick up the scattered pieces of broken glass.

The others stood looking at each other. Except for the clatter Pete made cleaning up, there was no sound. Maydene stepped from the group and headed toward the kitchen.

A minute later, she returned with a broom and dustpan. "Why don't you let me help you clean up? We can't put it back together, but we can gather the pieces so no one gets hurt —anymore."

"That'd be nice, Maydene. That'd be real nice. Thank you."

No one spoke as they cleaned, and he welcomed the quiet. He'd grown used to silence after living alone for so many years.

As they cleaned up the debris, Pete's thoughts returned to his son.

"Is Zak still in town and, if he is, where would he be? He probably won't want to see me, but I need to apologize."

Sitting back on his heels, Mick placed a shard of a broken glass into the tub Maydene had brought out.

"Oh, he's here, all right. But seeing you would be just about the worst thing for him right now."

"I expect nothing of him. I want that clear. I just need to apologize before ... well, before it's too late."

Mick crossed his arms across his chest. "For his sake or yours?"

The two men exchanged glares.

"Mitchell, this might not be a bad thing," Maydene said.

"Zak's gone off his nut, Maydene. He's talking to, and seeing, his dead wife. He lost his job because of it. And so did I."

Pete shifted on the floor. "I had no idea. I had hoped for better. I suspect at least some of the blame can be laid at my feet."

"Ya' think?" Mick asked, his face turning red again.

"Mitchell." Maydene stood and tapped her fingers on the righted table, her brow creasing.

"You can't be serious." Mick jabbed a finger toward Pete. "Him showing up like he's come back from the dead? Considering Zak's issues, how can that be a good thing?"

Mick stood, his shoulders hunched, and jaw clenched.

"I'd be angry, too, Mick," Pete said. "But from where I'm sitting, I might be the only one here who *can* help him."

Mick opened his mouth, but Pete went on.

"I'm the one who wandered out of here in an unstable fog twenty-five years ago. Why? Because my wife, who was everything to me, died too early. Sound familiar?"

Abe rose and set the tub of broken dishes on a table.

"Hey, here's an idea. We all want what's best for Zak, so let's stop bellyaching at each other." Abe scanned the room. "Does anyone know where he is?"

Mick mumbled something.

Abe turned toward Mick. "What'd you say?"

"He's not at home, or at least he's not answering his phone. I've tried to reach him the last couple of hours."

"But you haven't gone over there?" Pete asked.

"No, Pete, I haven't gone over there. He's not happy with me right now."

"Well, that makes two of us he won't want to see," Pete said. "So, who *will* he talk to?"

"Oh, for land's sake. I'll go." Maydene tore off her apron

and flipped the sign in the front window. "You boys are all talk and no action. Some people need to stop spitting and start purring, or this mouse will never be caught."

"You're right, Maydene," Pete said. "I'm going to go walk through our old neighborhood and check out that park next to the elementary school. He hid out there often enough when he was in trouble."

"I could go over to the paper and make sure he's not there collecting his stuff," Mick said. "Maybe stop by church and check there."

"You won't find him in any of those places."

All heads turned toward the voice coming from kitchen.

"Why do you say that, Jenny?" Maydene asked.

The young woman Maydene called Jenny held onto the doorframe. "He'll be by the river."

"SHALL we gather at the river? The beautiful, the beautiful river? Gather with the saints by the river? That flows by the throne of God?"

Sitting alone in his sanctuary, Zak sang the words as a dirge instead of the invitation the hymnwriter intended. His mother had often sung the song— her off-key, but comforting, soprano joyous as she prepared dinner. Zak had not inherited his mother's cheery disposition. He tended toward his father's melancholy.

Of all the things he could have left me.

Zak dismissed thoughts of his father, just as he had since he was eight.

Initially, he'd held out hope for his dad's return, but bit by bit, Zak had abandoned him too. He'd replaced his biological father with God, his spiritual father. Between Him and other godly men, Zak had found what he needed to become a Christian man.

Then Kay died, and God the Father was nowhere to be found.

It hurt but wasn't unexpected. Patterns tend to repeat.

Zak tossed a pebble into the river. Here, in his chapel of nature, his sanctuary of sorrow, he'd mourned his mother, hated his father, found God, proposed to Kay, celebrated his hiring as editor of *The Gazette*, and kissed Jenny.

He touched his lips hoping to ignite that spark once again. He was surprised his arms remembered her exact shape, and he could still feel her eager hands on his back as he pulled in for their first kiss.

He breathed deeply to clear those thoughts—those desires —from his mind. He wouldn't be kissing Jenny again, so why torture himself with the memories, the fantasies? Giving her up hurt, but also cemented his resolve.

It won't be so bad. Who knows, really, what to expect after all?

His hand played with the canister in his pocket. His fingers ran over it, absent-mindedly.

He had other things to think about in his last moments—his mother's singing, his father's airplane rides that had made young Zak giggle with equal parts exultation and hysteria, his first published letter to the editor, Kay as she walked down the aisle in her white dress, the euphoria of the positive pregnancy test and the dark bewilderment of loss three months later—his "coronation" as King of the Dead.

He shivered. He'd accidentally declared himself the king, but he could not seem to abdicate that throne. He was King of the Dead by divine right. After all these years, was it now time to ascend to his throne?

"God? If You're going to show up, You'd better do it now.

You and I have had an understanding for years. I don't blame You for all the crap I've had to deal with, and You leave me alone to live my life. I believe, I just don't embrace, because ... love hurts. Love costs too much."

He pulled the pill bottle out of his pocket and held it up to the sky.

"But our agreement is not working anymore. I need some answers. I'm asking You to answer for what You've done. Are You even there?"

Only the noises of the forest surrounded him.

Is it a sin? Is it a blessing? Does it matter?

He raised his head and took in the sights he loved best. Had he come to the end?

He opened the bottle and dumped the contents into his palm.

"I knew I'd find you here."

He started at Kay's voice and thrust his hand back into his pocket. She'd disappeared since the debacle at *The Gazette,* and Zak had assumed she was gone for good.

He stared at her, unsure what to say. She was different, somehow. More complete. Softer.

Is death the end of life? Death was the end of *this* life, certainly, but what about the afterlife? Was death, like Pastor Dave said at funerals, only the beginning?

"Don't I even get a hello?"

Zak shrugged. "I can't even say goodbye and you're wanting hello?"

Like an old man getting up from his recliner after a nap, Zak exhaled as he stood. He dusted off his rear, folded his arms across his chest, and stared into Kay's face—the face he'd always hoped would be the last thing he saw.

Now at what could be his end, she was here. Was it his sign?

He closed his eyes to gain a few seconds, breathed in to calm himself, and then opened his eyes again. "Hello, Kay. What brings you to the river?"

"You, of course. What has ever brought me anywhere since the day we met?"

Any other day, Zak would have believed her, but today, after everything, he wasn't sure what to believe. Even after the insane jealousy, the dramatic attitude, and the firing of Mick, he wanted to be with Kay.

He wanted to be with her more than he wanted his job back. More than he wanted to keep his friendship with her brother. More than he wanted Jenny.

But did he want to be with her more than he wanted to live?

He could no longer stand not being able to touch her. He had to join her or ask her to leave. How could he do either?

Zak turned away.

He thrust his hand back into his pocket and pulled out the sleeping pills he'd dumped there at the sound of her voice. He stared at them. Sleeping pills Doc Rawlings had prescribed after Kay died. Zak had taken them once or twice, then tossed them in a drawer. They'd represented weakness he couldn't afford.

But Zak was not so strong today. This morning, before the meeting, he'd pulled the bottle out and counted them. Twenty. If he lost his job at the meeting, would twenty be enough? Were they too old?

Kay peeked over his shoulder and it startled him. He tried to stuff the pills back into his pocket, but she saw them.

"Oh Zak, what are you thinking?"

He reached for her but pulled his trembling hand back. Her eyes held his, and what little strength he had left him.

"I ... it's just ... I miss ..."

He sank to his knees, his shoulders shaking from the sobs that wracked him inside and out.

"I can't do this without you. I can't continue ... I only want to be with you."

He turned to his right and looked at her again. A depth of understanding that had not been there since her death filled her eyes.

"Oh, my darling. My dearest one." She reached out her hand to stroke his head and Zak leaned into her touch, yearning for a physical connection she could not give.

"Take the pills and be done with it," a caustic voice urged. "Then we can be together forever."

Zak's head jerked to the left. "Kay?"

This was the Kay of recent days. Cold, hard, bitter. He whipped his head back to the right. Warm, soft, loving—the Kay he remembered from before.

Left. *Insensitive.*

Right. *Caring.*

Left. *Caustic.*

Right. *Empathetic.*

Zak's head spun and his vision narrowed to a pinpoint before blackness consumed him. ·

Chapter Twenty-Nine

S loan stewed at his desk. Things had gone sideways. He was *supposed* to be the editor now. He was *supposed* to be writing his first editorial, announcing changes at *The Gazette*. His smiling, yet enigmatic, photo was *supposed* to be on the front page. He had anticipated accepting the fake accolades from *his* staff at *his* paper.

But he wasn't editor. He was shuffling mundane bits of copy, as usual, instead of writing his editorial. Bill Perkins, the staff photographer, had grudgingly snapped a headshot of Sloan but there was no story to run with it.

And the staff avoided him like the plague. Worse, he'd heard them whispering behind his back.

"Pretentious opportunist," they'd called him. "Ungrateful slackard," another said. And those were the kind names.

"Sticks and stones, sticks and stones," Sloan muttered.

It was all Jonas Miller's fault. Oh yes it was.

"Let's just hold off on those things, *Sloan*" He mocked Clarity's man under his breath. "I want to be *sensitive* to Mr. Cooper's position."

Sloan wanted to smack a sensitive two-by-four against Miller's head.

Sensitivity did not get the job done. If he was only the editor.

Wait. He *was* the acting editor, wasn't he? Whenever Zak was unavailable someone had to make editorial decisions, right? That someone had always been him in the past, why not now? After all, he most certainly *would* become editor if the brass at Clarity had any brains.

This was a test. They wanted to see if he had what it took to be in charge—make the tough decisions. That had to be it. It made sense after all the posturing of the Clarity rep.

Sloan grabbed his phone and made the call.

"Hold Page One. We have a new lead story." He leaned back in his chair. "Says who? Says me, and if you want to keep your job, you'll say so too."

A rush of power overtook him. "Who's writing it? I am, of course. Perkins already took the photo of our new editor."

WHEN ZAK CAME to beside the river bank, he couldn't remember why he was there. His mind felt scrambled, out of sorts. He tried to connect the dots, but too many were missing, and the picture was incomplete. He checked at his watch. Two o'clock.

I missed deadline.

He reached into his pocket for his cell to call Sloan, but only came up with a handful of sleeping pills and the empty bottle they'd been in.

In the dining room, Maydene wiped off the tables a second time—or was it the third? The search party for Zak had left, each promising to call as soon as they found him. She'd volunteered to check his home and had then returned to the café in case he came by.

She considered opening the cafe to keep herself busy, but knew she couldn't both wait tables and cook if a mini crowd happened by.

She'd already rearranged the pie slices in the pie case, restocked all the napkin holders, straightened the pictures on the walls, and cleaned the coffee maker. Would she have to get out the mop also? Why hadn't anyone phoned in? Let her know what was going on?

Had they found him? Had Mick killed Pete yet? Those two were a spitting match waiting to happen. And what would happen when they did find Zak? Would Abe be able to talk sense into whoever most needed it?

She absolutely hated being outside of the action.

Worrying herself to distraction, Maydene scurried around to collect window-cleaning supplies. The trip to Zak's home had been fruitless. From peering in the windows, she could tell someone—a man—lived there. Not dirty, but it had the comfortable look of someone who had no reason, other than himself, to tidy up.

His empty garage was not unusual. The lawn needed mowing, but so did hers. He'd brought the mail in, but his copy of *The Gazette* waited on the stoop—only one day's copy. She'd left a note for him to call her ASAP.

She traded the spray bottle, squeegee, and cloth for the large canisters of salt and pepper. Wait, Jenny had filled the table shakers yesterday. She'd have to go back to the windows.

Devote yourself to prayer, being watchful and thankful.

What? Now? Oh, Lord, I couldn't possibly pray now. I'm

too wound up. There are too many things to think about and plan for. Too much to do.

Devote yourself to prayer, being watchful and thankful.

"Now, Lord, You know I've prayed about this endlessly—especially over the last several days." Maydene wagged her cloth at the ceiling.

But when His call was insistent, she'd learned to listen and respond. Even when she did not want to.

Devote yourself to prayer, being watchful and thankful.

"Yes, yes, all right. Prayer."

JONAS'S HEART pounded and his breaths came in short, ragged gasps.

"So, that's my story." Steve Tucker handed Jonas his Bible. "Without Jesus, without my wife's support, without counseling, I'd be sitting in your seat today, my life disintegrating around me. Just like yours. Think about it. He can do the same for you."

Steve's life mirrored his—and in some ways, Steve's was even worse. Yet his wife forgave and came back to him. A tiny hope for a future with Jen sparked—but at what cost? He left the inn's dining room and escaped to the gardens to think.

Jonas hadn't shared any specifics of how he had violated his marriage vows, but like Steve, he'd fallen into his first infidelity during a weak moment. The excitement of the forbidden, and his search for more, had consumed Jonas. Each time, he pushed the envelope more. How far could he go before Jenny caught him?

He, too, had become an expert at rationalizing his actions. He worked hard. Jen was preoccupied with Susan. The affairs weren't hurting anyone, and they relieved his stress. He had no emotional attachment to the other women, not like he did with Jen.

Jonas paced Steve's backyard, facing the darkness of his life —the shallowness of his actions. How could he have ignored what his actions meant to Jen? Steve's recounting of his wife's devastation when she'd learned of his double life had ripped Jonas wide open. Had he done the same to Jen?

Betty's love for Steve was evident, even more so now. According to Steve, it had taken her time and some serious work on his part, but she'd forgiven him. That forgiveness was part of the healing Jesus had brought. Would Jen do the same for him? Could he repair the damage he'd done? Jonas was not so sure of either answer.

And what about Steve's claim that Jesus had helped him? How had that worked? Jonas remembered little from his childhood years in church. "Jesus Loves Me," John 3:16, Noah and the ark.

But those were just stories. Pieces of fiction compiled into a book others used to keep people in line. Weren't they?

Jonas ran his thumb over the soft leather binding of Steve's Bible. He'd handed it to Jonas when he'd left him alone on the patio and he'd carried it into the gardens.

He opened the cover and flipped through the pages. Steve's highlighting, underlining, and notes in the margins were everywhere. He flipped to John 3:16. "For God so loved the world ..." In the margin, Steve had written, underlined, and circled, *Even me.*

On another page, one phrase was underlined, highlighted, asterisked, and a big arrow drawn in the margin, pointed to it. Steve had written, *Yes! Live this!* in large letters. "Be not conformed to the ways of this world but be transformed by the renewing of your mind. Then you will be able to test and approve what God's will is—his good, pleasing, and perfect will."

Be transformed was circled with another arrow pointing to the word *Then.*

Jonas sat on a nearby garden bench and glanced into the lush retreat Steve had created. Two squirrels chased each other through the garden behind the inn. They chased each other up and down trees, leaping from branch to branch, chattering in what sounded like a language based on laughter.

At first, he and Jen had had so much fun together. She'd laughed with him, encouraged him, believed in him. How had it gone so wrong?

With Jen, he'd been able to push his demons down, glossing over his darker, selfish side. From the time he'd met her in the library and quoted Shakespeare, she'd been different from any of the other girls he'd pursued. Even though she was attracted, she had resisted his attempts to woo her. He had requested for a date five times before she'd said yes. That had been unusual—and part of what drew him to her.

"Jonas, what're you thinking about?" Steve asked, coming up behind him, with his gardening toolbelt fastened around his waist.

"Jen." He closed the Bible with a *thwap* and laid it on the bench beside him.

Steve nodded and extended a can of cola. "Thirsty?"

Jonas swallowed hard and took the drink. "Oh yeah. Thanks."

Steve knelt down and pulled a few weeds in silence.

Jen's resistance to his charms, even though her attraction to him was obvious, had intrigued him. Challenged him. After a month of dating, Jen had fallen in love with him, and he had assumed she'd agree to be together. But she had always wanted more than a physical relationship.

So, he'd redoubled his efforts, spending as much time with her as possible. He was attentive, loving—anticipated her every need. She took him home to meet her mother. He went to church with her. She laughed at his jokes. He bought flowers. She listened to his dreams and shared her own. And Jonas fell in love with her.

"What have I done?"

Steve didn't pause his weeding. "Something incredibly stupid and pointless."

Jonas snorted, but it sounded more like a sob. "Astute."

"Yep, just call me Mr. Obvious." Steve tossed a handful of weeds into a small pile.

Jonas wiped the tears from his eyes and dried his fingers on his pants. "I'm going to win her back. I did it before. I can do it again."

Jonas spotted a weed and kneeled to pluck it. They worked together, side by side, clearing the weeds.

"You're going to have to tell her. All of it." Steve kept his eyes on his task.

"Yeah, I know." Jonas sat back on his heels. "If she hasn't flown off again."

"I mean *everything*." Steve gripped Jonas's shoulder. "You can't beat this on your own. You're not strong enough. You will fail."

"Thanks for the vote of confidence, man."

"You know what I mean."

Yes, he did. With a sigh, he picked up the Bible and handed it back to Steve. When Steve gave him the side eye, Jonas held up his hand.

"I already have one. Jen gave it to me when Susan was born."

Steve pulled a pair of hand shears from his belt. He

snipped off several bloomed flowers that were nearing their end.

"Why do you cut them off like that," Jonas asked.

"It's called deadheading."

"Great name."

Both men laughed.

"It is, but it's essential," Steve said. "Most flowers produce more blooms and are more productive if the older, faded ones are removed. Deadheading removes the unattractive flowers and—"

"—makes way for new growth."

"Exactly." Steve continued his pruning. "Do you believe in God, Jonas?"

"Yeah, I guess."

"Well, as I explained, I do too. I believe in Him, and I believe sometimes He orchestrates events for our benefit. Sometimes He lets us muddle through because there's a lesson we need to learn. Sometimes He prunes us back—clears a path for new growth."

Jonas leaned in. "What are you getting at?"

Steve eyed him as if taking his measure. "Not five minutes before you showed up here today, Jenny called asking for you. She wanted ..."

Jonas shot to his feet. "Where is she? I have to find her." He reached into his pocket for his car keys.

Steve stared him down until he dialed back his RPMs.

"She wanted to know if you had checked out yet. At that time, I wasn't sure if you'd be back."

Fighting to stay calm, Jonas glanced at his watch. Had it really been almost five hours since this morning's meeting at *The Gazette*? "So, what did she say? Where is she?"

Steve placed the shears back in the bucket and stood. "She

said if you showed up, I should tell you to stop by the café. There's something she wants to give back to you."

"Give back?" Jonas's engine sputtered and died.

Steve cupped Jonas's shoulders. "Those were her exact words."

Jonas shuffled through what things Jen had that she might want to give back. Keys to the Lexus? No, she'd thrown those at the windshield—and left a nice chip. Photos? Probably not. Only one thing seemed likely. Her wedding ring.

He covered his eyes.

Even if Jen was done with him, he had to see her. Talk to her. Apologize. Tell her that despite his screwups she had been —still was—the only woman he ever loved. "I guess I'm off to the cafe."

Steve tightened his grasp. "If she's not there, check at Dave Greene's house over on Third, near Concord. A little white house with a separate upstairs living quarters. I believe she's there. But ..."

Jonas held his breath, waiting for the bomb to drop and blow his hopes to ash.

"She has been seeing someone else. It's a new relationship, doesn't seem serious—yet. But they hit it off pretty well. He's a widower and works at the paper."

Jen was dating someone from *The Gazette* who was a widower? Zak. Was Jen seeing the man he had earlier envied? Jonas sprinted for the Lexus.

Jenny led the small group through the county park. Mick had called them a posse, but Pete said that wasn't accurate. They were a traveling intervention.

Jenny wished both of them would hush.

The two men snarled at each other like dogs facing off over a bone. Both had opinions on what should be done and who should do it, but neither wanted to take orders from the other.

Jenny, who would rather have stayed at the cafe and waited for Jonas, had said, "Oh, never mind! Just follow me."

Now she wished she'd thought to leave word for Jonas at the café.

"I'm not sure I know how to get where we're going," Jenny said to her entourage, which also included Pete. "I just remember it was down the main path and then by the river a ways. I'm hoping to recognize the point where we turned."

They were heading for the place where Zak had kissed her, though she was the only one who knew that fact.

He had called it his secret place that night.

"Maybe we should split up and just head for the river," Mick said. "One of us at one end of the park and another at the other end. Walk the river until we find him."

"No, that won't work," Pete said. "If only one of us finds him, he might spook. If he decides to run, we'll lose him all over again."

"He wouldn't run if it were me or Abe."

"You don't know that for sure."

"Do too."

Jenny stopped, her back stiff. She slowly twisted around with her best "Mother is mad, and you best behave" expression on her face.

"Before we all get lost together, Mick's suggestion isn't a bad one." She ignored his smirk of superiority directed at Pete. "Why don't you and I take the *far* edge of the park and work toward the middle. Abe? Will you do the same from the other end?"

Abe nodded.

"What about me?" Pete asked. "I'm not going to sit on the teeter-totter while you all search."

"You will go with Abe. If you find Zak, it will probably be best if you're with Abe—since Zak doesn't know you. He'll recognize the rest of us. Let's go."

~

PETE AND ABE hit the trail.

After a few minutes of amiable silence, Pete smiled. "I'm with you because Jenny doesn't trust me."

Abe nodded. "I reckon."

"I'm the wild card. She doesn't know what I'll do. What my intentions are. Why I'm here."

"Frankly, Pete, neither do I." Abe stopped walking and pulled Pete's arm. "Why *are* you here? What are you trying to prove?"

Pete shrugged off Abe's hand and stood silent, scanning the area near the river. It was a fair question, coming from the man who'd stepped in and taken Pete's place as much as possible.

"I would never harm my son, Abe."

"You mean more than you have?"

"No, I do not. I mean I would never harm my son. End of discussion."

"And yet you abandoned him. The boy cried for months after you left. Asked why you didn't love him anymore."

Abe turned and stared down into Pete's eyes, struggling with the memory of the pain Zak had endured.

"You broke that child's heart, Pete, and Zak has carried those pieces, unable to make sense of them or put them back together."

Pete pivoted and strode toward the river again. The crunching gravel assured him that Abe followed.

"You all act as though I left Oak Hill and turned my back on my son on purpose," Pete said. "It wasn't like that."

Abe remained silent after catching up with Pete.

"Have you ever lost anything important?"

"Well, sure. I lost a watch once."

Pete shook his head. "More important."

Abe shrugged his shoulders. "I nearly lost Maydene, as you know."

A couple with a stroller came around the bend in the path. As they passed, Pete nodded and smiled, waiting until they were out of earshot.

"Think of it this way, Abe. Let's say that young mother"—he tipped his head toward the woman several feet away—has a baby and a dog. She loves them both."

He sighed "This analogy isn't perfect, but bear with me. Say she loses the dog. What's she going to do?"

"Well, I reckon she'd go about the neighborhood hollering after the dog, maybe ask the neighbors about him."

"And if she really loved the dog, she might also put up some posters, visit the dog shelter, post on social media, and what not, right?"

"I suppose."

"How long will she look for the dog before giving up? A week, maybe two?"

Abe nodded.

Pete paused on the trail and shoved his hands in the pockets of his khakis. "Now suppose she lost her baby." He gave that time to sink in. "How long would she look? To what lengths would she go to find her child?"

Understanding filled his old friend's eyes.

"I'm not excusing my actions. I was wrong." He fought to control his emotions. "But I lost my baby, Abe. I had to do everything to find her."

Abe slung an arm around his shoulders. "Let's move on."

They walked on. Together.

"That's why I'm here," Pete said. "That and because Zak needs me."

The continued along the river, searching for Zak's clearing.

"I understand, Pete, and I don't," Abe said. "You didn't *lose* Carol. She died. Sad as that is, it happens. People die—and the world moves on."

"I told you it was imperfect. But it's the best way I've found to explain it." Pete squinted into the forest, as if sheer determination would reveal Zak. "When Carol died, my 'tendency toward melancholy,' as my counselor likes to say, clouded my mind. I couldn't accept her death."

"You walked out on Zak because you were sad? Did you think you were the only one? Zak loved Carol too. She died on him too—and then you were gone. That boy cried himself to sleep for months. He didn't really stop looking for you until, as an adult, he returned to Oak Hill as the newspaper's editor."

Though it was just, the accusation burned through him like a poisonous arrow. How did he expect Abe to understand when his own understanding was squirmy?

"It was more than sadness."

They approached a fork in the path.

"Which way?" Pete searched to the right as far as he could see and then the left. "You know these woods better than I do."

"Right hues closer to the river. Let's take that one."

Pete nodded and stepped onto the path. "That's sort of how it works too. Sometimes you have to go the way that seems most familiar, most true. When I left Oak Hill, and Zak, I had convinced myself that Carol wasn't dead. She'd simply wandered away and got lost. I had to find her. I had to find my wife and bring her home."

Pete turned to Abe, desperate for him to understand the

choices he'd made. "I couldn't, or wouldn't, accept the truth. We loved each other, and she left me. I just knew she was in trouble."

"So, you chose to disbelieve the truth of her death?"

"Chose is kind of strong, but yes. I suppose so, although it didn't feel like a choice."

As he relived the memories from those days, Pete was almost sucked back into the experiences again. But he fought back this time, with a strength not his own.

"Her death did not fit my reality. I regret to say there was no Zak in my mind. I'm not sure it would have changed my plan if there had been. Zak needed his mother too. I had to find Carol. Death was not a possibility."

Pete chanced a glance to his left and saw Abe chewing on the conversation.

"Maydene and I never had any children. Couldn't. Zak is the closest thing to a son we have."

When Abe stopped and sat on a fallen tree trunk on the side of the path, Pete hunkered down next to him and waited for him to speak.

"Sometimes, early on, I would see a boy fishing with his dad, or a little girl squealing in delight as her daddy spun her around, and I would imagine that was my life."

Pete nodded.

"But it was my imagination, Bud. Sometimes it felt real, but it wasn't. Do you see why I'm having trouble with this?"

"I can't explain it any better. I lived in my imagination, unable to face the truth."

"For twenty-eight years?"

"No, for four or five. The rest of the time I lived in fear. Fear of what people here thought of me. Fear of facing what I'd done. Fear that Zak hated me."

Abe plucked a stalk of foxtail grass and sheared the furry

tail off with his thumbnail until the head flew off and landed nearby.

"I told myself I'd be in the way, and he didn't need me. It was easier, for me, to let it lie. To not disrupt his life a second time."

"So why are you here now?"

"That's easier to answer. Over the years, God cleansed me of my fear. He gave me a new mind. One that's still prone to an overactive imagination, mind you, but one that is trained on Him. A year ago, while I was praying, God impressed Zak on me. I had to return because he needs me."

Abe stood and pulled Pete up. "Then we'd better get back to searching, because Zak's wife died in an automobile accident almost a year ago. And according to Maydene and Mick, he's been talking to her—seeing her."

"So, I'm right? He needs me?"

"I believe he does."

Chapter Thirty

Sitting on the riverbank in his special place, Zak laughed. He was unemployed, friendless, possibly certifiable. Now he contemplated suicide. Why not laugh?

Definitely looney. Definitely tooney. Definitely sorta buffooney.

The mix of two of his favorites, Looney Tunes and Dr. Seuss, made him laugh more.

Nothing should have been funny, but everything was humorous. Two Kays was a nice twist. Good Kay and Bad Kay.

He looked around and, sure enough, both were still there.

"One of these things is not like the other," he started singing, then stopped. "One of you ladies doesn't belong. Or maybe both?"

He raised his voice so they could hear. "I'll have to tell Harley Culp about you two. He could write me up and become famous." Another laugh.

In a blink, a heavy sadness fell on him, and his laughter became gut-wrenching sobs. He leaned against a tree and glared at the Kays through his tears. He hated them. Both. How could they sit there and do nothing while he suffered? How could they be so cold?

Kay's dead, Zak. You aren't.

Who said that? "Not *yet*."

He fished in his pocket to make sure the pills hadn't fallen out when he fainted. Holding them in his palm assured him he had an escape.

He looked around for the source of the voice he'd heard. There was no one. The Kays were quiet for once and the voice had been male. Was he talking to himself now? "That's not good."

You're not talking to yourself, Zak.

He looked up.

The voice had *sounded* like his in his mind.

"What do you mean, I'm not talking to myself. There's no one else here. Unless you count the dead gals."

Zak tipped his head left and right, like he was moving an antenna around, trying to pick up the strongest signal.

Who is this that darkens my counsel with words without knowledge?

Zak's mouth gaped open as he pushed his back against the trunk of the tree. To his left, Bad Kay sulked while on his right, Good Kay beamed. Neither spoke.

"Okay, I'll play along." He dug into his reporter instincts. "Hello, my name is Zak Cooper. I'm the editor, make that former editor, of *The Gazette*. I'm also a former son, former father, former husband, and nearly former human being. Who are you?"

Have the gates of death been shown to you? Have you seen the gates of the shadow of death? Tell me, if you know all this.

The words were familiar, but he couldn't place them.

He searched his memory. They had come from the Bible.

"The valley of the shadow of death." Not quite what he was saying, but close.

He thought back to his childhood coronation. Certainly, death had marked his life in many ways—but King? Others have lost loved ones. As an editor, he'd read stories about intensely tragic losses—worse even then his own.

"No, I guess I've never been to the gates of the shadow of death—wherever that is—but I've camped near them all my life. I've lost so many people I've loved, and who loved me. Why take more?"

Do you know the laws of the heavens? Can you set up God's dominion over earth?

God's dominion? Could he be talking to God?

Zak shrunk from the idea. He closed his eyes to avoid seeing Him. If there had been a cleft nearby, he'd have hidden himself in it.

Would you discredit my justice? Would you condemn me to justify yourself? Do you have an arm like God's, and can your voice thunder like his?

In the silence that followed, Zak's anger burned inside him.

"I have nothing to say to You," he lashed out. "I begged, pleaded, and cried out to You, yet You never bothered to answer. Never deigned to defend, let alone explain, Yourself."

Be not conformed to the ways of this world.

"What? What do you mean?"

But Zak understood. The world asked for signs and miracles, confirmation that God existed, then refused to see truth.

But this was different. This was his life. He deserved an answer.

"How can I reply?" Zak peered toward the heavens. "All my life I've heard *about* you, but have never heard *from* you—

until today. What do you want from me? That you haven't already taken."

Be transformed by the renewing of your mind.

"What does that even mean?" He lurched to his feet. "This is why people have trouble believing in You, you know?" If God was going to speak, why couldn't He speak plain?

But He said nothing more, either in Zak's head or out loud.

When he lifted his eyes, Kay—both Kays—had disappeared.

Yet, for the first time in a long time, Zak didn't feel alone.

He looked out over the river, seeing it with fresh eyes. His melancholy still hung on him like a shroud, but his burden was lightened by—what? —his experience with God?

If God had indeed spoken to him, why was he so depressed? And why did he still wish he could be with Kay— wherever she had gone—denying her death?

Then, words that Harley had shared in their session, returned.

"Clinical studies have shown there are roughly seven stages of grief that each person goes through ... You're moving through the stages, a little back and forth yet between denial and bargaining ..."

Was he grieving? Still stuck in denial?

"Now, you and I may not go through them in the same order or over the same length of time, but most people do process death in similar, if distinct, ways."

Zak had laughed at the counselor's "similar, if distinct" phrasing, but he owed Dr. Culp an apology, at least—and probably a phone call to set up an appointment.

"Yet you're talking to her. Why do you think you're doing that?"

What had he answered Harley? He searched his memories from that frightening day.

"Maybe because there isn't anyone else to talk to. Because I miss her. Because I love her."

Had his mind created the Kays as a means of denying Kay's death? Had he used bits and pieces of himself—and his memories—to keep her alive because he'd not invested in—or trusted—anyone else?

"I have a few issues yet to work through," Zak said to the river.

He had not yet come to terms with any of the deaths that littered his life. He would have to deal with those, but for today, the death of his denial was enough.

He opened his fist. Twenty little pills rested in his palm. In some ways, that path would be easier, but Zak couldn't kill himself. He still had hope, as irrational as it seemed. He couldn't be with Kay in this world, but was he ready to join her?

He didn't think so.

"I'll see you again, my love, and then we'll be together forever."

This prospect did not fill him with joy or confidence, but it offered a smidge of comfort. He walked to the river's edge and held his hand over the water. While his decisiveness held, he flipped his palm and dropped the pills.

As the current carried them away, a single swan floated out of a bramble on the far side. Breathtakingly beautiful in her white purity, she glided toward him, stopping mid-river. After glancing up and down the river while paddling in place, she turned her neck and honked softly behind her.

Out of the bramble came two—no, three—more swans. Each one with feathers nearly blindingly white in the sunlight that broke through the overcast sky. They swam to join the first.

Zak held his breath.

The leader looked again in his direction, then turned and swam with the current. The others followed.

Zak feared he was dreaming, but he wasn't. He named each one—Kay, Mom, Gram, Rachel—and watched them glide away until they were out of sight.

Only then did Zak wipe away his tears. He started to turn away, but a movement in the bramble caught his eye.

One more swan—this one black—peeked out. He moved to join the others, hesitated, then slid back into the bramble.

He peered at Zak and ventured out again, gliding a mere five feet from the bramble, eyes expectant, yet wary.

Dad?

Pete stared at the trail ahead.

"There's Jenny and Mick coming toward us. I don't see Zak." He waved at the two as they rounded the bend in the trail.

Jenny called out. "No luck?"

Pete shook his head. "What now?"

No one answered. Pete eyed the group. Abe, Mick, Jenny. His son had good friends—people who cared for him.

"You know, I wondered what state I'd find Zak in when I returned," Pete said. "If he'd be here at all. I can't tell you how glad I am to find that he has friends like you."

Pete met everyone's gaze, then gazed down. "As I was sharing with Abe while we walked, I loved my son—"

"Zak?" Mick said, surprised.

"Well, of course, Zak." He shook his head. "I don't have another son, do I?"

"What are you all doing here?" A surprised male voice spoke from behind Pete. "Especially you."

Pete turned around and stared into a familiar face, only with two days of stubble. "You look like your mother."

Confusion and recognition—and disgust—warred in his son's eyes. Pete stepped forward, arms wide. "Zak, I'm your fa—"

"Spare me the Star Wars speech, okay?" Zak held up his hand. "It's not been that kind of day. I know who you are—and who you aren't, *Dad*."

Pete lowered his head and stepped back.

Zak fought to control his emotions. He could not, must not, let that man touch him—physically or otherwise. He turned toward the others. "I'm ... touched that you all came searching for me. Thank you."

He glanced tentatively at Mick, and saw only love, acceptance, and concern. "I'm sorry, Mick. I'll make it right, somehow. I'm so sorry."

Zak folded his arms across his chest and turned his gaze to Pete. "Gram always said you'd show up one day. I hoped she was wrong. Hoped you were dead." An image of the black swan flashed in his mind, but he forced it aside. "Dead I could understand."

Someone touched his arm, and Zak spun around. Abe. He huffed out the breath trapped in his lungs.

"Zak, maybe you—"

"Not today. Please take my fa—this man back to town. There's a hotel near the highway where I'm sure he can find a bed."

Jenny stepped closer, her tone imploring. "At least talk to him. Maybe if you'd just talk to him ..."

Were they all fooled by his father's act of concern?

"Jenny, it may be hard for you to understand this because you had a real father." Zak did not even try to lower his voice. "But this man means nothing to me. Less than nothing. He's as unimportant as ... as the sock lint between my toes."

Zak chanced a glance at Pete. His father bowed his head, but he didn't cry. Didn't he care enough to argue? To fight for Zak? Fine, then. He turned to Abe again.

"Hotel. Edge of town. Now, please." A weariness overtook him. "I need to go home. Jenny, will you drive me back?"

Chapter Thirty-One

The Lexus squealed into a parking space across the street from the café, and Jonas threw the car into park and himself out the door. He raced across the street, trying to keep his emotions from getting ahead of him.

Jen had to be here. He desperately wanted this to be a new beginning, not an ending.

New beginning. New beginning.

Those words had become his refrain on the short drive from The Tuck Inn. He wouldn't allow himself to think about what else Jen wanted to give back to him. And, as much as he'd admired Zak Cooper, he didn't want the man taking his place in Jen's life.

He reached for the café door and was about to open it when he noticed the sign. *Closed: Please Come Again.*

"Why are they closed?"

He cupped his hands up to the glass and peered through the windows, but the café was empty—even though there was a cup of coffee sitting on the table nearest the front.

Before heading to Jen's home, he glanced down at the

newspaper box on the sidewalk and did a double take. *New Editor Named* screamed the headline of the top story. A secondary headline proclaimed *Former Editor Embraces Ghost*.

"He named himself editor? How ...? What ...?" Jonas dropped two quarters into the box and grabbed a paper and turned it over.

Below the fold, was another story. "Gazette Joins National Chain."

Jonas sighed. This is not part of the plan. His boss would not be pleased to discover Jonas had lost control of the situation.

He faced another crisis.

On the one hand, Jen. On the other, his future with Clarity. Jen? Clarity? Love? Success?

He looked once more into the café. No one. Jonas would have preferred to talk with his wife, but since she wasn't here, he'd take care of Sloan and try to save his career. It would be pointless to convince Jen to come back to an unemployed nobody. He'd go by the Greene's house afterward.

He pivoted away from the café and crossed the street to *The Gazette*. At least this problem had and easy fix.

ZAK HAD BEEN silent on the drive to his home, preoccupied with his thoughts, Jenny assumed. She welcomed the silence, because it gave her time to hone her arguments for why she and Zak couldn't be more than friends.

First, regardless of how tentative her marriage was at this point, she had a husband. She planned to talk with Jonas about reconciliation but wasn't sure where he stood or if they'd be able to work out their differences. Would he even be interested after the significant changes and commitments she would require from him, including levels of accountability he'd never been willing to submit to?

Second, Zak was tied to his deceased wife in unhealthy ways and needed to concentrate on getting his life together. But it was the third reason that convinced her not to pursue more with Zak.

Susan. Even if she and Jonas couldn't work things out, Susan needed a healthy relationship with her father. She wanted her daughter to invest her "Daddy needs" into her daddy, not another man, no matter how willing he was to pick up the slack.

As she pulled into Zak's driveway, Jenny sensed Zak had something he wanted to say. She shifted the car into park.

"Zak...?" Jenny started.

"Jenny...?" Zak said a half beat behind her.

They laughed.

He looked down at his hands in his lap and then up into her eyes. "May I?"

She couldn't make her voice work, so she nodded.

"I owe you an awful lot, more than I could ever begin to repay. I hope ..."

Jenny held up her hand to stop him, but Zak reached over and wove his fingers in hers.

"I hope that you will be able to forgive me." His lips swept the skin on the back of her hand.

"Forgive you? For what?"

"For ... many things. For taking advantage of you in the park. For not calling after." Then he released her hand and folded his into his lap. "But most of all, for telling you, now, after you led the search effort to find me, that I ..."

He closed his eyes and moisture filled hers.

When he looked at her again, a clarity that had been missing before shone in his eyes. "That I can't see you again."

She had been prepared to tell *him* that it was over but hadn't expected him to agree with her before she even gave her reasons. Even though this was what she wanted, the words stung her in an unexpected way.

"It's over?" It was out before she could stop it.

Place Me like a seal over your heart.

The words God spoke to her earlier returned. She said a quick prayer for strength.

"Yes. It must be. I am not—free—to pursue other relationships." Zak was more resolute than she. "I'm not over Kay yet—and maybe not ever. But, regardless of my reasons, you're married, and Susan has a father."

Jenny's mouth dropped open, and she made no effort to hide her shock. "You knew?"

"It's true, isn't it?"

"Well ... yes, but—you knew?"

Zak smiled again—a wondrous sight. "I am a reporter."

She reached across the car and smacked Zak's arm.

"Ow."

"When did you find out? How long did you string me along?"

Zak massaged his arm with exaggeration. "I didn't know until after we kiss ... until after the park. I *suspected* but didn't have proof."

"How did you find out?"

"Well, some things are elementary, my dear Watson. Susan, for one. It takes one man and one woman to make a child. Therefore, she has a father. That was the easy part."

Jenny leaned back against her car door, arms folded, and rolled her hand in a circle.

"Remember when Sloan came into the café behind me, fussing about the Puppy Paw Parade? He wanted to replace the parade on the front page with a story about Clarity Communications expanding into the Midwest."

"And I reacted."

"Yes, you did. I wondered why, but I didn't really think of it again until a certain Jonas Miller introduced himself this morning. That's when the tumblers fell into place and unlocked your secret."

"Well, it's not *exactly* a secret. Abe and Maydene know."

"I'm sorry I wasn't truthful with you." Jenny looked at Zak sitting in the passenger seat just as he had the night they'd met. *He seems unsettled still.* "There's more, isn't there?"

"No." He hesitated and shook his head. "No, that's all."

He opened the door and stepped out of her car. When he shut the door, she cranked the key. As she reached to put the car in reverse, he knocked on the passenger window.

She pressed the button and lowered the window before leaning across the seat.

Zak eyebrows drew together. "Is he a good man?"

"Jonas?"

He nodded.

Jenny bit her lip and returned to her seat. She stared straight ahead, her hands gripping the steering wheel. "He could be."

"But he's not?"

"Jonas cheats." Why was she telling Zak her secrets? "I've caught him twi ... No, it's three times now." She swallowed hard to avoid tears. "There are probably more, but I've chosen not to ask."

Zak hunkered down . "Do you love him?"

She shrugged. "He's my husband."

Zak shook his head. "Not what I asked. Do you love him? Because you could leave him, you know, biblically."

She gulped.

"Does he mean more to you than anything else?"

A cry escaped her, as tears flowed in spite of her efforts. "Yes, Zak. Yes, I think he does. Even when I wish he didn't."

Zak nodded and stood, then stepped away from the car. As Jenny put the car in reverse, he leaned down one last time and called into the window. "Fight for him, Jenny. He needs you."

She backed out of the driveway. In her rearview mirror, Zak stood in the street watching her leave.

Oh, dear God, what am I turning away from? What am I turning toward? Will You be there?

"You're fired."

Jonas had chosen to reward Sloan for his initiative in the newsroom—in a hastily called staff meeting. Everyone he could round up now circled the break area. Normally, he wouldn't fire someone publicly. Clarity frowned on that bad mojo. But he intended to make an example of Sloan—besides, he just didn't care for the man who was working his last nerve. Sloan's egregious actions begged for a little humiliation.

Sloan smirked and scanned the room.

"Sloan? Did you hear me?"

"Of course, Jo-, Mr. Miller. You certainly have the authority to fire any employee who is not performing to your expectations. It's one of the perks of management. Zakary fired Mitchell Sharp this morning."

"Zak fired the graphic artist?" This was news to him. "Aren't they brothers-in-law?"

"They were."

"Why would he do that?"

"Who knew why Zakary did anything these last several

months?" Sloan sniffed as he placed his phone and a thumb drive on his desk. "He was unstable. Surely, you saw that."

Several staff members whispered to each other and laughed behind their hands.

"Hmm. So ... Sloan. Shouldn't you be packing up your things? Go. Go, go."

Then comprehension dawned on Sloan's face, and grins broke out around the circle.

Jonas worked hard to maintain his professionalism.

"Me?" Sloan squeaked. "You're firing me?"

"Yes, you. Insubordination, officially. Your stunt with today's edition cannot be tolerated."

"It ... I ... A *small* misjudgment, Jo-, Mr. Miller," Sloan wheedled. "It was, ah, an emotional day for all of us. I assumed that ... I got caught up in the drama." He drew himself up. "*As acting editor,* I simply did what needed to be done."

"And as a representative of *the owner,* I couldn't have been clearer in my instructions about what you should do with the front page—and to take the authority on yourself to name yourself editor? I must say, I'm impressed with your, uh, machismo?" He leveled a glare at Sloan. "But you're still fired."

Sloan opened his mouth, probably to argue some small point, but Jonas had more to say. "As I said, insubordination will be the official reason, but did you really think Clarity could trust you after you'd proven willing to betray *The Gazette*'s leadership during this acquisition? Your video ridiculing a good man—one we hoped to keep in his position—was merely the last straw."

Sloan stammered, fumed, and lurched from his desk to the break table and back.

"Mr. White, don't make me call security to escort you from the building."

Sloan turned and walked toward the front door but swiveled on his heel to retrieve his phone and the drive from his desk.

"Oh, I'll need that thumb drive," Jonas said. "I'll need it if Mr. Cooper decides to sue the paper for defamation of character, you weasel."

Huffing with indignation, Sloan looked at the drive in his hand then tossed it on the floor at Jonas's feet. He spun and stormed out of the room.

Jonas faced the newsroom staff, but before he could open his mouth, Stan Becker started applauding. Kathe Siler and Nancy Lopez followed suit, and the clapping soon spread through the assembled staff.

"Thank you," Jonas said. "Thank you. I'll see you all in the morning."

As the staff broke off in clumps to dissect the latest development, Jonas called out. "Ms. Lopez? Please call Mitchell Sharp and rescind his termination. Let him know that as part of the team, I expect him here first thing tomorrow."

Several staffers shot each other wide-eyed glances. Jonas smiled. "I'm going to need all the help I can get if I'm going to serve as interim editor."

He turned to leave, his impatience to check Jen's home fueling his actions. Tomorrow would have plenty of challenges of its own—why worry about them tonight? On his way to the door, he leaned over Nancy Lopez's desk for one more instruction that couldn't wait.

"Nancy? Please keep this quiet, but can you can get Zak Cooper on the phone? I'd like to talk with him."

MAYDENE SAT at the front table of the café with her head bowed in prayer. Her cup of coffee had cooled beyond resuscitation when Abe returned with Mick and Pete. She'd stayed at her post diligently praying, except for the brief minutes she'd stepped into the Ladies Room. Even then, she'd stayed on task.

"What happened?" Maydene asked. Abe's face, so easy to read most days, was veiled. What was he keeping from her?

"Got any coffee, hon?"

Abe never drank coffee this late. Something happened. "I just cleaned the coffeemaker, but I can make a pot. Did you find him? Are you planning a late night?"

Her heart fluttered as the three men exchanged glances. None of them spoke.

"Abe?" she asked.

"I guess a pot would be a good thing." He nodded at the other men. "I'm having peach. Either of you want a piece of pie?"

Maydene narrowed her gaze at them.

Mick, who had been the subject of many of her chastisings while growing up, swallowed. "Yeah." He cleared his throat. "I'll take French Silk."

Maydene fumed as she threw a packet of coffee into the filter basket and tore the carafe off the drying rack.

"Pete? Pie?" Abe studiously kept his eyes off her.

Pete smiled, and she wanted to spit on him. *How dare they? Abe, at least, knows how badly I want to know.*

"Blueberry, please—and thank you."

Steam nearly escaped her ears as she poured the water into the machine.

"Abraham Lionel Gunderson, you tell me right now what you're up to. You made me stay here and have not said a useful word since you came back. I'm as anxious as a bird in a cage."

Abe's eyebrows pinched and released. He tilted his head, as if seeing her there for the first time.

There, just then, she saw the tiniest hint of a smirk.

"Well, honey, what would you like to know?" The snake couldn't even turn her way.

She reared back to the top of her five-foot-four-inch frame, nostrils flaring.

"What would I like to know? Only this." She scowled over her shoulder. "Is your will up to date?"

Abe smiled and walked to the coffeemaker. When he rested his hands on her shoulders, she shrugged them off.

"Were you curious, dear? I'm sorry. I guess I was distracted."

She heard one small snicker he was unable to cover.

She elbowed him right in the gut. Not as low as she would have liked, but it would do.

Pete and Mick guffawed between bites of the pie Abe had pulled from the case.

"Oh, Mitchell, you think that's funny, do you?" Maydene turned on her heel.

Mick grabbed his plate and bolted for the men's room.

"Don't think that will stop me."

"All right, boys." Abe spoke between shortened breaths. "We've pulled this prank. I can't keep it up any longer."

Maydene swatted him with her towel.

"I'm sorry, dear. Don't know what got into me." He winked and kissed her cheek. "Just ornery, I guess."

She crossed her arms over her chest. Her husband's continued giggles put the lie to his apology.

"Spill."

Abe sat on the end stool and pulled in a deep breath to calm the laughter. "Well, after we split into two teams, we walked the river side from one end to the other, meeting in the middle. We didn't find Zak."

Maydene gasped.

"We were all gathered together trying to determine where to go next, when he came up behind us."

Maydene leaned forward. "Who?"

"Who what?"

"Who came up behind you?"

"Why, Zak, of course."

Maydene took the deepest breath she'd had since Mick first came in at lunch and sunk to the nearest chair. "So he's alive ..."

"Ah, yeah. Seems to be." Abe forked a bite of his peach pie.

Maydene waited for more, but Abe just continued eating. "And then?"

"Jenny took him home, and we came here for coffee and pie."

Maydene's eyes nearly popped out of her head. "*Jenny* took him home?"

"Yep, he asked her to give him a ride. After he apologized to Mick and promised to make it right. Oh, he also asked me to take Bud to the hotel, but I told Bud he could bunk in at our place instead. Zak wasn't too happy to see him."

"Jenny took Zak home?"

"Yes, dear." He glanced at Pete and Mick, who had skulked back to the counter. "Am I not speaking English?"

Maydene whirled in her chair to grill Pete.

"Did you tell him who you were?"

"I tried to, Maydene. But he didn't really want to talk to me."

She stood and walked over to Mick, leaning in closely. "What are these buzzards not telling me?"

Mick scrunched his mouth and looked up to the right.

"Nothing, Maydene. Yep, I think that's about it." He stuffed the last bit of his pie in his mouth and sighed.

She straightened. Looked at Abe. Pete. Mick. And shook her head. "Mars, my great aunt, men are from Pluto." She sighed. "I'm calling Jenny, and she had *better* be home."

Chapter Thirty-Two

Jenny parked her car in the driveway and slumped behind the wheel. The emotions of the day, after an intense week, had drained her. She wanted a hot bath and a mug of chai.

As she walked to the back of the garage and the stairs leading up to her apartment, she saw a note taped on the handrail.

We've taken Susan for pizza and miniature golf. Enjoy! - Yvonne

"Hallelujah," Jenny softly whispered. If she'd had the strength, she would have shouted.

She climbed the stairs, counting each one in her head. At the landing after the first nine stairs, she paused to gaze over the back yard. No fancy gardens, flowers, or vegetables, but Dave and Yvonne had a swing set left over from when their children lived at home. A backboard hung from the garage, the basketball discarded next to the drive.

In the time she'd lived there, she'd never seen Dave play. She'd have to remind Susan to put the ball away in the morning. She was too tired to go back down and do it tonight. She turned to the second rise of stairs.

Nine more steps, and she'd be home. The white oleander bath oils she'd been saving for the right occasion called to her.

Ten. Eleven. Twelve.

Maybe she'd make the chai before her bath, then she could sip on it while she soaked.

Thirteen. Fourteen. Fifteen.

A little Bach on the CD player, mixed with Debussy? No, her soundtrack from the movie *Somewhere in Time*. That's the ticket. Her muscles unwound at the promise of the evening before her.

Sixteen. Seventeen. Eigh—

"Hello, Jen."

If a hand hadn't grabbed hers, Jenny would have plunged to the landing from the fright. "Jonas?"

JENNY FELT like she'd walked into a maze—one with hidden trapdoors that would swing open and drop her into the abyss if she took one wrong step. Jonas was not supposed to be here. Not in *her* house. Not yet.

She just wanted her bath.

Instead, her husband hovered around her like a great moth, arms and mouth flapping nervously. Amusement tickled her, as he worked so hard to connect, yet remained out of his element. Despite her surprise at finding him here—Yvonne had let him in after Susan assured her that he was, indeed, her daddy—the upper hand was Jenny's to take. And she intended to do just that.

"Jonas." She held up her "stop" hand, the same one she uses with Susan to get her to slow down. "Hush. I am going to take a bath. It's been an exhausting day. You may wait out here, or not. At this point, I really don't care."

His mouth hanging open as he'd formed the next word of that now forgotten sentence she'd interrupted.

"But—"

"Shh." She placed her finger on his warm and familiar lips. "No talking."

She indicated he should sit on the couch, and he did.

"We don't have cable. Can't afford it. But you can usually get a decent picture on Channel 16." She handed him the TV section from the Sunday paper. "I will be a while. If Susan gets home, you can put her to bed."

"She won't."

"She will if you read her a story."

"No, I meant she won't be here tonight." His eyes sparkled with their familiar mischief. "I asked your landlady to keep her. All night."

Jenny's jaw dropped. "You can't .... I ..." She shook her head and pulled her hair back in a sloppy bun. "You best do some serious rethinking while I'm in the bathroom, Jonas."

"Want me to wash your back?" He was undaunted and persistent—at least nothing had changed in that area.

"I certainly do not," she said. "But there are two things I *would* like you to do."

"Anything, Jen. You name it."

"In half an hour—that's thirty minutes, set a timer on your phone—start a kettle of water boiling. Get the large white mug that should remind you of our flower garden back home out of the cabinet to the right of the sink."

Jonas nodded, eyes smiling.

"In that mug, place two tablespoons of the chai mix you'll find in the pantry, second shelf, add the boiling water, and stir.

Leave it on the table next to the box of Girl Scout Thin Mint cookies—also in the pantry, third shelf."

Jenny paused, then headed toward the bathroom. *I wanted my chai during my soak.*

As she reached for the doorknob, Jonas called, and the sound of her name in his voice almost made her cry. *I've got to get a grip.*

"Jen? You said there were two things ...?"

"Oh, right" She turned with a smile. "Good, you *are* listening."

She walked back to the couch and leaned down to crook her finger under Jonas's chin, raising his face until his eyes met hers.

"There's a small bucket of ice in the freezer." She twisted her hair around her finger. "Take it out and use it in whatever way you need to cool yourself down. You are nowhere near returning to my bed."

Jonas's jaw fell. Jenny whirled around and bit her lip to keep from giggling at the astonishment on her husband's face. She crossed the room laughing under her breath and entered the bathroom, making sure to lock the door behind her.

Maydene sat at the desk in the kitchen office. Abe, Pete, and Mick remained in the dining room, carrying on about how they'd played her and teased her about the "Zak Search."

Men do not understand the importance of these things.

To get the whole truth of what happened, she'd have to call Jenny. She leafed through a couple of invoices, planning next week's purchases, while dialing the number and waiting for Jenny to answer.

"Hello?" A male voice answered.

Maydene started and pulled the handset from her ear.

"I'm sorry, I must have the wrong number," Maydene said. "Please excuse me."

"No problem. Bye."

She hung up, embarrassed to have dialed the wrong number. After all the times she'd called Jenny, her fingers practically knew the number from muscle memory. She set aside the invoices and dialed again.

"Hello?"

She frowned. The same male voice.

"Um, hello. Um, me again," Maydene stammered. "I'm sorry to bother you, but I thought I had called Jenny Miller's home."

"You did. She's, uh, indisposed at the moment."

Maydene's mind whirled. Who would be at Jenny's house? Where was Susan? The voice was vaguely familiar, but she couldn't place it. Then a fearful certainty entered her mind.

"Zak? Is that you?"

"Who is this?"

"This is Maydene."

"Oh, hi, Maydene. I thought your voice sounded familiar."

Her dander rose. *To be so cavalier!*

"Zakary Cooper! What are you doing there? Jenny's husband is in town, and it seems to me you ought to have more to do than woo a married woman!"

"I'm not ... What do you mean 'woo'?"

"You haven't answered *my* question yet. What are you doing there?" Was Zak laughing?

"Just waiting for Jenny to come out of the bath so I can put lotion on her back."

Maydene stared at the phone in her hand as though it were a foreign object.

"Maydene?" came out of the handset. She heard him as she hung up.

~

"Put down that coffeepot!"

The laughter ceased, and three pairs of eyes turned to the kitchen's swinging door, which had smacked against the pie case.

Abe and Mick sat in one of the booths and Pete, who had stood to fill his coffee mug, froze at the coffeemaker.

As Mick and Pete stared wide-eyed at Maydene, Abe stood, hands in his pockets and head bowed.

"Maydene, we said we were sorry for playing that trick on you."

Maydene smiled at her husband, but her insides were boiling.

"As well you should be. But we have a crisis on our hands, and I need the posse to make another trip. But this time"—she planted her hands on her hips—"I'm going along."

~

Zak sat on the loveseat in his living room, an auto race he wasn't watching roared by on ESPN. Instead, he replayed the mental loop of his day—over and over.

Waking up to what seemed like insanity.

Firing Mick.

The meeting with the videotape—and quitting his job.

Contemplating suicide by the river—and choosing to live.

Encountering God.

The swans.

Being "rescued" by his friends.

310

Seeing his father again—and rejecting him.

Setting Jenny free when his heart cried against losing her too.

Not running after her as she drove away.

Coming home—alone—again.

Each time the loop played, tears came.

Where are you, Kay? I need you.

But she was gone. Had been for almost a year. And he couldn't bring her back. His grief, in a real sense, was just beginning, and tonight, it enveloped him like the humidity of a July afternoon. Each breath was an effort he wasn't sure was worth it.

For distraction, Zak picked up the day's edition of *The Gazette* that had been lying on his porch when he got home. He bypassed the screaming headlines on the front page. *Read the book, saw the movie.* He wished they had been more circumspect, but the word wasn't in Sloan's vocabulary.

He flipped to the national news and read about the war overseas and the President's assurances that democracy would bring peace. In local news, the board of the library announced plans to open a branch—their first—on the north side of town. He browsed the financials, then turned to sports, glad *The Gazette's* commitment to prep sports remained intact.

Finally, the comics. Most were amusing, but a few stiffed completely, at least for him. His favorite never failed to bring a laugh, however, and today was no exception.

When he'd become editor of *The Gazette*, he'd been amazed that the obituaries and the comics garnered the most comments from readers. Get a fact wrong in a news story, and *maybe* one person would notice. But changing a comic—with or without notice—resulted in mailboxes—both digital and analog —stuffed with letters to the editor. For weeks.

Early on, he'd removed the *Peanuts*. It was tired and dated and, what with Charles Schultz's death, the timing seemed right. But the letters poured in demanding the strip's return. He later learned that, nationwide, the response from *Peanuts* fans had been the same.

So, when the syndicate started offering *Classic Peanuts*, reruns basically, he'd put the comic back in—and the public unrest had quelled. He remembered thinking how morbid that was and wondered why people couldn't just let go.

He didn't wonder anymore, but still thought it morbid and unhealthy.

I'm going to cancel that contract on Monday—complaints or not.

Then he remembered he was unemployed, and the comics were now Sloan's responsibility.

He put the paper down and looked up. The race was over, and ESPN had switched to some sports commentary show with a male host who had spiky hair and the unfortunate habit of interrupting his guests as they were about to make their point. Zak switched off the set.

Time for bed. He couldn't avoid it any longer. Sleeping alone had been one of his biggest challenges since Kay's death, but he desperately needed rest. He rose from the loveseat, unbuttoning his shirt as he went, and switched off lights in the living room.

His steps slowed as he neared the bedroom, but he forced his feet across the threshold. He tossed his shirt into the hamper outside the closet—and missed. He fought to keep his thoughts on task. He tossed his pants after the shirt and walked into the bathroom.

He brushed his teeth, surveyed his aging, sagging body in the mirror while doing so, and sighed. He *could* pinch an inch —and more. No arguing that point. He stepped onto the scale and hopped right off when he read the numbers. As he finished getting ready, his anxiety abated as his body prepared for the sleep it craved.

After turning off the bathroom light, Zak headed for bed. He pulled back the comforter—and was overcome with Kay's scent.

Which was ridiculous. He'd washed the bed linens multiple times since her death. The scent was in his memory, not the comforter. Nevertheless, he pulled the comforter back up over the pillows with effort and crossed the room to the dresser. Tonight, he'd sleep in the guest room.

He dug out a T-shirt, pulled it over his head, and headed for the hall. He hit the light switch and glanced over his shoulder. A shimmer of light played on Kay's pillow. Was it the glow from his neighbor's security light—or something more?

Regardless, Zak raised his right hand to his mouth and blew a kiss in that direction. Then he shuffled down the hall.

Chapter Thirty-Three

The last of her bathwater swirled down the drain. She'd been in the bathroom nearly an hour. Maybe Jonas had left?

She wanted—needed—to talk to him, but tonight? Tonight, she was exhausted. After the soothing bath, her body begged for some much-needed rest. Besides, she hadn't processed the conversation she'd had with Zak.

But of course, Jonas was still there. Watching television.

Fortunately, she had left her bathrobe in the bathroom. She tightened it around her waist and crossed to her bedroom. As she walked through the living room, Jonas leaped to his feet and switched off the television.

He grinned and pointed toward the kitchen. Her chai and cookies waited on the table just as she'd asked—along with a vase of flowers. She really didn't want him to be nice to her tonight—not when she was nearly asleep on her feet.

"I'll be right back," she said. "I'm going to change into something more comfortable."

She mentally smacked herself, afraid Jonas would get the

wrong idea from her comment. But when she came out of the bedroom wearing an oversized sweatshirt and baggy sweatpants, he gave her a natural, good-to-be-with-you smile. She relaxed.

"Your friend, Maydene, called while you were in the bath. Twice. Never did say what she wanted, but she thought I was, uh, someone else."

"Really? Who?"

"Zak Cooper." He looked over her head.

Her face heated.

"Jen? It's okay. I didn't give you much reason not to ... test the waters."

"It is not okay. I knew better."

An uneasy silence hung between them. Jenny fiddled with the knick-knacks on her étagère. Jonas examined the framed photos of Susan on the living room wall. Jenny said a quick prayer, asking for wisdom and compassion. When she turned around to apologize, Jonas's fingers gently stroked Susan's face in her latest school picture.

"She grew so much." His voice thickened with regret.

"I'm so sorry I left without talking to you. I should not ..."

He held up his hand. "I hate to say this, but I didn't miss you. Correction, I didn't *admit* I missed you for the first three months. I didn't have much occasion to miss you, I'm afraid."

They were entering territory she didn't want to talk about—least not tonight. Silence again held sway.

"But we don't need to talk about that, not tonight." He rotated to face her. "I'm glad to be talking with you at all, Jen."

His consideration took her by surprise. He seemed to be giving her what she needed.

"I may need to reheat your chai." He shrugged. "You were longer than I anticipated."

He stuck his pinkie finger in the drink and sucked the

liquid from his finger. He made a face like the tea was poison. Jenny smiled as he set the mug in the microwave. His disdain for any hot drink that didn't contain coffee hadn't changed. After thirty seconds, he placed the mug on the table with a little flourish.

"Thank you." Jenny sat and wrapped her hands around the mug, grateful for the chai *and* the conversation shift. "You still hate chai, I see."

He chuckled. "Indeed."

Jonas had not just set the box of cookies on the table. He'd taken out a plate—one—and placed three cookies on it. But the box was nearby if she wanted more.

"Jen? I'm sorry about what I said earlier." His ears turned red. "Given the circumstances, that was entirely inexcusable. Thank you for not throwing me out. I will behave—without the need of ice."

She nodded, gazing into his eyes from over the top of her mug. She would like to have Jonas back in her life to that extent, but experience had taught her not to trust his pretty words.

He backed out of the room. "If there's nothing else ..."

She could think of nothing to say that wouldn't give her away, but as he willingly returned to the living room, she called out. "Jonas? Would you like a cookie?"

His shoulders relaxed. "Yes." He turned around, eyes moist. "Yes, I most certainly would like a cookie."

❧

"Maydene, darlin,' this is silly." Abe hissed under his breath. "We should all be home and in bed."

"Just hush," she said. "If the three of you had done the job right the first time, we wouldn't be here now."

She stood on Jenny's landing, with the three stooges behind her. They were a motley crew—two geezers, an old woman, and an unemployed artist. Talk about an improbable mission. She looked up at Jenny's kitchen window. The silhouette on the blind showed a woman *and* a man seated at the table. No sign of a child.

"Maydene, I agree with Abe," Mick whispered from behind Pete. "Zak's car isn't here. I think you jumped to a wrong conclusion."

"Mitchell, if there's ever an opening on the police force, don't apply." She'd had about enough of their skepticism. "Of course Zak's car isn't here. Jenny drove *him* home from the park, remember? For all we know, his car is still at the paper. But *hers* is here, and look at the window." She pointed toward the shadows.

"That's not Zak's profile," Pete said.

"And just how would *you* know what Zak's profile looks like?" She glared down the stairs. "Now, here's the plan—"

Headlights illuminated the detached garage, and the crunch of gravel under tires filled the night as a car swung onto the driveway.

"Oh, great," Maydene said. "Pastor's home."

"This is going to make an embarrassing sermon illustration," Abe said.

"Is it too late to pray?" Mick asked.

Maydene ignored them.

"Lord, have mercy on our souls. Amen," Pete took Mick's suggestion. "It's never too late to pray, Mitchell."

"Just stand there—and don't make a sound," Maydene hissed. "They'll walk from the garage to the back door and will have no reason to look up here."

Pastor Dave pulled into the garage and three people exited

the car. Yolanda and Susan were talking about their miniature golf game.

"Dave, sweetie, will you grab that basketball?" Yolanda said, as she approached the back door. "Jonas must have left it out after playing with Susan earlier."

Maydene turned to Abe and mouthed "Jonas?" He pointed his finger at her, as if to say, "I told you."

Dave retrieved the ball and tossed it in the garage before pressing the button to lower the door.

"Is my Daddy still here, Yolanda?" Susan asked. "Can I go see him?"

All three of them looked toward the apartment window. Yolanda nudged Dave and pointed. "It looks like he's still here, Susie. But Mommy and Daddy need to talk, *so let's leave them alone tonight.*" Yolanda spoke the final words loud enough for the whole backyard to hear.

"Okay," Susan said. "I like to sleep at your house. Hi, Maydene. Hi, Mr. Mick."

Mick waved sheepishly as Susan skipped beside Yolanda. When they entered the house, Yolanda's laughter reached the stairs and tinkled like windchimes. Maydene covered her eyes with her hands.

Dave walked over to the bottom of the stairs and looked up at his parishioners—and one extra. He snorted.

"Your pillar of salt imitations need a bit of work." A huge grin spread over his face.

"Oh, hush Pastor. Honestly, we were—"

"Nope. Don't want to know. Believe me, it's *much better* this way," Dave said. "I can make up whatever I want for an illustration." He tipped his head. "Goodnight, now. Sweet dreams."

"G'night, Pastor," the stooges chorused as they slunk down the stairs.

Maydene followed behind them without a word.

~

Pete couldn't sleep. After the misguided mission to Jenny's, Mick had gone home. Abe, and a strangely quiet Maydene, had brought Pete to their home, made up a bed for him in the guest room, and excused themselves for the night.

Sleep eluded Pete. His reunion with Zak had been a dismal failure, and the sting of his son's rebuke, though expected, had cut deeper than he'd been prepared for.

Before the Gunderson's had gone to bed, Pete had tried to talk with them about the situation, but they were too tired to give him much attention. Maydene suggested that he could go across the street and invite his son to breakfast in the morning.

"Maybe if there aren't so many people standing around watching, he'll be more open to you." She pointed to a house. "That's where he lives."

On the one hand, approaching Zak at home, where he was most comfortable, made sense. On the other hand, tomorrow was a world away. The urgency that had dogged Pete's heels all evening frightened him.

Maybe a glass of milk and a cookie or two would settle his mind enough to shut off.

He wandered into the dark hallway in search of the kitchen. On his way through the living room, he glanced across the street. A light glowed inside Zak's house. Maybe he should go over there?

Before he could talk himself out of it, Pete opened the front door. The crisp evening air clarified his thoughts—and his vision. Zak stood at the window, staring out over the side yard.

Pete stepped off the porch and onto the driveway. He

would count on his forward momentum to get him across the street.

~

AFTER AN HOUR on the guestroom bed, Zak was glad he never had guests. He'd hate for them to sleep on the knotty mattress. But it wasn't just the mattress that kept him awake.

Every time he closed his eyes, that black swan peered at him from the safety of the brambles, wondering if the river was safe. Wondering if he dared live the life he was born into. Hesitating out of his hiding place, only to paddle right back in.

Zak crawled out of bed and walked to the window. He was unprepared for how lonely he was now that Kay was really gone. He had no job, had fired his best friend—he intended to fix that—and encouraged a potential girlfriend to return to her husband.

Why was the swan hiding in the brambles?

Because the other swans had left him behind and he was afraid? No, that wasn't right. He hadn't been hiding at all. He had come out looking for something but retreated to the safety of his nest *because* of fear. What did he fear, though?

What he had seen, of course. The swan had looked at Zak when it retreated. What had frightened it?

The doorbell rang, and Zak jumped. He'd been so engrossed contemplating the swan, he'd lost track of his surroundings. In his rush to the door, he stubbed his toe on the ottoman.

"Ow. Dadgone it." Doorbells and telephones. Gram always said when they rang at night, they never carried good news.

He hobbled to the front door, cursing under his breath, and flipped on the porch light. Squinting through the peephole, he saw his father.

Oh crud. He sighed and wished he hadn't turned on the light. But he opened the door and scowled at his father.

"Evening, Zak." Pete dipped his head in a nod. "May I come in? I know it's late, but we're both up and—"

"Gram was right, as usual." Zak stared at Pete a moment before stepping to the side and motioning him in. He hobbled away.

"You're bleeding, Zakary."

"Great parenting instincts there, *Dad.*" He dumped a healthy dose of sarcasm into the last word. "Bleeding generally happens when you stub your toe in the middle of the night rushing to open the door for a stranger. Have a seat." He waved a hand toward the couch. "I've got to get this cleaned up and bandaged."

JENNY AND JONAS finished a whole sleeve of cookies and started on a second as they reminisced. It had been a mutual, unannounced, decision to concentrate only on happy memories —they were both too tired for anything beyond that. Besides, they were having such an enjoyable time, it would have been a shame to interrupt it. There would be time later.

She held her second cup of chai, and Jonas had downed almost a half-gallon of milk, when Jenny yawned. Even as he smiled, Jonas's yawn-echo betrayed his exhaustion.

Jenny looked at her husband through new eyes. There was a particular intimacy that occurred when people stay up too late together. False faces and carefully constructed facades fell away, and glimpses of the true self could be found. Jenny liked what she saw in Jonas. The same man who had wooed her with lines from Shakespeare and pure attention sat at her table tonight.

Cradling his hand in hers, she traced the tendons on the back of it with her finger. The conversation lulled. She'd always loved his hands. Not big, but strong. Lightly freckled with a soft coat of fur, as she'd frequently teased. It reminded her of his chest, where she used to rest her head each night before falling asleep. She closed her eyes.

He took both of her hands in his and brought them to his lips, kissing the back of each—once. "I've got to go. It's getting late."

Jenny nodded and stood to gather the dishes. He went to the living room and sat on the couch to put on his shoes. He was leaning over to tie the last one when she entered the room.

"Jonas?" She placed her palm on his shoulder. "Will you stay?"

He looked up with an expression she couldn't quite read.

"On the couch, I mean," she stammered. "I ... Susan would love finding you here in the morning when she returns."

He stood, his eyes filling with joy, desire, and ... was that regret? But when he took her hands again, a resolve clarified on his face.

"I would stay, Jen." He took several uneven breaths, and Jenny's heart leaped. "But I wouldn't be able to sleep on the couch, and that wouldn't be fair to either of us. So, no, I won't stay. Not tonight."

She nodded.

He pulled her closer and kissed the top of her head. She placed one hand on his chest between them and stepped into his arms, laying her head on his shoulder. She desperately wanted him to hold her. And he did, for a moment, then stepped back from her embrace.

She gazed into his eyes and her struggle reflected there.

"Will you come for breakfast? I don't have to work until the evening tomorrow, and Susan will be back early, I'm sure."

"Yes, Jen, I will come back." He ambled toward the door. "But tomorrow ... well, it will be tough and unpleasant."

Jenny cocked her head.

"I have to tell you the truth about ... me." He paused with his hand on the doorknob. "Do you still pray?"

She nodded.

"Good. Pray for me ... for us. I'll see you in the morning."

As he walked out the door and down the steps, she was wide awake. "Well, Lord, is now a good time?"

Chapter Thirty-Four

S loan eyed his copy of the Zak film. He didn't quite know what he'd use it for but was certain it would come in handy. He was glad he'd made a copy. One couldn't be too careful.

"Yes, the golden boy, that's Zak. The favored child." Sloan cracked his knuckles. "Zee's a good man. Jonas said so, and he'd know. Let's keep Zak around."

He sat in the wingback chair in his study, plotting. When he'd returned home from *The Gazette,* he packed up his stuff in a frenzy. It was 1:00 a.m. on the day after the end of the world, but everything important was packed in a single suitcase. Everything he cared about. Everything that *meant* anything. His camera, some cash, a few favorite videos—including *The Ghost and Mr. Cooper*—which was destined to be a classic.

In one hand, he held a bus ticket. Couldn't take the car. They could trace the car. And they surely would, wouldn't they?

The other held, well, something else altogether.

Sloan had four hours before the bus left Templeton.

One more job. Would the ninnies at *The Gazette* thank him? No. They'd never thanked him or even recognized his accomplishments before. Why should this be different? But he'd have to time it right.

Zak had bandaged the big toe on his right foot and stopped the bleeding. Pete said it might be broken and insisted he elevate his foot on several pillows stacked on the coffee table. The throbbing had tapered off, thanks in part to the large dose of pain reliever he'd swallowed down. Talking with his father was enough pain. He was willing to medicate the rest. They'd made small talk for almost half an hour, but Zak wanted some answers.

"Why are you here, Pete? And why do you keep staring at my foot?"

A small smile flashed on his face. "The second one is easiest to answer." Pete leaned forward.

"You were six."

"Ah, Memory Lane. Quaint."

A flicker of rejection appeared on his father's face, and he sat back.

Like the swan.

"Sorry," Zak said. "That was rude."

"Yes. But I should expect it, I suppose."

Zak extended his hand. "Please, go on."

Pete sighed and gazed at the ceiling as if seeing the memory there.

"You were six. It was a Saturday. Your mother was at the grocery, and I was gardening. You were running around outside, barefoot, doing whatever six-year-old boys do in July."

He was a natural-born storyteller. "I always liked your feet, so like your mothers. Narrow and perfect in every way."

Sitting there in his boxers and T-shirt, Zak felt exposed. He wished he'd taken the time to get dressed, but had hoped for a quick, painless visit.

"Anyway, you were running around, as I said, and stubbed your toe—same one if I remember right—on an exposed tree root. Oh, the cry that went up. You'd have thought someone cut off your foot entirely."

Despite himself, Zak laughed. He still had no tolerance for pain. Kay had always teased him about it.

"I lifted you up and rushed you into the kitchen. Set you on the counter next to the sink. Stuck your foot right under the rushing cold water and used your mother's dishrag to clean out the dirt. Boy, did I hear about that from her."

Zak had to admit having someone other than himself remember his life was nice.

"I don't know whether it was the water, my roughness, or the absence of your mother—perhaps all three—but you would not be comforted. So I said, 'Looks like we'll just have to take it off.'"

"You didn't."

"Didn't take it off? No, of course not." He swept a hand toward Zak's foot. "There it is, all bandaged up again. But I did *say* that. Your eyes got big as saucers back then too. 'How?' you asked, all scared. And I said the first thing that popped into my head. 'I'll just bite it off.' Then I grabbed your foot, stuck your toe in my mouth, and pretended to bite."

Pete's laughter roared through the room.

"I thought you were going to faint. I really did. I said, 'Mmm. Strawberry.' You looked at me in much the same way you are now—like I'd lost my mind. 'Yep. Strawberry,' I said.

'Your toe jam is strawberry. My favorite.' And then you like to bust a gut laughing and there was no more crying."

Both men laughed. Pete quieted first.

"Do you know how many times I've thought of that over the years?" he said, and Zak had to strain to hear his words. "Do you know how much I would have given, what price I would have paid, to see those toes again?"

Another chuckle escaped. "Now I have, and they're still perfect."

Zak cleared his throat and started to rise, uneasy with how familiar this little chat had become. "Um, I think I'll get dressed. I mean, if we're going to be up for a while."

Pete beat him up and put his hand on Zak's shoulder, keeping him in place.

"Son, it's okay. I've lived in places where it was a good day when the guys put their pants on—let alone shirts. Besides, you used to run around the backyard starkers to play in the sprinkler. I've seen it all."

"Maybe, but not lately."

"No, I dare say you couldn't do that now, at least not without drawing a crowd."

The laughter returned.

Pete looked at his watch. "You have no idea how much I've enjoyed this, but it's nearly 1:30. I suppose I ought to head back. We both need to get some sleep. Tomorrow's coming, but I hope we can do this again."

Zak smiled, but neither man moved. He looked at his father, struck by the physical similarities—and the differences—between them. They would never win the Look-A-Like contests *The Gazette* ran each Father's Day, but there was no denying he was Pete Cooper's son either. A part of him couldn't believe his father was here. How soon would the day come when, for whatever reason, the wind blew him away again?

"Don't leave," Zak found himself saying. "You haven't answered the rest of my question yet ... Dad."

Pete looked up when Zak called him Dad. "What question was that?"

"Why are you here? Why now?"

Pete narrowed his eyes and pursed his lips. "Well, there's a simple answer and a much more complicated one."

"Start simple."

"You may not like it."

"Why?"

"It's rather ... harsh."

Zak was intrigued and a little frightened. But what could his father say that would make Zak leery? "I'll consider myself warned."

Pete placed his hand on Zak's shin. "You need me."

He squirmed under his father's unexpected touch, and Pete removed his hand.

"Well, that's hardly simple, is it?"

"Oh, I don't know. Maybe not, but it is true," Pete said, before Zak could interrupt him again. "I didn't know about Kay before I came. I just knew you needed me."

Zak waited for him to go on.

"Do you know anyone else who lost his wife at a young age?" Pete said.

Now Zak regretted his question. "You know, maybe this isn't su—"

"Do you know anyone else who lost touch with reality when his wife died?"

"Okay, see—"

"Do you know anyone else who is afraid to live life like you are? Like *we* are?"

Zak stood, and the throbbing in his toe returned. But that pain he could disregard. That pain would go away—would heal. Pete's finger poked at a deeper wound.

Zak spoke through teeth clenched against the pain—physical and mental. "Do you have any idea how much nerve it takes for you to say that to me?" He struggled to control his anger.

"I am *not* afraid to live. I could have killed myself at the park today—yesterday, whatever. Thought about it. Wanted to. But I didn't. I'm still here. I threw the pills in the water."

"That only proves you're more afraid to die than you are to live."

Zak's chest heaved with every breath he fought to control.

"Are you saying I should have done it? Should have killed myself? That would have rid you of the burden of abandoning me."

Pete flinched. "Go on, lash out at me. I understand. All I'm saying is that not dying is *not* the same as living—living fully alive. In a real sense, part of you died with Kay, which is normal. But that part of you stayed dead, which is not."

"What do you know about normal?"

"Not much. Only what I hear. But I know all there is to know about living as though you're dead because it happened to me."

Zak turned his back on his father and hobbled down the hall, determined to get away— anywhere.

"Where have I been all these years, Zak?" Pete's voice rose as he followed. "Didn't you ever wonder?"

Zak whirled. "Only daily, every year, until my high school graduation when I decided to tell everyone, including myself, that you were dead."

Pete reared back as if Zak had struck a nerve. "Well, you were right. I have been dead—or as good as."

"Not quite as good as," Zak murmured as he continued down the hall.

"For many years, I went so deep into my grief I didn't know who I was. When I came out of that, I was still mostly dead. I let my fear of living prevent me from coming back for you. From coming back to *our life*."

"Oh, that's rich. What life would that be, *Dad*?" His sarcasm didn't slow his father down a bit.

"I didn't come back, because if *you* died and left me, too, what would I do? Does that sound familiar?"

The hair on the back of Zak's neck rose. The similarities between him and his father were more than physical. "I'm not dead."

Pete reached a hand toward him, but Zak pulled back.

"No," his father said. "You're not. But the life we could have had together is. That life is dead, along with a part of me and a part of you. I killed it when I allowed my fear to convince me I was too late."

"Well, maybe you were."

"Perhaps, Zak. That life we could have had is dead and gone. We can never have that again. But we're both still physically alive. We *could* have *a* life together."

His father sighed and walked to the entryway.

Zak slumped against the wall, afraid he'd never see him again. Too afraid to stop him from leaving.

"Zakary," Pete opened the door and turned around once more. "This may sound ridiculous coming from me, but I do believe in God. I do believe He will guide his children if we only ask Him to.

"But, if you never hear another word I say, I pray you hear this. Not dying is not the same as living. Don't be so afraid to live again, to love again, that you may as well be dead. That's no kind of life. I know that for a fact." He stepped outside and closed the door behind him.

Zak hobbled to the door. Grabbed the knob. Tried to force himself to open it. Failed.

He leaned his head against the jamb, tears flowing freely. His father had not lied, because he felt dead. He reached his hand up, as if to his father's face.

"Daddy," he cried from his fearful heart.

Exhaustion hit Zak as soon as Pete left, but the throbbing pain in his toe would not let him sleep. He limped back into the living room and collapsed on the loveseat.

Was his father right? Was he so afraid of life, of love, that he may as well be dead? He loved. He did, didn't he? He'd loved his mother. His father—at one time. Gram. Rachel. Kay, of course.

All dead. None his fault, but dead, or as good as, nonetheless.

But that was proof he could love, right? There were people still alive that he loved. What about Mick?

I love Mick.

You fired Mick.

Jenny then. He'd loved Jenny, hadn't he? Or he would have given more time. Before Jenny, Kay had been only a soothing presence—a crutch to help him move on.

Harley had said it wasn't all bad that he was talking to Kay. She'd been helping him get over her death—sort of. But why had Kay turned evil and menacing as soon as he'd started feeling better and began taking steps toward a new life?

Was his mind forcing him to create distance from Jenny? A way to protect himself from further hurt and abandonment?

"I'm seeing a pattern here, Sherlock."

And this midnight visit from Pete? Was it a case of same scene, different cast?

"Oh, dear God."

What was it God had said to him in the park?

"Something about the world. Not being like the world. The ways of the world."

Zak's frustration angered him. He'd always been like that. Easily frustrated, easily angered. Frustration was like a gateway straight to his ...

Gateway. Bible Gateway. Yes.

He opened the search engine on his phone and entered the words.

The site loaded, and Zak typed *conform* and *world*.

With the touch of the return key, the verse he'd heard by the river, the one God had spoken to him, appeared.

"Romans 12:2. That's it. 'Do not conform any longer to the pattern of this world but be transformed by the renewing of your mind. Then you will be able to test and approve what God's will is—his good, pleasing, and perfect will.' That's the verse."

He hit the link to view the verse in context.

That's why the verse had sounded so familiar at the park. It was part of the "living sacrifices" one—his mother's life verse.

"You'll never know what God's will is, Zak, until you ask him from the right perspective and with the right motives," his mother had said one afternoon before she died. Then she'd quoted Romans 12:1-2 from memory.

His eight-year-old mind tried to understand how his mother dying could be God's will—and why she was so calm when his father appeared to be losing his grip.

"I can't explain it too well, honey, except to say when you know God's will, you'll know."

Her answer had left him more confused than before—and it still was less than satisfactory. But he believed he was coming to understand.

He didn't know what God's will for his life was, but he knew what it wasn't. It wasn't that he throw the rest of his life away living in the past.

Could he really move on?

Zak glanced at the green light blinking on his answering machine. Proof the real world was still calling. He pushed *play*.

"Zak? Are you there? Please pick up. It's Nancy. Are you okay? Are you there? Pick up if you're there."

Zak smiled. Nancy knew he ignored messages until he felt like listening to them.

"Well, okay. Mr. Miller, with Clarity, our new owner, would like to meet with you. Can you come in? Please? We're all worried. Call me."

Zak looked at his watch; 2:30 a.m. Nancy was home fast asleep.

Well, it was a cinch he wasn't going to sleep—not after his father's visit and Nancy's call. He may as well get dressed and go pack up his office, save Nancy the trouble.

Who knew what God's will was for the future? But it didn't likely involve *The Gazette*.

Chapter Thirty-Five

Not that he'd expected anyone to change the locks, but Zak breathed a sigh of relief when his key unlocked the front door of *The Gazette*. He wasn't clear if law enforcement considered a former employee using an unreturned key breaking and entering, but he was glad not to actually break in.

He stood in the newsroom, soaking everything in. Despite what he'd said yesterday, he'd come to retrieve more than his father's chair. So he would quietly pick those items up and wait for someone to ship the chair.

The sounds of the newspaper echoed in his mind. Phone conversations, clacking keyboards, the hum of the small press in the back.

Before he grew too morose, Zak headed toward his office. He loved this office and would miss it, perhaps most. Knowing he would occupy it had sealed the door on his decision to come back home.

Over his etched-into-the-glass name, someone had taped a sheet of paper that must have read at one time, *Sloan White, Editor*. Zak rolled his eyes. Typical. Claiming something that wasn't his to claim. Someone had torn the paper in half, leaving only "hite, Editor" behind. Zak removed the rest and tossed it into a nearby trashcan.

He twisted the knob to open the door, but it was locked. Sloan, no doubt.

Again, his key worked fine. He crossed to the windows and lowered the blinds of the two directly behind the desk. No one would see him through the third window. While he was reasonably sure his being here was okay, why take chances?

He surveyed the room filled with treasured memories as well as a few personal items of value to no one but him. His First Place award from the Associated Press for editorial writing. His stuffed Bill the Cat doll—a present from Kay on his thirtieth birthday. The framed Letter to the Editor—the first he'd received in his new position at *The Gazette*—pointing out that the paper had used *compliment* when they should have used *complement* in a news story. The reader had asked if he actually *had* a dictionary or if he was just stupid.

His mementos were small beans, however, compared to what he couldn't take. The adrenaline rush of deadline news. The creative high of writing the right lead on an important feature story. The camaraderie of disparate people coming together as a team—every day—to produce an entire newspaper —even with the occasional complementary error.

Zak sat at his desk one last time. The massive metal desk Waxman hadn't seen the need to replace. The one Kay had always teased was big enough to run laps around. His desk.

Imagining Sloan at *his* desk made his lips curl in distaste. He crumpled a sticky note with Sloan's spidery scrawl and aimed for the round file. But then the content of the note, *send done.docx file to Esch* made him pause.

Esch was the power-hungry president of Clarity Communications, which had purchased the paper. Surely

Clarity wasn't monitoring the paper's content? It would be Jonas's job to move *The Gazette* into the Clarity format.

Zak hit the space bar on the computer to wake it up. He shook his head when the prompt for a password didn't come up. Sloan's pride had probably convinced him he didn't need one.

His screen confirmed Sloan had wasted no time in moving in. Instead of Zak's wallpaper with a favorite cartoon, the Clarity logo loomed. Ignoring that invasion, he opened My Computer and selected the Search function, telling it to search in all folders and subfolders for any file name that included the word *done*.

This search will retrieve more than five hundred documents. Do you want to continue?

Oops. Each time he edited a file, Zak had tacked *done* to the end of it. It wasn't original, but it prevented him from opening a file he'd already gone over.

He reformulated the search so that it would retrieve only files exactly named "done," and hit enter. He looked at the clock on the wall: four-fifteen. Zak was running out of time. Ben Weller, his wire editor, was supposed to come in at 4:30, although 4:45 was more normal.

Your search found one document. Do you want to open it?

"No. I asked you to search so I could know it was there. Of course, I want to open it."

Sometimes computers drove him nuts. He clicked *Yes*.

What he saw open on the screen made his blood boil. He reviewed it a little, confirming that it was what it purported to be—a list of misdeeds and errors Sloan had committed over the past several months—then closed the file and opened the e-mail program, starting a new message to his private email account. After attaching the file to the message, the front door of the paper opened and clicked shut.

Ben entered, an unbelievable five minutes early.

Zak ducked into the kneehole of his desk to avoid detection. When he'd given Ben a minute to reach his workspace, he peered over the edge, eyes level with the desktop, and snaked his right index finger toward the send button.

A crash of breaking glass was followed by a thud of something hitting his office floor.

He punched the send button as an explosion *kawhumped* in front of him. The percussion shattered the remaining windows and lifted his massive desk an inch off the floor, striking him square in the forehead. His world went black.

"Now that should make page one."

Sloan chuckled as he bulleted out of Oak Hill and up the road to Templeton. He'd abandon his car there in his second cousin's auto graveyard down the road from the bus station.

"Now what, Jonas?"

He'd specifically targeted the editor's office. If he couldn't have it, no one would. The explosion had been bigger than he'd intended, true. He'd barely made it back to his car, which he'd left running, before it went off. Rocked the car a little, it did.

"Lazy Ben is never in on time, but what a story he'll have when he ambles in."

He frowned. The damage would prevent *The Gazette* from covering its own demise, but *The Tribune* in Templeton would be all over this story. And the local television crew. Maybe even one out of South Bend or Fort Wayne.

"Film at eleven."

As USUAL, Maydene and Abe arrived at the café at 4:00 a.m. She'd already started the coffee as Abe prepped for breakfast.

Maydene's mind churned. She hadn't slept well. Her discomfort had little to do with the embarrassment she was sure to suffer about their escapade last night. Nor was she unsettled by the events of the last couple of days. Zak was back from his disappearance. Jenny and Jonas were talking about salvaging their marriage—that's what she assumed they were doing last night. And Pete had talked to Zak.

She'd found Pete asleep in the rocker facing Zak's house. She woke him to send him to bed, but also to learn how things went with Zak.

"I just hope I made an impression." Pete got up out of the rocker. "I've done what I came for, and it's time to go."

She'd told him he ought not give up so easily and he was welcome to stay with them longer. He'd nodded, said "Well, thank-you," and gone to his room.

That man irritated her. She hoped he'd stop by the café on his way out of town. Maybe she could help him see his way clear to stay a bit longer.

"He gives up too quickly," she said. "Zak is here. Why would he leave?"

She set out the fresh Danish and sighed. She owed Zak an apology for assuming the worst about him, without reason to do so. How had she mistaken Jonas's voice for his? If Zak was anything, he was honorable.

But she'd stumbled again on the thorn in her flesh—rumor and gossip. She'd gotten herself in trouble with it before, but somehow, never could resist its entanglements. The conviction unsettled her. The Lord was hammering home how wrong she'd been.

Abe had tried to get her to see reason, but she'd paid no attention to him last night. After all, she knew what she knew.

And she was justified in confronting those who were sinning. Which is what she'd meant to do by leading the posse to Jenny's house. She hadn't gone over there to protect her friend.

She would at least admit that.

Abe came into the dining room wiping his hands on a kitchen towel. "I thought you'd quit and gone home." He smiled. "It's so quiet out here. Normally, you're humming some chorus or whistling some hymn. What happened to my radio this morning?"

She set down the sugar bowl she'd been refilling with white, yellow, and pink packets and looked at her husband, her tears flowing.

He dropped his towel on the table and took her into his arms. "Now, now, darlin.' What's troubling you?"

She punched him lightly because he already knew the answer and was going to make her say it.

She rested her head on his chest. "The Lord is chastising me for my actions last night, and I am seeing the not-so-pretty side of myself—again."

"Maydene, you are beautiful in my sight—and in the Lord's." He stroked her hair. "Perfect? Not so much. But beautiful, nonetheless."

She punched him again.

He held her closer.

"Yes, beautiful, nonetheless. I daresay, if you were perfect, you wouldn't love me."

"That's for sure." She sniffled. "But I do love you, old man."

They stood there, Abe stroking her hair as she soaked in his love and care.

A boom like a muffled cannon shook the windows of the café.

Maydene clutched Abe's shirt. "What was that?"

"I don't know, but I'm gonna find out." He sat her down at the table and headed for the door.

"I'm not sitting here."

He fastened the sternest look she'd ever seen on her. "Yes, you'd better." Then he was out the door.

By now, Maydene could see flames shooting out of *The Gazette* across the street. Had the chemicals from the ink somehow caught fire or the furnace exploded?

She rose and went to the window.

The fire blazed in Zak's office. It was bound to spread, but for now it seemed contained to the office itself.

She gripped the door handle, hesitated remembering Abe's warning, then went outside.

Though she stood across the street, the heat warmed her like a campfire. But the smoke was awful. She reached into her apron pocket, took out her damp towel, and placed it over her mouth and nose.

Where was Abe? Eyes watering, she squinted. She didn't see him anywhere. "Abe? Abe?"

Someone tapped her on the shoulder, and she spun around with relief only to see Barry Sasser.

"You should be inside, Maydene."

She shook her head. "Abe's out here somewhere."

"We'll find him. Please go back insi ..." Barry's gaze slid past her, his eyes big as saucers.

She whirled.

Stumbling out of the smoke, Abe carried a body in his arms.

Barry ran to him, with Maydene right behind, and took the body.

She tried to see who it was, but the sirens signaling the arrival of the fire department turned her focus back toward Abe.

He stumbled and fell to the ground.

"Abe, we have to move farther away."

He didn't respond.

Barry worked on the body Abe had carried while everyone else just looky-looed about. So she lifted her husband with a strength that was not hers and dragged him to the curb on the opposite side of the street. "Abe, honey. Speak to me."

His eyes fluttered open, and she was able to take another breath.

"Zak ..." He coughed, clutching her hand. "Found Zak in the office ... had to reach ... would've died."

He must be mistaken. Why would Zak be at the paper when he'd quit yesterday?

Then the man Barry was helping coughed, and Maydene glanced at him. He was coming to.

"Sloan," Zak said.

Maydene wheeled back to Abe to assure him Zak was alive. He clutched her apron, pulling her closer.

She could hardly breathe from the exertion, but she tried to help Abe. "Don't speak, old man. Just breathe. In and out. In and out." Without taking her eyes from her husband, she shouted at Barry. "We need a doctor over here."

Abe tugged on her apron. She kneeled and took him in her arms.

"Maydene." His eyes rolled upward. "Love."

She clutched him to her breast, willing her heart to beat for his.

Chapter Thirty-Six

Jenny bustled around the kitchen, preparing breakfast for her family for the first time in almost two years. As she worked, she whistled "You Are My Sunshine," a tune from her childhood. She sailed around the kitchen, memories from the night before awakening hope for an even better future.

Eggs scrambled in one pan and strips of bacon sizzled in another. Biscuits were in the oven, the juice was poured, and the coffee—not chai—brewed. Her joy in providing for her family lifted her spirits. This whole reconciliation thing may just work out—yes, it may.

Outside, gravel spewed from under tires. Jonas had arrived. He drove a tick or two over the speed limit, as if he were on the Grand Prix circuit. His car door slammed, and she peeked out the window as he bounded up the stairs.

She waited for him to knock, so she could answer and invite him in—to her apartment and her life. The door banged open, and Jonas barreled in

"Well, come on in, I guess. Make yourself at—"

"Someone bombed the paper. Ben Weller called Charles

Waxman who called me. Get dressed. We gotta get down there."

Jenny's body froze as her heart raced.

"What? Was anyone hurt?"

"At least two, maybe more. You need to get dressed. Now. Can we leave Susan downstairs?"

"Yes, I suppose. I'll call Yolanda." She headed for the phone. "Wait, our breakfast." She did an about-face and rushed into the kitchen to salvage whatever she could for later.

"Jen? Clothes?"

His impatience irritated her, even though his coming for her first, before heading to the paper, should have made her happy—and did. "Okay, but you'll have to save breakfast."

"I can do that."

Jenny couldn't focus. "Jonas, why ...? How ...?"

"I don't know anything yet," he called from the kitchen. "Only that we need to get in the car."

"Can you call downstairs and explain what's going on? Yolanda's number is on the list beside the phone."

When the phone rang, she ran to it and grabbed the unit from its base.

"Hello?"

"Jenny? I need you," the quivering voice said.

"Maydene? What's happened?" She shushed Jonas as he tried to hurry her along and crossed to her bedroom. "What's the matter? Are you okay?"

Jenny held the phone to her ear with her shoulder while she sat on the bed to pull on her jeans.

"Can you come to the café?"

"Of course, we're on our way down there now. We heard about the explosion at the paper. Is the café okay? Are *you* okay?"

"He ... he's gone, Jenny. I couldn't save him."

"Who? Who's gone, Maydene?" Jenny yanked open a drawer and grabbed an old, oversized T-shirt to throw on.

"I tried ... I pulled him back, but it was too late."

"Maydene? Who's gone?" Jenny's voice rose with her panic.

She grabbed her hairbrush off the bureau, with the plan to yank it through her hair as Jonas drove.

Maydene broke into wracking sobs.

Please no, Lord. Not ... She couldn't get his name out. Refused to put it out there, even in her head.

"Abe. Abe's dead. What am I going to do?"

"Oh, Maydene. What happened?" Jenny sat down on the edge of the bed. When Jonas came to the bedroom door, she mouthed "Abe's dead."

His eyes widened.

"And Zak ..." Maydene stammered.

Jenny's heart stopped briefly. She didn't mouth anything to Jonas.

"Zak's injured," Maydene said. "Abe ... Abe saved him."

The world, which had been level five minutes ago, tilted under her. "We'll be right there."

The line went dead. Jonas entered her room, concern etched on his face.

"Abe's dead. In the explosion somehow. I need to get down there. And Zak—Zak's been injured."

Jonas took her in his arms as her shock gave way to grief.

And she let him hold her up, be her strength.

BEFORE JONAS PULLED to a complete stop, Jenny leaped out of the car and raced into the café in search of Maydene. She'd prepared herself to comfort a weeping, possibly angry, woman.

Maydene sat inside the door, cradling Abe's apron in her hands.

"Maydene?" Jenny reached out a hand.

Maydene clasped it and held it tight between her hands and the apron, as Jenny sat beside her.

"I've no right to be surprised, or angry." Maydene's eyes were red and moist but clear. "Abe has long been a hero, even if I didn't always recognize it."

Jenny nodded, her hand stroking Maydene's, their gazes meeting.

"Why *wouldn't* he try to save Zak? Why wouldn't he?" A tear pooled in Maydene's left eye, eventually sliding down her cheek to fall onto the apron she clutched. "In small ways, God has used him to pull people out of fires, me included. He gave to others, more than he took."

She choked on a small sob. "Unlike me, Jenny. My sins made me look for the worst in others."

"Maydene, that's not true."

"Well, you're wrong."

"What about the woman who told me about her ability to take the measure of someone in a glance?"

"Doesn't that sound judgmental to you?"

"Well, no. It sounds like, oh, discernment." Jenny rubbed Maydene's hands, warding off the chill that settled in them. "A good trait to have. A spiritual gift."

Maydene got up. "Do you want a piece of pie or a salad?" She turned toward the kitchen. "Abe, old man, bri ..."

Her hands flew to her mouth, and her eyes widened. "Oh, listen how I talked to him. Like he was my servant, some employee I assigned tasks to. Oh, my love, my love. What have I done?"

Jenny stood and wrapped an arm around Maydene's shoulders to lead her back to the chair. "It wasn't like that. You and Abe were married so long, you had your own language. It's sweet, not harsh."

Maydene's face aged a decade. "You said 'were.' How that one word breaks the heart."

The women sat at the table in silence. Maydene stared out the window, and Jenny watched her.

Though wrapped in sorrow, Maydene's strength and unwavering faith remained. Her unflagging belief in her husband's goodness, his commitment to others, and Jenny's memories of Abe's caring ways brought tears to her eyes.

Where were her similar memories of Jonas? What if he had been the one to die?

Memories of Abe flashed through her mind. His "warning" to her about Maydene the day they'd met. Dancing The Electric Skillet. His gentle response to her uncalled-for tongue-lashing about unfaithful husbands. Abe had taken her anger and frustration over Jonas's actions and given back love.

Then the rough fabric of Abe's apron brushed Jenny's cheek as Maydene wiped her tears. The floodgates opened, and Jenny fell into Maydene's arms. Both women wept. Jenny for Abe and his death, but also for the time she and Jonas had wasted.

Jonas stared at the remains of the fire. The building wasn't a total loss. Both the pressroom and the computer server had escaped unscathed. Based on Zak's single remark, investigators were searching for Sloan White. Jonas had been happy to explain Sloan's firing yesterday.

According to sources at the hospital, Zak was hurt but not in any danger. Barry Sasser had described him as "a little sooty, but all right" when he'd spoken to the television crews. Zak would be in the hospital a few days to allow his lungs to clear and his burns to be treated but would make a full recovery. Abe had saved him from more serious injuries.

ZAK AWOKE IN BED, certain the episode had been a bad dream—a nightmare. If that was dreaming, maybe exhaustion was better.

When he opened his eyes, neither the room nor the bed was his—and Jenny sat in a chair beside him, reading a book. He stirred, tried to move, and her head jerked up.

"Zak? Are you here?"

Of course, I'm here. Why are you here? Where was here?

She stood and looked into his eyes. "Zak?"

"Hello." His voice scraped like sandpaper.

"Hi. How are you?"

"Don' know. Tell me." Words were tough to get out. The *inside* of his throat felt sunburned.

Jenny held up a finger. "I'll be right back. Don't go anywhere."

Where was he going to go?

She left the room and Zak looked around. Antiseptic white walls. Industrial curtains on a window. Guardrails on the bed. Hospital.

Panic rose a little in his chest. He'd been here, done that, didn't want a repeat.

"Jonas. Pete." Jenny's calls in the hall bounced around the room. "Where's Mick?"

Dad's still here?

"He's awake and talking," Jenny hollered down the hall.

Bet the nurses loved all the racquet Jenny was making. Zak's chuckle died at the pain in his chest.

"Praise God," said a voice that sounded like Pete's.

The door opened, and four anxious faces peered into the room.

Zak tried to smile, but the effort hurt.

"How are ya,' buddy?" Mick walked in.

"Tired, mostly." But Zak focused his attention on his father. He had to get one message across. "Don't go."

Pete shook his head. "I'm not going anywhere."

Jenny put her arm around Pete's shoulder.

"Everything's okay, Zak," Jonas said.

Jenny gave Jonas a sideways glance. That girl was horrible at masking her emotions.

"Um, why don't you get some rest?" Jonas shifted his feet. "The paper is doing fine."

Zak nodded. Sleep had undeniable appeal.

Jonas shrugged his shoulders at Jenny before Zak closed his eyes.

"He doesn't know," Jenny whispered.

Zak was glad when sleep took him.

WHEN ZAK AWOKE NEXT, a nurse applied some sort of salve to his legs. She glanced at him, her brown eyes determined, but kind.

"Almost done." She wiped her hands on a towel and wrote something on his chart at the end of the bed. "Sorry I woke you."

He nodded.

"If you need anything, my name is Emily." She finished with his legs, replaced his blanket, and put her materials on the small cart behind her.

"I'll show you how to apply this yourself soon, Mr. Cooper."

"Zak, please. You can call me Zak."

She nodded and smiled as she pushed her cart toward the door.

"Emily?"

She turned around. "Yes, Mr. ... Zak?"

"Um. I was, uh, wondering ..." He glanced at the sheet she'd covered his legs with. "How badly am I hurt?"

She narrowed her eyes and shook her head. "You'll have to ask your doctor about that, Mr. Cooper."

His face heated. "It's Zak. And that's not what I meant, Emily. Sorry. I meant how bad are my burns."

Her cheeks glowed pink as she fidgeted with items on her tray. "I'm sorry, too, Zak. However, your doctor will advise you fully. But it's my understanding that with the proper treatment and follow-up, you'll recover."

Something—fright?—lingered underneath her air of professionalism. Her eyes seemed ... wary. What was she afraid of? "Thank you, Emily. I value your opinion."

She turned and walked through the door. "Men," she grumbled as she left.

He smiled.

WHILE ZAK WAS in the hospital, Pete rarely left his side. He drank in the sight of his son, slaking his thirst for the face that had parched his heart for more than two decades. As he kept watch, he was grateful Zak had asked him to stay. He thanked Jesus for that unexpected gift.

But he could not figure out how to tell Zak what had happened without risking his fragile state.

Pete stood and walked to the window. Why did such tragedy happen? Who could fathom the mind of God to understand why one man had died while another was spared? He stared outside, contemplating things he could not—would not ever—understand. Did Zak know about Abe's death? No one could tell for sure, and none of them was willing to ask, but Pete figured Zak knew on some level. Would the knowledge send his son back into denial?

As he turned to check on Zak again, his son watched him. Zak's eyes were open and clear—and troubled.

"I'm going to get a dog," Pete said. "We could both use the extra love."

Zak looked at him as if he'd lost his mind. "What kind of dog?"

"Four legs. Fur. Barks loud when someone knocks on the door. Piddles on the floor. You know, a dog dog." He winked, and Zak shook his head.

"I'm thinking an Irish Setter, Mr. News Editor, Mr. Just the Facts Please. Found her at the shelter in Templeton. She'd been picked up and was about to be put down. Her name's Flynn. What do you think?"

Zak shrugged and turned his head away.

Pete let the idea wane when Zak didn't ask more questions.

"I've been keeping the house and yard up as best I can," Pete said. "I don't want you to be ashamed of it when you come home."

"Thanks."

"I'm staying there. Hope that's okay. In the guest room."

"That's fine."

Pete walked to the other side of the bed, to see Zak's face. "Jonas wants to talk with you about the paper. When you feel up to it. I think he wants you to come back."

Pete smiled at the flicker interest in his son's eyes.

"It's still there?"

"The paper? Oh yeah. Waxman was publishing within two days." Pete moved away from the bed, determined to make Zak seek more information.

"How'd he do that? There had to be at least some smoke damage," Zak said. "I mean, outside of my ... the editor's office."

"Oh, there was, but Charles made an arrangement with the Templeton Trib. But the damage wasn't as bad as everyone expected." Pete shifted closer again. "Except for your office, which is basically gutted."

"You keep saying 'Waxman did this or that.' What about the Clarity people? Or Jonas?"

Pete could not keep a little smile from teasing the corners of his mouth.

"Simple. After the, uh, incident, Clarity canceled the purchase—money had not changed hands yet—and fired Jonas. Something about him not handling a volatile situation well? And Charles was more than happy to have his family's paper back. He hired Jonas as interim editor—until the, um, right person returns."

Zak retreated again, his eyes betraying his pain. "And Sloan?"

Pete met his son's gaze, but said nothing.

"They got him, didn't they? Dad?"

Pete sat on the edge of the bed.

"Not yet. But they're working on it. There were no witnesses and no family to speak of—just a distant cousin in Templeton—so no one knows where he might have gone, or even why. The police think he got on a bus headed west, but they're just guessing."

Zak appeared ready to drift back to sleep and Pete hoped he would—before the real questions started. This whole explaining things was starting to get a little dicey. But Zak only sighed and turned his gaze toward the window.

"Don't you want to know about your injuries?" Pete asked.

Zak shook his head.

"It's not as bad as it could have been. That desk of yours probably saved your life."

He kicked himself internally. The discussion of what, or who, saved Zak was, he hoped, at least a couple days off.

He cracked his knuckles and stood to stretch his back. Hospital furniture was not comfortable for the family, but it did the job. He looked again at Zak. The rise and fall of his chest was not one of peaceful sleep. His sobs were silent but deep.

Pete walked over and kissed his son on the forehead. A tear slid down Zak's face and another followed. Pete rested his hand on his son's arm, but wished he could hold him—assure him he was not alone. Pete was here to stay for as long as Zak—and God—allowed.

"Dad? I need something."

"Anything, Zak. "

When Zak turned his way, the depth of pain in his eyes tore at Pete, and for the millionth time, he wished Carol were still alive. A mother's comforting touch was what Zak needed.

"Please ask Maydene to come see me."

When he finally did fall asleep, Pete cried.

Later that afternoon, Zak finally asked his father about his injuries. Most of the facts he'd already heard when the others thought he was asleep. He'd discovered that skill last time he was in the hospital.

He'd heard enough that he wasn't worried about his physical recovery. But he was concerned about his mental healing. As King of the Dead, he'd lost several people he loved too early. But this was the first time someone he loved had died *because* of him.

"I still miss Kay, you know," he said.

Pete put down the sports page he was reading in the chair opposite the bed and moved closer. "I should think so. I still miss your mother in many ways."

Pete's constant presence reminded Zak of the black swan he'd seen on the river that day. He'd watched Kay's swan sail off down the river with the others. It had hurt too when she left, deeply, but seeing her move on had also encouraged him. But the black swan had stayed behind, watching him, waiting. Waiting for what?

Zak glanced at his father and saw his concern and his love. "Why did this happen? Why now?"

Pete stared down at him.

"I cannot give you the answer to those questions, son," he said. "If I could, it would have saved me a lot of grief too. I suggest you ask the One who does know, but be prepared for an unsatisfactory answer."

Zak turned his head away. "Well, that's not a helpful answer, Dad. I deal in questions and answers every day. I mean, what kind of answer is it to say there is no answer?"

"I didn't say there was no answer. I said there was no satisfactory answer—not here on earth. Sometimes God asks us to just trust Him."

"Great. Trusting God was Kay's thing, not mine."

Belief? Sure. Worship? Absolutely. But trust? On what basis? Trust had always been the bugaboo in Zak's life, thanks in large part to the father who now stood beside him.

It wasn't that Zak didn't trust. It was more that he trusted so rarely—and so deeply. Once someone earned his trust, they never lost it. But the earning was the hard part. Pete was trying. Could Zak ever trust him again? Did he even want to?

He made a mental note to call Pastor Dave and ask him to come by when—*if*—Maydene visited. He had a hunch the pastor's insight would be helpful, and he had a few other things he hoped Dave could clarify.

"Hey, Dad?"

Pete looked up again from his reading.

"Welcome home."

Chapter Thirty-Seven

Maydene hung up the phone and sank back into the cushions of her couch. Of course, she needed to visit Zak. She should have gone without waiting for him to ask. And she wanted to see him—had tried to make herself go several times. She wasn't angry, certainly not with Zak, but her emotions changed almost hourly.

Since the funeral two days ago, forcing herself to do anything had been a chore. Particularly anything that reminded her of Abe. How could visiting Zak not remind her, regardless of her love for the boy?

Abe had always been the one to put action to her good intentions. But she had to do this, told Pete she would. He was going to drive her to the hospital in the morning.

She understood how and why Zak had kept Kay alive—as well as why things had gone so badly. Sometimes Abe's presence was so real that she found herself looking around for him, certain he had simply fallen asleep in the other room.

Or she'd hear him speaking in that deep voice of his that had rumbled through her life for so many decades. She'd already spotted him once in a crowd, but of course it wasn't him. Couldn't be him no matter how much she wanted it. It was her heart seeing what it wanted to see, was used to seeing.

That's how it had started for Zak, she was sure of it. But his mind had taken those echoes of reality and converted them *into* reality.

"You know what Abe would say." She stood, hands on her waist the way he had done so many times when giving her a hard truth. "'Maydene, you need to get to work. You're not doing anyone any good sitting here and moping.'"

Returning to the café would be difficult. But if she didn't find a way to keep busy, she wouldn't have to wait long to join Abe. Not that she was despondent, or a suicide risk, but she'd read about, and was acquainted with, couples that had happened to. Carrie and Orba Shively had died within a year and a day of each other. They'd been so devoted Carrie had been lost without Orb.

Part of her was attracted to the romance of the Shively's story. Even though she was ready to die from an eternal perspective, Maydene did not want to die. She had more life to live—and she was glad. So she would visit Zak, even knowing the pain it would cause her. And she would return to the café, even though doing so would remind her daily of Abe's absence.

Life was a grand gift from God, and Maydene wasn't going to sit and squander that gift without squeezing every bit of *oomph* out of it.

She stood and headed for the kitchen, determined to sample another of the many casseroles the women from church had brought over. Most didn't compare to her cooking, but she was a professional. What she enjoyed tasting most was the care put into each bite.

As she got to the kitchen, the phone rang—again.

"Hello?"

"Hi Maydene, it's Jenny. Just calling to check on you."

Was it two o'clock already? Jenny called every day after the lunch rush cleared. Maydene had closed the café for several days after Abe's death, but Jenny had run it since the funeral—putting in long hours. She had to be exhausted, but never complained. Some people cried through their grief. Jenny worked.

"Hello, dear, how're things today?"

"Oh, things are great here. We had a rush for about a half hour around noon, but then it quieted down. Steady, but manageable."

Maydene had never had a daughter, but Jenny came close to one.

"I'll be coming back day after tomorrow. I've just decided."

"Oh, Maydene, while I'd love that, do you think it's wise? There's no need to rush. You should take your time. I have everything under control."

"Of course, you do, dear. That café is where my life is. Where some of my best memories of Abe are. It's time."

"Well, if you're sure ..."

"I am. Besides, I'm going to see Zakary in the hospital tomorrow and will probably need the distraction afterward."

The pause on the phone lasted a tad too long.

"That's ... good. He's doing well, last I heard. Tell him I said hello—and Jonas, of course."

"I'll do that. How're things going with Jonas? Have you had the talk yet?"

"No, not yet. Things, life, just keeps happening."

Maydene understood, but sometimes life just ended, abruptly and without warning.

"Jonas told you he needed to tell you the truth about himself—isn't that how you put it the other day?"

"Yes, and I'm starting to wish I hadn't told you."

Maydene smiled, amused at Jenny's defensive tone. "When a man wants to tell a truth, it's best he be allowed to tell it quickly, Jenny. Encouraged, even. Clear the air and move on. Otherwise, it festers inside him, and he may have second thoughts. Besides, how can you move forward without this talk?"

"I know. You're right, as always. It's just—"

"You aren't sure what you want yet."

From the silence on the phone, Maydene might have taken a step too far. She had to learn to control her tongue.

"Yes, I know," Jenny finally spoke. "I thought I knew, was sure I knew, and then Zak was injured, and I feared I wouldn't ever know—for sure, I mean—how I felt."

Maydene pushed. "You know you're not being fair to Jonas? Or Susan?"

"I do. I've been kept awake nights about it."

A comfortable silence filled the space between them.

"Maydene? I love Jonas. I do. But ..."

"But you're not sure you can ever trust him to be true, to be faithful. To keep his horse in his own barn, as my mother used to say."

Jenny laughed and brought a smile to Maydene's lips.

"Exactly. Your mother was a wise woman."

"Yes, she was."

"Jenny, there's only one way you can trust that man again." Maydene moved into full mother mode. "Oh, there are things you may ask him to do and then wait and see if he does them. Or there may be systems you put in place, checks and balances, to help him be true. All of those are important."

She drew on her experience—on the experience of Abe resolving to trust her again. "But none of those things can happen or have a chance to succeed until you decide to trust him enough to give him the chance. And you can't do that until you find out what he has to tell you."

For a long time, Jenny didn't respond. "You're right, of course you are." Her soft voice came from the other end of the line. "And I will. I will do that."

"Make it a priority, Jenny. Don't put it off."

MAYDENE SAT in Pete's car, preoccupied with concerns about her visit. She didn't want Zak blaming himself for Abe's death when it was not his fault. But she also didn't want him to miss the lesson of Abe's death.

Pete had been considerate when he picked her up—asking how she was doing, sharing a nice long-ago memory of Abe that she'd forgotten, holding open her car door.

For an instant, she'd almost cried because Abe had always held the door for her. It was something men of a certain age and temperament just did—and the gesture was as natural for Pete, as it had been for Abe. She knew it meant nothing, but it also meant the world.

Pete, bless him, had tried to engage her in conversation, but her apprehension over the visit undid his best intentions. Besides, it was not a sin to be so comfortable with someone that words weren't required. She and Abe had grown up with Pete —and Carol. They'd gone to school together, attended church together, and lived within blocks of each other as young families.

"Life's funny, Pete," she said as he pulled into the hospital garage and headed for a space. She weighed her words. "It's funny, sad, precious, yet so often treated cavalierly."

Pete nodded, turned off the car, and faced her, lips set.

She touch his hand resting on the steering wheel. "Thank you."

He cocked his head, relaxing. "You're welcome. But for what?"

"For coming back."

~

ZAK, Mick, and Pastor Dave roared at Emily's jibe aimed at Zak as she left the room.

"I've got a great nurse, haven't I?"

"Well, she won't put up with anything from you, that's for sure," Dave said.

"And she gives as good as—no, better—than she gets," Mick added.

Zak laughed again, then put on a scowl of mock offense.

"I'm crushed, Cut down, and by my bestest friend. Who'd of thunk it?"

"She certainly knows the value of laughter as a healing balm," Dave said.

"Ha 'Pattycake, pattycake.'" Zak repeated Emily's exit line. The men exploded in laughter again.

"Oh, laughing is a blessing, as the Proverbs teach," Dave said, as the silliness cleared a bit. "'A joyful heart brightens one's face.'"

"Yes, it does, Pastor," Mick agreed.

But Zak's countenance had darkened while they laughed. While the laughter felt good, it had also made him feel uneasy.

"It does. But it also feels odd—uncomfortable—to be laughing," Zak said. "I mean, when you think on it, what do I have to be laughing about?"

"I'm not sure I follow you. From what I know of your

situation, the bigger question is why wouldn't you be laughing?"

He gaped at Dave as if he'd lost his mind. He slid over to the edge of the hospital bed. It was time for his exercises, and he needed to move. But then he remembered his hospital gown and its revealing nature.

Tough. He was cleared to stand. He was going to stand. The boys would just have to ignore any accidental peep shows.

"Well, let's start with the little things. Second degree burns over 25 percent of my body. Raspy voice and shortness of breath from smoke inhalation. Unemployed. And alone in this world." His feet dangled in the air.

"And now, with a little help from my able assistant," he extended his hand to Mick who did a passable supporting lady flourish and helped him stand.

"And if that's not enough, I caused, even if inadvertently, a good man's death. Okay, all together now, everybody laugh, because that's funny. I don't care who you are."

Zak stood and raised his hands above his head, fists clenched in mock victory.

Dave scowled. "Zakary, you have a negative slant on life that is not healthy. Why *shouldn't* you be joyous and laugh? You're alive."

The pastor spread his hands and stared at Zak over his glasses. "That's no small feat, given the circumstances. Your injuries will fade. You have begun, slowly but surely, to heal from Kay's death. You have many good friends and a father who returned to you practically from the dead. And from what I hear, you have a job waiting for you if you want it."

Then Dave did his own not nearly as passable flourish. "Plus you have at least one young woman making goo-goo eyes at you."

Zak flopped back down on the bed. Walking would have to wait.

"Dave, I need to make something clear to you. I withdrew from Jenny's life because she needed to try to make her marriage work. She still loves her husband."

"Yes, I remember. Very noble of you—and right-minded, I might add. I believe she loves him."

"So ...? Okay, Lucy, 'splain.'"

Dave grinned his biggest grin, looked at the other guys, and together they all brought their hands together as if to clap.

"Pattycake, pattycake," they chorused.

MAYDENE WALKED down the hall beside Pete, silent. He stopped in front of Zak's door and raised his hand to knock, but Maydene placed a hand on his shoulder to restrain him.

"I'd prefer to go in alone, if you don't mind," she said. "It just seems right that way. At least at first."

"Of course." A trace of doubt clouded his face. "There's a little visitors alcove near the elevator. I'll wait there."

He turned to go but pivoted back as she reached for the door handle. "I love my boy, Maydene."

She nodded. "So do I, Bud. Never, not once, have I blamed Zak for Abe's death. He would have gone in after *anyone*. That's who he was."

Pete nodded and spun to go. Maydene watched him walk down the hallway, and saw again, the man she'd known before Carol's death and Zak's abandonment. Had she really thrown a pile of coins at him once?

"Amazing grace, how sweet the sound," she whispered. Then she knocked on the door.

"Come in," a voice said from inside.

Chapter Thirty-Eight

Even though he knew she was coming, and had prepared, Maydene's appearance constricted Zak's throat, making his breathing ragged, and brought fresh tears to his eyes.

Maydene stepped in tentatively and nodded to Pastor Dave and Mick, who stood to the side of Zak's bed. As she approached Zak, Maydene reached into her purse and pulled out a handkerchief. She dabbed at his eyes, even as hers clouded over.

Giving up on the handkerchief, she grasped his head in both her hands and turned his face upward, toward hers. She kissed the tears off his cheeks and the floodgates opened for them both. Maydene held him.

"Shh," she said. "Shh. It's okay, Zakary. It's okay."

When their tears subsided, Maydene sat in the chair beside Zak. She took his hand and stroked it. His mother had comforted him similarly many times, holding him in her lap while he cried.

Even as she lay dying, she'd tried to assuage his grief.

Maydene's embrace felt the same. Though she was in pain, she tried to heal his.

Zak glanced toward Dave and Mick. Their eyes were closed and their lips moved as they prayed.

He knew he had to say something, but anything would be inadequate.

"Maydene. I don't know what ...," Zak said. "I shouldn't even have been in the office that day and—"

"Zakary, don't even think it. You know Abe. It wouldn't have mattered who was there—you, Ben Weller, or—or Sloan White. That man would have gone in regardless."

"I wouldn't have gone in for Sloan," Mick muttered.

Zak opened his mouth to respond to Maydene, closed it, then forged on. "But it was *me*, Maydene. It wasn't Ben or—or anyone else. It was me. Abe sacrificed his life for me."

"Yes, it was. And what does that mean to you?"

The question caught him off guard. He'd been prepared for her to talk about what Abe had meant to her. Or about Abe's life—even the way he died. But she was talking about *him*. What did Abe's sacrifice mean to *him*?

The door opened, and Pete peeked in.

"Is it okay?" he asked. "I can go back to the lounge ..."

Maydene raised an eyebrow at Zak.

"Sure, Dad. It's fine. C'mon in."

"The more the merrier, eh? Have a sit, Pete." Mick stood and offered his chair to Pete, moving to lean against the wall. "I'm getting D.B. Disease, anyway."

Dave turned to Mick. "You not feeling well?"

"D.B. Disease, Pastor." Mick grinned. "It just means I want to stand awhile, Dave. My posterior's getting numb."

Zak shook his head and turned to Maydene. "I'm not sure I follow. What does Abe's death mean to me? It means I have another death on my head that I'm going to have to try and live with."

His father glared at Maydene, but she waved him off with a flutter of her hand.

"Not Abe's death, Zak. You have life today because Abe, acting as an agent of God, sacrificed his life to save yours—does that not mean something to you?"

Zak was silent as he stared at his sheets.

"John 15:13," Pastor Dave said. "'Greater love hath no man than this—"

"That he lay down his life for his friends," Zak finished.

The room grew silent.

"But I always thought ... Wasn't that ...? I mean, isn't that a reference to Jesus?"

"Of course," Dave said. "But it's more than that. It's an instruction in how to live *your* life. How, as Christians, we are expected to live sacrificially *because* Christ did the same for us. To show such love for others that, if necessary, we're willing to die for them."

Zak stared straight ahead. Maydene let go of his hand and walked over to the window looking out on the hospital parking lot.

"I would have died for Kay. I still would if it would bring her back." His voice sounded a million miles away.

Maydene whirled from the window. "That is not a choice that was given to you, Zakary. You can't fault yourself for actions you didn't take—that you *couldn't* have taken."

Dave moved his chair closer. "Furthermore, you did all you could to prevent her from going to Templeton that day."

"No, I didn't. I could have insisted—demanded—she not go. But I was in too much of a hurry to get to work. I was *late* for *work* —and she died." His voice fell. "I didn't even get to say goodbye."

"You're not thinking clearly, Zakary," Maydene said. "We are each responsible for the choices we make. Did you have a choice to go to work that day or stay home?"

"Yes, but ..." His mind flipped back to that bittersweet morning when he'd chosen to linger in bed with Kay.

Maydene continued. "But as the editor it was your *responsibility* to be there, yes? You did what you had to do. So, it was with Kay. Did she have a choice? Of course, but she had an appointment, and it was her job—her *responsibility*—to be there."

Pastor Dave held his head in his hands. "This is a huge struggle—for Christians *and* for those who don't yet believe. It's a struggle of mine." He looked up. "Why do bad things happen? If God is so great, why do His people suffer? What is the nature of evil?"

Zak leaned closer. "And the answer is ..."

Dave ran his hand through his hair. "It's an unsatisfactory answer, Zak. In the end, we have to trust that God knows what He's doing."

Zak didn't look away from Dave as the whole room waited for his answer.

"You already know this," Dave said with a bemused smile. "At least you should if you've listened to me preach at all."

Looking around the room, Zak saw they were all waiting for Dave to share the secrets of the world with them.

Inclining his head and extending a hand, Zak urged Dave to continue.

"We live in a fallen world. Sin is real." Dave spread his hands. "God created us, each of us, with free will—and too often we choose the bad, the evil, the easy way out. We choose, consciously, something that is less than the good."

Dave stood and turned away, his mouth pursed. "I never know how to word this adequately. It's tough for pastors too.

We have no more access to spiritual truths than you do. Degrees in theology don't come with all the keys to the kingdom."

"Blame it all on sin," Mick said. "When in doubt, it's sin's fault."

Zak sat straighter in his bed. "Are you saying Kay's choosing to go to Templeton for her appointment was evil? That she chose something less than good and that's why she's dead? Because if that's what you're saying, then Christianity is not for me, and I'm outta here."

Dave placed his hand on Zak's arm. "No, of course not. It's not that simple—and yet it is."

He stood and walked around the room.

Pete stood. "It's just the way the world is, son. It's broken, *fallen* is the theological term Dave used, I think, but broken works better for me. When things are broken, they don't work right. Oh, they may function a little. May still do some of the things they're supposed to. Doesn't mean they're not broken. You follow?"

Zak nodded.

"It's nothing that we *do*, it's the way the world *is*. When Carol ... when your mother died, it was a result of the same brokenness." Pete's voice broke. "Until that moment, my life had been perfect, blessed. How could it not be? I was a child of God. Protected under His wing."

A sad laugh escaped Pete as he wheeled from the window. "We can be so blind."

Maydene placed a hand on Pete's back, he smiled weakly at her before returning his gaze to Zak.

"If I'd had someone point out to me the fallen nature of the world, I might have been able to stay and work through my grief. But instead, I went in search of my own truth. Your mother wasn't dead, she'd just wandered off."

Zak spoke, more to himself than to his father. "I did that too. I created Kay out of bits and pieces of the brokenness in me … but I didn't recreate Kay as much as I gave life to my dark self."

"Um. Are you all going to be getting any deeper?" Mick asked. "Because I feel like I'm in a huge hole, you know, and looking up."

"Here's another angle I've heard," Dave said. "We're all wounded healers. The brokenness in our lives—our wounds—creates scars that only the Great Physician can heal. But when you're weak and I'm stronger, I can share my strength, which comes from God. And one day you'll return the favor or pass the healing on to someone else."

As the room fell silent, Zak was surprised to feel blessed. It was a terrible, awful, blessing—but it could not be denied. He got to live with these wonderful people longer. Together, they would stumble on, helping each other as best as they could.

"Maydene? You asked me what it meant that Abe had sacrificed his life for me," Zak said. "I think I'm closer to an answer now, but it may take me a lifetime to understand it."

Her smile strengthened him.

"Life is for the living," Zak continued. "I can't avoid my brokenness—or the world's—by refusing to see it or putting on a mask. One of the best things I *can* do is see my scars, acknowledge them, and help others find the same healing I have found."

For the first time since the river, he felt Kay's presence in a positive way. She would have understood all of this inherently.

"For the past year or so, I've been too absorbed in my wound. Poking it, probing it, trying to figure out the why of it as if knowing that would make it disappear. Instead, I should have been doing the work of cleaning it out like you did with my toe that one day even though it hurt and made me scream."

Pete chuckled. "Strawberry."

"Exactly. You were a good father. You cleaned my hurt, put medicine on it, and distracted me from the pain. That's what we need to do for each other—as often as necessary."

After a knock on the door, Emily entered with Zak's pain medications.

"Am I interrupting something?" She glanced at everyone before her gaze landed on Zak. "Ya'll are awful quiet in here."

He smiled at her and held his hand out for his pill. "No Ma'am, Nurse Perkins, we're all just healing in here. Would you like a little?"

Emily's eyes narrowed. "Well, that's good. This *is* a hospital, so I guess healing is encouraged—just do it quietly. If the director comes in, some of you are going to have to hide in the toilet. Only three visitors per room."

She noted the time Zak had taken his pill on the chart and turned to go but stopped at the door. "Oh, Mr. Cooper, the doctor plans to release you. He'll be in later to give you the details and to talk about what to do when you get home."

"That's great news," Zak said.

"Yes, it is." She looked down. "So, I guess this is goodbye, Mr. Cooper." She opened the door. "I've enjoyed being your nurse. You take care of yourself."

She stepped into the hall.

"Emily?" He called after her and returned to the doorway. "It's Zak, remember?"

"You take care of yourself, Zak." She smiled and shook her head.

As the door closed behind her, Zak turned back to the others, who wore beaming smiles.

"What?" he asked, feeling the heat rise to his face. "She ... it's just ... I mean."

They all roared with laughter.

Epilogue

Zak sat in his recliner, glad to be home. Today had been long, but good. Even after being back on the job six months, he enjoyed being active again. He had a new desk and a new chair in his new office. The desk he was grateful for, even though the metal behemoth had likely saved his life. But he missed his dad's chair.

Jonas stayed on at *The Gazette* as a reporter, eager to hone his skills. Zak had been concerned about bringing him on full-time. They went through some rough days working through the whole Jenny issue, but overall, they were functioning. Especially after Jonas had learned Zak had encouraged Jenny to give Jonas another chance.

However, Zak remained worried about the couple. Once his presence no longer threatened Jonas, the younger man had begun confiding in Zak as he would an older brother. He'd shared snatches of his past and indicated, obliquely, that he was meeting with Steve Tucker and his group at church. And, he was glad to see, Susan seemed to be thriving with both parents around.

Emily's increasing presence in his life brightened Zak's days considerably. They weren't an item yet, but Zak hoped they soon would be. For now, he enjoyed having a female friend to go to movies with, talk to over dinner, and take walks with.

Last week, during a walk together, he'd reached for her hand—and she'd willingly given it. Her warm skin gave him the shivers. He hoped it wouldn't be long before they grew closer, and he could kiss her. But he was not in a rush and neither, it seemed, was she. Slow was good.

His weariness today came from his appointment with Harley Culp. These weekly times nearly always wore him out. He wasn't seeing Kay anymore, or even talking to her, really, but moving on challenged him. Harley said many of his difficulties came from the unorthodox way he had grieved.

Zak found dealing with Kay's death especially difficult after spending time with Emily. She looked nothing like Kay— was brunette where Kay had been blonde, had green eyes, instead of Kay's blue, contemplative instead of spontaneous.

Yet sometimes the things she'd *do* just screamed Kay at him. Those were the days when letting go—or holding on, for that matter—became difficult.

Emily could often tell when he had slipped into what she called "Kay mode," and he knew that was hard for her. She understood the time it would take to work through his grief. But when she felt like she was competing with a shadow, their relationship had bogged down. Zak redoubled his efforts with Harley.

Under Harley's guidance, Zak stepped through the stages of grief properly. His "departure from the norm," as Harley put it, had distanced him from the actual event of Kay's death and made dealing with her loss even harder. But consistency was helping him make satisfactory progress—at least according to Harley.

Today's session had been especially challenging. Discussion had led to the day Kay had become real. Harley suggested Zak watch the recording of *How the Grinch Stole Christmas* again.

Harley believed seeing the report again and reacting to it anew from his current, healthier position—would help. Zak feared viewing the news report again, but Harley hadn't steered him wrong yet.

So, there he sat, in his recliner, the recording queued up in the menu, and the remote in his hand. He only had to push the button and the movie would begin. *Just push the button.*

"Push the Play button and get it over with," Zak said. "How bad can it be?"

Of course, that was the answer he feared.

He held the remote, massaged the buttons with his thumb. Watched the panel light up every time he touched another one. Flipped through the broadcast channels, where nothing caught his interest, and ended up back where he started.

He threw up a prayer for strength.

Place me like a seal over your heart, like a seal on your arm.

He jerked out of his recliner. His breathing doubled. He whirled around, looking for the owner of the voice.

It wasn't God speaking—the voice had been feminine. Besides, God had not audibly spoken to him since that day by the river, and Zak preferred it that way. What he heard in his mind was different—more like an echo from the past.

Place me like a seal over your heart, like a seal on your arm. For love is as strong as death, its jealousy unyielding as the grave.

He knew that voice. Kay. His heart raced, and fear made

the hair on his neck stand up straight. The last time he'd heard her voice, nothing good had come of it.

It burns like blazing fire, like a mighty flame.

He almost called Harley to chastise him for pushing too hard. But after the initial shock, the voice brought comfort, not fear. And her words were familiar.

The passage came from the Song of Solomon. Kay had read it to him on the last Valentine's Day she'd been alive.

"Zak, listen to this," Kay had said. "Dreama told me about it. She read it to Mick one night and now he's always asking her to read it again."

They had giggled at the thought of Mick enraptured by the Song of Solomon.

Zak sat on the couch again and looked at the remote in his hand. Was the memory a sign? He took a deep breath and pressed Play. He'd always appreciated *The Grinch*. Had watched it every year as a child and never failed to be touched by the story of the transforming power of love.

Zak had his own grinchy moments, when all he wanted was to crawl into his cave and curse those around him for their ability to be happy. Why wouldn't they be? They had normal homes with living mothers and fathers who cared. What if they lost it all?

Every year, when Cindy-Lou Who came into the picture and touched the Grinch's heart with her innocent trust, when the townspeople awoke on Christmas morning full of joy, Zak's heart leaped at the possibility of love—at the certainty of a love that could transcend circumstance and appearance and point the way to joy.

Kay had been his Cindy-Lou Who, trusting the feel-good fibs he'd told her about being happy, but Christmas morning had never come in Zak's heart. Though he wasn't as cold and isolated, in many ways Zak continued to grinch along in his cave at the top of the mountain, coveting the joy other people appeared to have that he couldn't feel. Yearning to hear, but certain he wouldn't, the joyful strains of "Welcome, Christmas."

Zak became lost in the story again, giving himself over to its seductive claim on his life. He forgot why he was watching. He forgot the pain. He walked with the Grinch through his misguided attempt to stop Christmas from coming, waiting to experience the joy vicariously.

When the newsbreak about the accident appeared on his screen just before the end of the program, Zak stiffened. The newsreader came on with a report of a Christmas tragedy and then the images he feared appeared on the screen again.

He saw with fresh eyes the mangled mess of Kay's Accord and College Boy's Chevy, and his heart rebelled.

The news reporter's words didn't change. "Excessive speed and alcohol certainly played a role in this tragic scene."

Zak sat riveted to his seat. This was where he'd shut off the tape, and Kay had made her first appearance over a year ago.

This time, however, the tape played on.

"Thanks, Trey," Scout said. "A sad tale, indeed. Tune in at eleven for more on this story, including an interview with a witness on the scene."

There had been a witness? Zak had never heard about a witness. But what did it matter now? He sighed and returned to the end of the show.

The Who's were gathering around the Christmas tree singing "Welcome, Christmas." They were celebrating love— despite the theft of the trimmings. They celebrated because love was what mattered. Not lights, tinsel, gifts, or roast beast. Love was *the* reason, not a reason.

And Zak finally understood. Real joy, founded in love, was the reason Maydene could rejoice—even when losing her husband—that Zak lived. It explained how Jenny could forgive Jonas and offer him another chance. It made sense of Pete's return after all those years.

"Joy comes from choosing love," he said in wonder. "Choosing to love in spite of the circumstances."

It made real what he'd always heard at church.

"The greatest of these is love."

"Bear one another's burdens in love."

"For God so loved ..."

He turned off the television and stood. The light in the house seemed brighter, clearer. He walked into his bedroom, looking for his Bible. When he couldn't find it, he retrieved Kay's, still on her nightstand where she'd left it.

As he sat there, he caught a faint aroma of the past. It soothed, rather than frightened. He opened Kay's Bible and thumbed through it. The margins were filled with notes and highlights of various hues, giving the pages the feel of a watercolor.

Kay had left a sticky note protruding from one section. On it she'd written *My Zak* with an arrow pointing to the Song of Solomon verses. He'd never seen it, though it had been there all the time.

He read them out loud. "Place me like a seal over your heart, like a seal on your arm. For love is as strong as death, its jealousy unyielding as the grave. It burns like blazing fire, like a mighty flame."

He paused at the power in those words. Why had he not noticed them before? They'd just been a silly story to tell about Mick. Now they were more. Now they painted an accurate description of the love he and Kay had shared. If the passage were to be believed, it was not a love that would ever pass.

Zak would always love Kay. Always. Whether he married

again or not—and that was okay. Any new love would be just that—a *new* love, not a replacement.

He didn't have to get over her. He had to deal with the reality that she was physically gone. But in a healthy way, Kay would be a part of him forever.

"Now, that's joy."

Zak gazed at the photo collage over their headboard. Kay had placed their posed wedding photo in the center, but other photos of him and Kay, together and separate, at various times in their lives surrounded it.

He reached up, took the collage off the wall, and set it on the bed. He ran his fingers over the images, remembering what her hair had felt like, how her eyes had danced, the way her laughter had so often set his world right.

Oh, he would miss her. But he could move on now because, in ways beyond his understanding, Kay would always be with him.

He picked up the Bible, still open to the Song. He looked at the Kay from their wedding day as he read further.

"Many waters cannot quench love; rivers cannot wash it away. If one were to give all the wealth of his house for love, it would be utterly scorned."

He closed the Bible and set it aside.

"Katharine Renee Sharp Cooper"—he said into the tender air—"wait there for me, my love. We'll find each other again."

Then he lay down on their marriage bed and let her scent cradle him into his first peaceful sleep in a year.

Acknowledgments

To my Lord, Jesus, who told me (through his apostle, Paul) not to conform to the ways of this world, but to be transformed by the renewing of my mind. As usual, You are right.

To my love, Deb, without whom this writing thing would be impossible. None of "this" (motions widely around himself) would be possible. "Set me as a seal upon your heart, as a seal upon your arm, for Love is as strong as death." Song of Songs 8:6

About the Author

Michael Ehret has accepted God's invitation to write and is also a freelance editor at WritingOnTheFineLine.com. In addition, he's worked as editor-in-chief of the *ACFW Journal* magazine for the American Christian Fiction Writers (ACFW), was editor-in-chief of the Christian Writers Guild, and he pays the bills as the bookstore coordinator for Indy Library Store. Michael sharpened his writing and editing skills as a reporter for *The Indianapolis News* and *The Indianapolis Star*.

He's been married for 43 years to Deb and they have three children, one dog (a Goldendoodle named Toby), and a granddog. Since he writes fiction by the seat of his pants, who knows what's next? Connect with him at https://writingonthe fineline.com or on Facebook.

Also by Michael Ehret

Big Love

A Novella

Berly Charles remembers the days before her father was a successful business tycoon in Indianapolis. Growing up a razor's edge from homelessness planted a tiny desire for home in her heart that she now, as the owner of Le Petite Maison, LLC, fills for others by building their tiny home ideals. Now she has the opportunity to take her tiny house company big time—is this the chance she's been waiting for?

Nathan "Rafe" Rafferty is a writer for a nationally reputed architecture journal who is used to calling his own shots and covering the biggest and the best architectural accomplishments of the modern world. But when his hipster, much younger, editor assigns him to cover a new trend—tiny houses—the assignment stirs unpleasant memories and thoughts of revenge.

This novella was originally published in *Coming Home: A Tiny House Collection* on May 15, 2017. This edition is revised with an all-new ending.

Get your copy here:

https://scrivenings.link/biglove

Stay up-to-date on your favorite books and authors with our free e-newsletters.

ScriveningsPress.com

www.ingramcontent.com/pod-product-compliance
Lightning Source LLC
Chambersburg PA
CBHW060615100726
47907CB00006B/1626